# The Witch

## By Cheryl Potter

# Part 1: Terra

# He Comes ...

It was the chosen evening, Kate knew. All day she had fought the tremor in her hands, denied the urge to scan the horizon – part of her knowing, the rest of her racked with unknowing.

Jack had sensed her restlessness. His usual gentle handling of the ewes had been barbed with impatient nips. The dog now sat at the foot of the ladder, willing her to come down from the roof.

Kate cursed herself for not fetching the short scaling ladder from the outhouse as she had intended. Like so much else today it had slipped from her mind. Forgetfulness had earned her grazed knuckles and elbows in an ungainly scramble to the ridge.

She sat astride a half-round ridge tile and stared through a gaping hole into the room below. Five tiles had blown off and the old thatch beneath crumbled at her touch. She groaned inwardly. It was going to take more than a hessian sack to patch this one up. Still, it would have to do for now.

Untying an old grain sack from her shoulders, she began teasing it under the tiles around the hole. A whine escaped Jack and he stretched his black and white body up the ladder.

Kate sat bolt upright on the roof, the hessian left flapping in the breeze. Below, the fields rolled away to the Welsh border, the unseen mountains imagined through the blue haze. She turned to look over her left shoulder, towards Bristol, the ports and the boats....

In her mind's eye she saw a cargo ship. For a moment she seemed to be steadying herself on the swaying deck, staring high above the port to the hills beyond. The vision lasted a moment only, then a cold shudder brought her back to roof and Jack's whines.

With hasty stabs of her foot she pushed the sacking home then crawled backwards to the ladder, more than grateful to feel its solid rungs under her boots.

Jack leapt up at her excitedly when she took her cloak and crook from the hook on the back of the kitchen door. A last look at the folds was unusual for August. Kate did not however reach the folds. She ran to Blackwood Top. There, commanding Jack to silence, she waited knee deep in bracken.

She saw *him* through a bank of vermillion poppies. No more than a black dot at first, obscured and revealed by the dancing flowers. She watched the dot grow and take the shape of a man. He was tall and heavily built and carried no baggage, that much she could discern. As for the rest, the fading light connived to keep her ignorant.

She held Jack by the scruff, knowing only too well his instinct to protect her. Heavy feet crushed a path through the bracken, ascending the hillside. Then stopped.

He stood before her; a black figure, silhouetted against the night sky, the last of the sun's rays blazing from behind his shoulders.

'I've come a long way, Kate Gurney,' he said. It was a voice she had never heard – a coarse voice with a foreign lilt, yet he used her name with all the familiarity of one coming home.

She felt rather than heard Jack's deep growl.

'Hush you old fool! Your name sir?'

'Ah Kate, you do not know?'

'No, I cannot say that I do.'

'Swear to it.'

'By all that is holy, I swear I do not know you.'

'A curious oath for one such as you,' he said, moving closer.

Kate flinched, acutely aware of the old wounds; chilled by the knowing in his voice.

'Send the dog away,' he whispered with undeniable authority. 'I've come a long way.'

'She hesitated before issuing the command and had to repeat it before Jack skulked into the shadows.

'He will come if I call,' she said, immediately feeling foolish. He gave a short burst of covering laughter before winding his knuckle in her sleeve and jerking her towards him.

'And if you do, I will snap his neck like a twig. Now Kate, have a care. I have not come to harm you. You know that, why else are you here waiting for me?'

'Who are you?'

'Find me in yourself Kate. I am there. In the mind of the child ... and even now, though less often, in the mind of the woman. Why do you tremble?'

Kate's hand went to her forehead in confusion. How much did he know, this man? How could he know? It had happened so long ago. Twenty years ... more. She forced the memories, stark ugly memories, from her mind, feeling strangely exposed to him.

'They have been talking about me,' she blustered, feeling self-control melting. 'What right–'

'Fight on Kate, you will not defeat me.' His voice blended with the rustling of the aspens in the wood below. For a moment she wondered if he was there at all, this man, or merely the working of her imagination. But there was nothing imagined about the big hand which slid over her face. He laughed softly as she recoiled, then clapped the hand over hers and crushed her flat palm first against one heavily browed eye, then the other; over the fleshy nose and parted lips, heavy with saliva, to a stubbly chin.

'Feel me Kate Gurney, that you might know me well.'

She gasped with sudden pain as he released his grip on her hand. Her mind worked furiously, sifting through them all; the gossips, the self-righteous men, the stone-throwing children. Which of them had he spoken to? They all knew the ins and outs of Kate Gurney, damn them. What better sport than to sling mud at that strange who lived alone near Blackwood Top?

'Damn them all!' she spat, unaware that she had spoken her thoughts.

'The good people of the town?' he mocked. 'Why so bitter Kate? Did they drive you away, or deny you a living?'

'I wish they had. Least then I might have made a new life somewhere. A place where they might respect a creature for hard work, not scorn her for her name and rob her blind come shearing when there are fleeces to be sold.'

'They fear you, Kate.'

She laughed ironically, 'They scorn me.'

'You scorn yourself girl. You could have them at your feet.' Again his voice melted into the rustling of leaves. Kate's head began to swim and she was keenly aware of hunger.

'I have little enough to offer, but you are welcome to eat at my cottage. After your journey,' she said.

'Not tonight ... I have work to do.'

'You are leaving?'

'Does that trouble you?'

She stayed silent. She did not know his name, who he was, where he came from. He frightened her. Yet she wanted him to stay. This was the chosen evening, she knew.


Later....

Lying fully dressed on the hard inn bed, he stretched and smiled contentedly. She would do, he reflected. In fact, Kate Gurney was tailor made for his purposes. An outsider and younger than he had expected. The landlord had guessed at eight years when the mother was hanged, and that before Cromwell and his cronies. Talkative in his cups was mine host, a mine of information.

She was in her thirties then, a good forty years younger than Mother Sutton and most of the others he had come across. Lacking in real resentment but he could remedy that. Oh yes, he could remedy that – virgin soil this one.

Suddenly the door of the shabby room creaked ajar. Instinctively he reached for the knife in his boot. Polly, the taproom girl, sidled in with a knowing giggle. She locked the door and moved to the bedside.

In one furious movement he grabbed a handful of her tousled hair and jerked the squealing servant to her knees.

'Never walk in without knocking again, do you hear?' He pressed the flat of his blade against her pink cheek.

Polly showered him with terrified nods. And from deep in his throat there came a rumbling laugh.

# The Absolution ...

The tupping had not gone smoothly this year. Both of Kates's veteran rams had died last winter leaving her no choice but to put first-year rams in with the ewes. She had given the young males free rein among the seasoned ewes before letting them loose on the yearlings. It had been a fumbling, long-winded business, needing more than a little encouragement from her. Now that each of her *ladies* was at last marked with a smudge of blue dye, she gave a sigh of relief.

The work seemed to tax her strength more this year. The hurdles for making the folds seemed heavier; the trek to the wood to collect them, further; and the sheep themselves seemed just a little more awkward.

That she, who had always prided herself on her strength and laughed off the petty ailments that drove other women to their sickbeds, should wheeze with the effort of turning a ewe, maddened Kate. She refused to give in to the aches that crept into her joints, knowing that once she did, there would be no turning back. It was a downhill slide into old age and the almshouse.

Her day's work done, and the last of the lambs extricated from the brambles, she tied a hurdle gate across the entrance to the fold. It had been an oppressively hot day, so humid that the red dress she wore still clung uncomfortably to her skin. Turning from the fold she decided against going straight to the cottage.

Invigorated by the cool of early evening Jack romped after her, over the plank bridge and into the wood. He disappeared into the undergrowth as she picked her way between the trees, confident that he would find her again at the secluded lake a short way on.

'No Jack, you wait there, least till I'm done. You'll only stir up the mud.' She laughed, forcing the dog's hind quarters to the floor and gratefully kicked off her boots and stockings.

Warm sunshine filtered through the mellow autumn leaves bathing her nakedness as she washed soiled dress and stockings in the water. Wringing them with strong hands, she tossed the clothes onto a rock and plunged into the clearer water further on.

Kate rolled on to her back and stared up at the ribbons of pink-edged cloud. As always the water took away the heaviness of mind and body. Four whole days had come and gone since his coming; four days without a word from him to fill the hours of torment. The certainty that had planted her on Blackwood Top that night had begun to crumble. After all the anticipation it seemed that nothing had changed, except for the return of the nightmares.

Now though, all anxiety drifted away. The water held her in its arms and she felt as light as a rolling cloud.

She had floated into a twilight world, neither awake, nor asleep when Jack's warning bark startled her. Sunset had come and gone unnoticed and as she swam back to her clothes, night was casting its shadows over the wood.

'Where are you dog?' she called, dragging herself on to springy grass. 'Jack?' She felt for the clothes and with an involuntary shiver shook the dress before stepping into it. It hung in wet creases about her. Pushing the stockings into her pocket, she thrust her feet into the boots and reached for her shepherding knife.

A sudden movement in the undergrowth jerked her to attention. 'Jack?' she whispered.

'He can't hear you. He has gone hunting.' The reply was as unexpected as the hand which, coming from behind, took the knife from her grip. Kate stifled a cry.

'I thought you had gone,' she said, her throat suddenly cracked dry. She forced herself to turn, sensing him close behind her. Yet when she looked he was several feet away, stooping by the water's edge. He was staring at the moon's reflection, his dark hair tied back.

'You called me to you Kate.'

She stared at sharply the defined profile, the deep forehead and jutting chin.

'Who are you?'

He turned his face towards her in silent contemplation, then drew himself to his full height and held out his hand.

'Come.'

From deep in the wood there came the shrill cry of a vixen. The cry of a will dominated, a cry of pain. Kate walked towards the outstretched hand. She rubbed her face against the warmth of its palm and folded into an unyielding embrace. A strange hand gripped the back of her head and guided her face inside the folds of jacket and unbuttoned shirt to the naked chest beneath; all warmth and powerful heartbeat.

'I will make you strong Kate. I have power enough for both of us.' The words wafted dreamlike over her. He held her so tightly that she was struggling to breathe. Her head throbbed with the pounding of both hearts. 'We will repay evil for evil.'

'Sweet Lord, what is happening?' she yelped, summoning all her strength to pull her head free. Her eyes glittered up into his face as she strained against the bruising hold he kept on her waist.

'Bitterness is in your heart, Kate. How many times have you wished damnation on your tormentors?'

''No,' she groaned in anguish. 'Not meant.'

'Ah Kate, you know that it is so. The women who turn you from their door – the witch's bastard, they call you. The men who call you whore, yet slaver with lust. The priest who delights to condemn you from the pulpit, driving you from the church. The lord who rides his hounds through your folds and shoots your ewes should they stray on to his land.'

'No!' she choked. 'No more. It is just punishment.'

'For what, eh? The testimony of a confused and frightened child? Elizabeth Gurney – *your mother* – stood condemned of witchery. She was lost before ever she came to trial.'

Kate seemed to shrink into herself. She closed her eyes and turned her face from his.

'With or without your evidence, she was doomed.' His voice changed to a chilling imitation of the gossips. '*She* killed the old man, the Gurney woman. Crossed her he did, refused to buy her cloth. Vowed she would make him rue the day. You know, the loose one with a *bastard*.'

He had uttered the last word with such relish that Kate clawed at his face, screaming with fury.

He stood rock-like through her outburst, tightening the punishing grip on her waist, unmoving though she could feel broken skin and sticky blood under her nails. At last she flagged, her breath rasping in her throat, strength exhausted.

'Damn them woman! Turn your hate on them, not on yourself. You poor fool, you did not kill your mother – it was them, all of them.'

'*She* was strong, not me. She spat in their eye, even though they tortured her.' Her face hardened. 'Stuck her with pins, trussed her up and threw her in the river, kept her awake even when she begged for sleep. She scorned them all.'

'She knew she would die.'

A racking sob shuddered through Kate's body. Her sides ached under the pressure of his hands.

'They said I must save her soul. Only I could do it.'

A hand seized her chin and forced her to look into the deep brown of his eyes. When he spoke his voice was deep with anger.

'What did you tell them?'

'No, I cannot remember. Please–'

'Tell me now!'

'I cannot–' Before the words were out of her mouth he grabbed her wet hair and pulled her backwards under the water. There had been no warning. No time to snatch air. Just a terrible weight across her pelvis. She reached down and tried to thrust his knee away but succeeded only in gulping water. She spluttered and the watery image of the moon was lost in a cloud of bubbles.

He glanced casually across the water, counting the trees lining the lake, waiting for her kicking legs to weaken enough. It happened when he reached the thirty-ninth, an oak he supposed. He snatched her up, all bronchial splutters and greedy for air, and carried her to a fallen log.

She lay face down for several minutes, choking away the water. He sat by her head, his face streaked with blood, his eyes set in an unseeing stare. At length she asked hoarsely, 'Do you want my soul?'

He gave a short laugh. 'Is it yours to barter?'

'All my life I have harboured this ... guilt.'

'And you play right into their hands; you did as a child; you do even now. Out your secret fears, those memories that worm into your power.' He brushed his fingers over her cheek, gently caressing.

'I have never spoken of such things before ... never. Am I then to tell you, who have no name?'

'You have no choice Kate,' he said bluntly. 'I shall out this canker. It destroys the purity of your inheritance.'

'Inheritance? What power do you speak of?' An incredulous laugh escaped her. 'For pity's sake, I am no witch.'

'But you are. You are the daughter of a true witch; her only daughter. Until now guilt has suppressed your talent. It was always there. How else did you come to be on Blackwood Top?'

Kate fell silent. She *had* known he was coming just as she knew when a ewe would bear twins. As she sometimes knew the manner of a man's death, years before the event. This much she shared with her mother. 'You have the sight, child,' she would say. ''Tis a rare gift, if troublesome.' But if that made Kate a witch, she had never practised the craft.

After the hanging of her mother Parson Ellson had taken her in. He had read to her from his treasured collection of woodcut pamphlets the lurid confessions of convicted witches; their pacts with the Evil One, the waxen effigies, the Sabbath dancing. For the good of her soul he had said, but she kept with her the vivid memory of the face that gloated most unpriest-like over the gruesome tortures and executions of those wretched women. She had secretly vowed to be as virtuous as goodwife Ellson herself.

'Believe it,' his voice cut across her thoughts, 'there lies your strength.'

'To be a witch is to be cursed!' she whispered, rubbing her cheek against the grainy bark of the log. 'My mother was murdered for it.'

'She demands vengeance.'

Kate closed her eyes and she was there, in the foetid cell at Gloucester gaol, her mother's bewildered green eyes boring into hers.

'I betrayed her,' she murmured. 'You were right, she knew she would hang, like so many more. I could not accept ... I prayed. Then he came to me.'

'Who?'

'The gaoler. He gave me food and said I could save her. If I said she had done things, she would be beaten and allowed to live.'

'What things?'

'His breath stank of ale. He had a great wart under his eye, and his fingers – fat as swollen sausages – crawling over my arms and legs. I let him touch and poke because I wanted her to live. He talked about devils who came to women as animals or men, to suck their privates and make them slaves. Fat fingers drew pictures in the sawdust; vile pictures – a man and a woman, a dog and a woman, a ram.'

'Until you were convinced it had truly happened.'

'He put the pictures in my mind. My mother had lain with the Devil, had made an effigy of the old man at his command. It was not her fault. Evil would be beaten out of her, and then we would be as we had been before they came for her.'

She lay listening to the leaves stirring like a gentle sea, powerfully aware of his closeness, of his raw strength. She swung her legs round to sitting.

'I was made to repeat my story to the judge at the assize court. I could see her in the corner of my eye, sitting ... head bowed ... there was a faraway look in her eyes ... I swear that until I saw her eyes I did not know what I had done.'

'The twist of the knife,' he said coldly. 'An old trick. Not enough that they had condemned her, they must have her spirit broken – penitent before she reached the gallows. You were the only weak link in her armoury.'

Kate said thickly, 'I denounced them all; the judge, the gaoler, the mob who leered as she hung in the gibbet. I hated them all.'

'And God?' Again his voice seemed no more than the rustle of leaves.

'Yes,' she said grimly, 'even Him.'

He stroked her hair, saying quietly, 'Then it is settled. You shall be absolved of guilt.' He walked pensively towards the water's edge, hands clasped behind his coat.

Kate rose from the log. 'Tell me how.'

He sighed heavily, then held the knife out to her. 'Go fetch me a hazel rod.'

'For what?' she asked unsteadily.

He put the knife handle into her palm and closed her fingers around it. 'Kate the child offended. The child shall be duly punished. Fetch the rod.'

Kate shivered. She was to be beaten. The certain knowledge set her heart straining against her rib-cage. Her legs weakened under her as she moved through the trees, yet she obeyed his command. She trusted him, as she had never trusted anyone before.

The gnarled hazel tree by the stream was bathed in silvery light. She stepped into the light and cut a strong branch. With deft sweeps of the blade she stripped it of leaves and nipped out the bright new growth.

He was waiting for her by the lake. His jacket lay across the log and the full sleeves of his white shirt were rolled back to the biceps. She gave him the branch and he ran his hand down it.

'Kneel over the log,' he said quietly. Kate stepped out of her boots and dropped trembling to the springy grass. There was a moment of absolute still. No wind in the trees, no animal cries, nothing. She turned her face to the moon, the silence pressing against her ears.

Out of the void there came a sudden wave of euphoria. The fear and uncertainty snuffed out. She was on the threshold of rebirth. He had brought her there, would take her beyond. All that barred her way was this baptism of pain. The realization exploded in Kate. Blood seared red-hot through her veins.

He thrust the rod to her lips and she kissed it. He pushed her over the log so that she came to rest on her forearms on the other side and whipped back the dress to expose the white flesh of her buttocks. With his left foot squarely planted in the middle of her back he unleashed six merciless strokes. Then paused.

Over her quiet groans he said, 'Kate Gurney, you are absolved of your childhood folly, by these strokes I free you.'

He delivered six more stinging blows.

'Denounce all those who have ever harmed you, Kate, damn them to everlasting hellfire!'

'I damn them,' she laughed and sobbed at once. 'Damn them all!'

Through the consuming pain of the last six strokes, she was dimly aware of his voice.

'Tuum nomen sanctificetur,' he intoned. 'Caelis in es qui noster Pater.' The words echoed incomprehensively in her mind. At last he said, 'And now Kate, you are mine.'

An hour later....

Something woke Polly the taproom girl. She surfaced through heavy layers of sleep and lay listening to the sharp pattering against her window. That fool Jabez come alley-catting no doubt. Well she was going to deal with him once and for all. She pulled a woollen shawl around her shoulders and threw back the shutters.

'Go home to your wife, Jabez you old mongrel!' she yelled at the dark figure below. 'Coming here at this ungodly hour.' She went to slam the shutters closed again, but checked. The figure had not moved and as her bleary eyes focused she realized her mistake. 'O-oh, it's you,' she stammered. 'I thought ... Master Sutton, he said you'd paid up and gone.'

'Unfinished business, eh Polly?'

The girl giggled nervously, pulling the shawl tighter round her shoulders. Fond of rough sport was this one. More than that, there was something about him; something she could not fathom, something that frightened, yet intrigued her. Still he rewarded her more than generously.

'Ah,' he concurred, 'an ungodly hour ... I shall leave you to your sleep.' He turned to go.

'No!' Polly urged, fingering the emerald scroll brooch pinned to her shawl. 'Wait, I'm coming down.'

He glanced across the street. The house fronts were ghosted with the shadows of trees and in the moonlight a cat stalked some unseen prey. Polly emerged from a side entrance, a froth of loose curls and billowing cloak. She padded barefoot towards him, the wind parting the cloak to her nakedness beneath.

# Possession ...


Basking in his sleepy warmth, Kate trailed her fingertips over his shoulder muscles and down to the base of his spine. A laugh, soft and wondering gurgled in her throat as she contemplated his nakedness, their nakedness.

Glimpses of the night's events taunted her – disjointed images as in a dream; a watery moon, grave words that had no meaning, and pain – searing, yet welcome. But she had no memory of coming back to the cottage, nor of how she came to be sharing her pallet with him.

She lay quite still, afraid to disturb him, tuning her breathing to the slow rise and fall of his shoulder. The muted light of dawn filtered through knotholes and crevices in the window shutter, outlining the dresser and the pile of fleeces she had stacked in the corner, the discarded clothes draped over the high-backed chair under the window.

*And him.* His presence – the very smell of his skin, dominated the room. It breathed new life into things familiar; into Kate herself. She rolled on to her back and stretched awakening into tingling limbs. A slight stiffness in her thighs and buttocks triggered another glimpse of the night's dream and with it a shiver of exhilaration.

'Are you cold?' he asked, without turning.

Kate released the stretch, startled by his awareness. 'No, not cold ... not now.' She brushed her lips against his shoulder and peered over the tousled dark hair at his sleep-creased profile. Not cold, she reflected, new, reborn, vital – anything but cold.

'You are woman, made new. Virgin soil ready to be planted,' he breathed, his eyes set in an unseeing stare. In one vicious movement he spun into her and trapped her hair against the bolster ticking. 'Take me to you now and I will demand all. Do you hear me Katharine Gurney, witch's bastard? *All.*' With rough hands he kneaded her breasts, the well of her stomach. His dark eyes bore down on her, lips stretched into a thin smile.

'All,' Kate acquiesced. She was fixed in his unrelenting stare, tormented by hands that seemed to burn her flesh. 'I know.'

'Know what?' he demanded, gripping her chin in between his fingers. 'Tell me.'

'That you will own me.'

'Body and soul.'

'Body ... and soul.'

'You will do my bidding in all, as mistress, servant, slave if need be?'

'I vow it.'

'And if you abide by all this, Kate, I shall cast down your enemies and raise you to riches, the like you have never dreamed of.'

'I'll gladly swear my pact on the Book,' she urged, flicking a glance at the dust-laden Bible on the dresser.

'This?' Springing from the pallet, he knocked the book to the floor with a derisive blow. The thud set Jack snuffling and whining outside the door. 'I'll have a binding seal on our pact or none at all.'

He snatched a knife from the pile of clothes on the chair and rubbed his thumb across the keen blade. Gripping her wrist, he swung her up to kneel on the blankets. Then holding the blade upright between them, he pulled her tight against him, trapping the sharp edges between his chest and her heaving breasts.

'There will be no turning back,' he growled.

'I know,' she answered hoarsely.

'Ah,' he smiled slowly, circling his arms around her trembling shoulders, 'I think you do.' Their mouths locked in a savage, biting kiss. Then he jerked her shoulders forwards.

Kate collapsed breathlessly to the bed, lightheaded with new sensation. She reached up to touch the oozing gash on his chest, tasted the blood – warm on her fingers. Strength welled within her; strength and confidence. Clasping his head between her bloodied hands she drew him down to her own fresh wound.

His voice, strangely far off, whispered her name over and over again. His tongue caressed and cleaned the cut. Bloodied lips and chin came up to her neck forcing her head back. Hands trembling with restrained power, explored breasts and inner thighs. Fiery pangs shot through her loins, her ribs, even her neck. A strange numbness crept up the base of her skull and Kate's parched senses quivered with expectation. But just as she reached the brink of this new sensuality, when she feared she must explode, he pulled away from her.

Confused, she searched his face. His eyes, concealed beneath closed lids flicked once, then stayed quite still. His lips, slightly apart and streaked with blood, sank towards each other, as though he were drifting asleep.

Trembling, Kate clawed her fingers past his chest wound, down to the dark hair of his lower abdomen. She saw the eyelids snap open, met with defiance the wildness in his eyes and laughed as he seized her shoulders, not caring that his fingernails bit into her soft flesh, that his teeth gnawed at her neck, throttling the laugh out of her. Then a tumble of arms and legs, his weight bearing down on her, a rushing like waves crashing on rocks and cries, very much like her own, as the waves lapped over her head, drowning her.

Afterwards, lying in the crook of her arm, she snatched greedy breaths until the weakness in her shaking limbs gradually subsided. He lay quietly staring into the shadows of the ceiling timbers, his rage spent. From outside the latched door came Jack's soft howling.

'He knows I must up and tend the ewes,' she said at last. When he did not reply she swung her legs to the floor and padded barefoot across to the window, flinging back the shutters.

'The dog grudges you a lover,' he said, sitting up to study her. She was staring across the ridge and furrow grassland to the wooded hillside where she had first met him. Her elbows rested on the uneven windowsill, fingers linked, her chin resting pensively on her thumbs.

'I know Jack better than that,' she said, smiling softly at the half-reclined figure on the bed. 'Not you though ... for all I've tried to *see* you. You're just not there. A name would do ... anything.'

'What use is a name?'

'Something to call you by, at least.'

'No need for titles, no given names. *Feel me,* woman. Sense me. You are part of me now.' The intensity of his words compelled her to turn and face him. She moved towards his outstretched hand and knelt beside the pallet, obeying his wordless command. She forced her head into hands that gently massaged her neck and temples, and brushed her lips against his thick wrists. His eyes, dark and unswerving, lured her thoughts from everyday concerns. New folds, fresh grazing, hooves and fleece to be checked – all this drifted from her mind as his voice, like gentle waves breaking on shingle, filled her head.

'Feel the strength in me, Kate. You are an empty vessel. Take me into you. Feel the fire of my strength in your shoulders ... your arms ... the tips of your fingers and toes. Know me. For good or evil, I am your master.'

He seized a handful of her hair and flung her so hard that her skull banged against the floorboards. Kate choked with pain and tried to lift herself up but was forced down to her knees under his weight. The second coupling was as unexpected as it was savage. A hand clamped her screaming mouth, another clawed at her hanging breasts. Kate's nails splintered the wooden floor. She felt herself drowning in a frenzied, stormy sea. Overwhelmed by pain and nausea, gasping for air – for life itself, the room, the floorboards swam out of focus....

*The morning light suddenly gave way to silvery moonlight. Above her head was a canopy of leaves. Below her she saw a young woman; eyes bulging with terror, her mouth twisted into a soundless scream, spread-eagled half-naked in the undergrowth....*

It was a fleeting vision – no more than a glimpse, but the horror of it stretched the moment. Then, at last, reality thrust itself back upon her consciousness. The room rushed back at her. And he now lay heavily on her doubled body, impassioned groans stuttering in his throat.

'Where were you?' he rasped, throwing himself off her at last. Kate bit her bottom lip to stop it trembling and rolled on to her side, hugging her knees. Her eyes followed him from the window where he had filled his lungs with air, to the chair where his clothes lay. 'Well?' he demanded, buttoning his shirt.

The image of the girl in the wood was still vivid in Kate's mind. Her brain reeled with it. 'I – I'm not sure ... *trees ... a girl.*'

His fingers ceased buttoning. In one easy movement he lifted her on to the edge of the bed and roughly pushed the hair from her eyes.

'What of this girl?' His eyes shone with interest.

Kate shook her head. 'She was so afraid.'

'Of what?'

'I don't know,' she whispered, with a shiver. He scrutinized her for several seconds, then turned away to finish dressing. Kate eased her cramped legs down to the floor. Her shift and woollen stockings lay in a crumpled heap by the chair. She pulled them on, taking deep breaths to ease a wave of nausea.

'Did you know this girl?' he asked, casually straightening his cuffs. Kate knelt down by the door and rummaged through the contents of a chest under fleeces stacked in the corner.

'There was death in her face,' she said, staring distractedly into the chest. 'Poor wretch, she was out of her wits.'

'Did you know her?' he repeated dryly.

Kate shook her head, 'No, I didn't.' She pulled a beige day dress from the chest and shook out the folds before stepping into it.

'These visions,' he said, lacing the back of her bodice for her, 'do they come to you often?'

'They come when they will,' she answered softly. 'Sometimes three in a week, sometimes none for a year. Mind, I rarely understand what I see. Only now and again, a face I know, or maybe a place.'

'Like Blackwood Top?' he remarked.

Kate lay her head back against his chest and sighed, 'Yes.'

'You are no longer alone with your gift, Kate. From this hour forth you will tell me everything you see. Withhold the most trivial of details and I shall know, believe me.' With peculiar tenderness, he folded her into his arms and pressed his cheek against her uncombed hair. 'Strength comes out of pain, Kate ... remember that.' He exhaled warm breath into her hair. 'And you are rare among women, or I would not have chosen you.' He tilted her face up and stared steadily into her searching eyes. 'But you know that, don't you?'

Kate gave a ragged sigh. 'Stay with me.'

'You have your flock to tend – even the dog knows that, listen to his whining. And I have matters of my own to attend to.' He moved to unlatch the door.

'When will you come back?' she urged, recalling his prolonged absence after their first meeting, with dread. 'There's room enough for us both here....'

'Be strong, Kate. If I stayed under your roof, how long before tongues began to wag? Secrecy is a powerful ally,' he said deliberately. 'I shall come to you soon enough. Come-' he said, back-handing boisterous Jack aside and guiding her along the shady landing to the narrow stairs, 'it is many hours since  last ate.'

Kate scraped what little she had from the larder; bread, some butter and fat bacon, a jug of frothy ale from the cask. They breakfasted in silence at a small table by the range, Jack forcing his head ingratiatingly against Kate's legs.

After he had eaten the best part of a loaf and swallowed the last drop of beer, he sighed and leaned back in his chair. Wiping his greasy fingers on a towel she had brought to him, he asked, 'What do you know of Samuel Grafton?'

'That he is the eldest son of Sir Hilary Grafton,' she offered. 'They say the old man is a bit touched in the head these days. Spends most of his time locked in his London house, or taking the waters at Bath.' She added ruefully, 'Master Samuel runs this estate now.'

'The old man, Sir Hilary, wasn't he the justice who condemned your mother?' He cast her a sideways glance.

Kate pushed her plate away and wiped her mouth clean. 'Yes,' she said, meeting his gaze, 'he was one of them.' She snorted ironically.

'What of the son?' he demanded.

'Samuel's bailiff rode up here a month back. Tom Clarke, tipped chin and starched collar these days he is, doing his master's dirty work. No more than a ragged-arsed bully when we sat in the parson's schoolroom together.' She laughed scornfully. '*Master* Samuel thinks three shillings an acre a meagre enough return on this land. He'll have another shilling or come autumn I'll be out.'

'Knowing that you can't afford to pay,' he observed, drumming the table with his nails. 'So, have you contested the new rent?'

Kate shook her head dolefully. 'What good would have come of it? Besides, there was little enough time to go traipsing up to the guildhall during shearing. Samuel Grafton is set on selling this land. That one has more than his share of gambling debts. Clarke made no bones about it, I am a thorn in Samuel's side, he said, *Devil take him.'*

He leaned back in his chair, fists clenched and pressed together. After a moment his stern features stretched into a grim smile and he said quietly, 'Yes, indeed.'

*He* stood, the only quiet figure, in a cursing, swearing crowd, drawn to the cockpit behind the Buck and Bowstring by a series of bills advertising the event. He surveyed the assembly of gamblers critically. It was the usual motley gathering of work-soiled craftsmen, grubby apprentices, a smattering of gentry trading their midday repast for a taste of blood. Bets had been laid and recorded on slate in chalky scrawl. Bodies were surging, all eyes fixed on the trestle table below, where the one-eyed black champion was painting crimson streaks across the throat of his speckled opponent.

'Gritty old bugger, I'll say that much for him,' hissed a voice close to his ear. 'Though I dare say you've put your crown on Black Jack, eh?'

He shot the companionable punter a cursory glance, taking in the Grafton livery and crooked grin, then returned to the warring cocks. 'I'll wager you never backed a dunghill brood, gritty or not.'

The punter snorted agreeably. 'Not me–'

The clamour of the crowd rose to fever pitch. Amid a fluster of downy feathers, Black Jack – straddled across the speckled's still darting head – his razor-sharp bill plunging and tearing, was spraying ring-siders with blood. Black Jack caught and bagged, was declared the victor. The crowd roared its satisfaction.

'Black-hearted demon,' spat the punter, rubbing his hands gleefully. 'Well,' he sighed, pulling on his gloves, 'no rest for the wicked. Messages to be delivered, horses to be fed. Just have to collect my winnings next time.'

'A shilling says you can't secure us a table and a pot of ale at the Buck before that fair establishment is overrun,' he said with a wry smile.

The punter checked, pulled off his gloves and winked. 'That, sir, is a fair wager.'

# The Familiar ...

In the amber light of a September evening, Samuel Grafton's groom rode over to Kate's smallholding. Finding the cottage empty, he remounted and went in search of the folds. Beyond the copse and across the brook to Kingsmead, according to the gentleman's directions.

Emerging from the copse, he coaxed his horse up a sharp hillside to the hurdle enclosure on higher ground. The nearest ewes eyed his approach with suspicion, before bolting from the edge of the fold. Kate, who was securing the gate hurdle on the far side of the fold, looked up.

'Are you Mistress Gurney?' he called, skirting the enclosure.

Kate shielded her eyes against the last of the sun's light. 'I am,' she said sharply. 'Who wants me at this late hour?'

He reined his horse in close to her and, with obvious reluctance, removed his hat and dismounted. The witch's brat, they called her – tarred, it was said, with the same brush as her mother. He had imagined her to be one of those malicious looking hags he had seen in the pamphlets. It confused him to find that she was a comely enough wench with no aversion to staring him straight in the eye.

Though he had been working as a stable lad in another county at the time of the execution of Elizabeth Gurney, the details of her crime had reached him. It had kept tongues wagging for weeks; how she had put the Evil Eye on a merchant called Laurence Tyler because he had gone to another weaver for the cloth which she had previously supplied. They said that she had fashioned an image of him; that she had put the effigy in a glove stolen from Tyler and having burnt the lot in the kitchen grate, fed the ashes to her sow. Shortly after, Tyler had died of a raging fever. He shuddered mentally. Given a choice he would not have come within a mile of this place or this woman.

'William Kerry, head-groom to the Grafton family ...' he grunted, adding hastily, 'though it's not as such I've come here.'

'What is your business then, William Kerry?' she prompted impatiently. She scolded Jack who sat, hackles raised and growling, between his mistress and the stranger.

'I was told that you had a way with ailing creatures. A gentleman I met at the pit, name of Marsden, recommended you.'

'Marsden?' she queried. 'I know no-one of that name-'

He cleared his throat uncomfortably. 'This gentleman said you had common blood.'

Suddenly she understood. *The knife, the crushing embrace.* It was him, she knew it had to be him. And now there was a name. Marsden.

Kerry backed away.

'Wait,' she said quickly, 'I must be weary to have forgotten kinsman Marsden. That's who it will be. Sent you here, did he?'

He nodded stiffly. 'Be obliged if you'd come up to the manor to cast an eye over the master's horse,' he grunted. 'There's a half-crown in it for you.'

'If it's lame you'd better fetch the horse-surgeon,' she said doubtfully.

'He's away in London, same as Master Samuel and his family,' he grunted. 'Now, will you come or not?'

Kate shrugged. 'It's a long walk up to Apescross.'

William Kerry folded his hands across the pommel of his saddle and sighed. It had gone against his better judgement to come at all. Comely she might be, but she still sent a shiver up his spine and now he was forced to share a saddle with the woman. Why he had ridden the master's favourite hunter back from the Buck, sotted with ale, he would never know. Ridden it half to death, he had, and in the dark. Next morning he had come to on a bale of straw next to Prince Rupert, cannon fire in his head, the Prince's hoof swollen obscenely. None of the usual poultices had worked and now the wretched horse had gone off his fodder. It could not have gone worse what with the family expected back from London any day.

He watched irritably as she threw a woollen shawl around her shoulders and fastened it in her belt. Then pulled himself into the saddle and stretched out his hand to lift her up behind.

Later, while Kerry went in search of a lantern, Kate stood alone in the stableyard, gazing up at the reflected glow of the setting sun in the window glass of Apescross Manor. The air was still save for the restive whinnying of the horses and from somewhere in the house, the sound of a girl's laughter.

More than once during the journey, she had been on the verge of asking Kerry to take her back to the cottage. What earthly use was it her looking at a valuable horse? All she knew was sheep. To attempt a cure was to take responsibility for the animal. And it would surely have to be in a bad way for the groom to have resorted to seeking help from her.

But as she stood in the cobbled yard, she felt calm again. *He* had suggested she come. That was enough.

As she gazed, the reflection from a window on the second floor of the house vanished. In the dark opening she could just make out the outline of a person standing at the window.

'What are you doing there?' It was the voice of a young woman, by her demanding tone, a lady of the house.

Kate stayed quite still. Kerry had sworn her to secrecy, now this woman threatened to alert the whole household.

The question was repeated, this time with indignation. Somewhere a dog began to bark. Kate guessed there were twenty paces between her and the stableyard gate. She tensed herself, ready for flight then, to her relief, Kerry rushed back with the lantern and hurried her towards the Prince's stable.

'Ah-ha!' exclaimed the voice from the house. 'So, Will has a sweetheart.' Chuckles echoed around the yard. Kerry swore under his breath. He bundled Kate inside, then turned to scan the shadowy building. 'Beware the clap,' hissed the voice.

'I will if you will, Miss Barbara,' he muttered. With exaggerated movements he pressed a finger to his lips and bowed away into the stable. Once inside, he pointed Kate towards the injured animal, then threw the bolt.

Kate found the Prince lying listlessly in the corner of the stable furthest from the door. He was a well-proportioned horse, but his chestnut coat glistened with sweat in the lamp-light and his breath came in harsh snorts. A poultice had been strapped to the pastern of his swollen right front leg, giving it the appearance of a large white boot. She touched it gently and the horse twitched away with a snort of protest.

Instructing Kerry to hold him, she quickly cut away the poultice and inspected the swollen flesh and hoof. The inner hoof had become convex with swelling and was very painful to the touch. Holding the lantern directly over the upturned hoof, she pored over it until she came to a small irregularity; a tiny pit in the throbbing surface. Without once taking her eyes off the tiny incurve, she lowered the lantern until Prince could bear its heat no closer. Though the tissue had swollen almost completely over it, she noticed a minute flicker in the hole; a reflection of the lamp-light as she moved it back and forth.

'There's something bedded in the hoof,' she murmured. 'It will have to come out before it festers.'

The groom wiped his brow and nodded.

She said briskly, 'I'll need pincers, hot water and another pair of hands to hold him.'

She watched him go, then exhausted, too tired even to stand, eased herself down between Prince and the stable wall, and yielded to sleep.

Minutes later, she was jolted awake by footsteps and a voice with a familiar lilt.

'A gambling man like you, Will?' said the newcomer, with a derisory laugh. 'Come, let the woman do her bit, what harm can come of it?'

Kate scrambled to her feet and stared at the starched white collar and the stylish cut of his black coat. 'Kinsman Marsden,' she said, dry-mouthed.

'Ah, Mistress Gurney,' he greeted expansively. 'Come, show Master Kerry here that you can mend this poor creature. I've a crown resting on it.' He raised an eyebrow expectantly, and began to unbutton his coat.

Swallowing hard, Kate pulled the shepherding knife and a small, flat tin from her pocket. She flicked the tin open and ground the blade against the worn oilstone inside, using extra force to steady her shaking hands.

Her thoughts raced. How did he come to be at the manor? That very morning he had taxed her about the Graftons as though he knew nothing about the family.

Dragging her mind back to the horse, she swilled the sharpened knife in the bowl of scalding water Kerry had brought. Then, as steadily as she could, she pared the tough flesh away from the incurve until the shiny tip of the hard object within, was well exposed.

The groom held the hind quarters, worry etched into his features. His livelihood she knew, depended on the survival of the horse.

She had her back to Marsden, who held the head, but she was keenly aware of his soft whispering and the effect this seemed to have on Prince.

The squealing, writhing horse had become quiet as a lamb; had not stirred, even when she cut into the inflamed flesh. She turned, fearing that fever had reached the brain, rendering the horse senseless. Instead she found him quite alert and relaxed under Marsden's manipulative fingers.

Easing the pincers around the shiny head she clamped them tight and pulled firmly. Prince gasped and Kerry pressed himself across the trembling flanks to prevent sudden movement.

Kate's eyes widened as a metal spike, the length of her thumb joint, emerged. Laying it aside, she applied thumb pressure to the open wound and cleaned away the blood and puss that oozed from it. Then smeared on it a layer of green ointment; a concoction she always carried against foot rot in the ewes.

'To stop it festering,' she said in answer to a quizzical stare from Kerry. 'Tomorrow I'll bathe it with feverfew to bring down the swelling.'

The groom picked up the spike and stared at it. 'First thing I looked for,' he said, shaking his head. 'Even had Smithy Cobshaw's lad come look at it. I'd have wagered there was nothing stuck in there.' Running his hand over the horse's side he scrutinized Kate for several seconds, then sighed. 'Ah well, if it has done the trick–'

Marsden snorted. 'I didn't take you for a churl,' he said ironically. 'I daresay Mistress Gurney has keener eyes than you.'

'Ah,' the groom agreed grudgingly, 'that may be.' He gave the horse an affectionate slap, then threw a blanket over it.

Marsden glanced at Kate, his eyes intensely conspiratorial. It was a look of deep familiarity and infinite knowing that warmed and filled her with longing. Then it passed and a sideways flick of his eyes commanded her to leave.

She washed her hands in what water remained and began to gather her things. She was pushing tins and knife into her pocket when the stable door was flung back. A young woman, tightly clutching a scarlet cloak around her, picked her way across the straw. The flame in her lamp guttered as she moved towards them.

'So,' cried the young woman, staring wide-eyed at Kate, 'this is where you've disappeared to, Marsden.'

Kate looked at the dark ringlets and powdered cheeks. For all the paint it was a young face – no more than a girl. Too young to address *him* so carelessly, to shout taunts at a groom from a second-storey window. From Kerry's earlier grumblings she supposed that this was Barbara Canard. Perhaps, after all, the tales she had heard about Grafton's niece and ward, were not unfounded. Kate looked from the girl to Marsden, who was buttoning his coat with an affable smile.

'Needed a pair of strong shoulders, miss,' explained Kerry, rubbing his hand across the Prince's shivering flank. 'The old boy was in a sorry way, weren't you my old beauty?'

'What business does she have here?' demanded the girl, casting Kate a withering glance. 'Aunt Henrietta won't be at all pleased to know that her guest had sloped off to some *ménage-à-trois.*'

Marsden snorted a laugh and folded his arm around Barbara's shoulders. Kate alone saw the momentary flicker of his eyes – a dark shadow corrupting his genial features. A suggestion of moonlit woods and soundless terror.

He paused in the stable doorway and glanced from Kate to the groom. 'Worth a crown of any man's money, eh Kerry?' He laughed and Barbara laughed with him, her eyes glazed with triumph. Kate turned away, her face burning with humiliation, and finished pushing her things into her pocket.

She heard the door swing idly shut and when Kerry asked if she would come again tomorrow, she could only bring herself to grunt a reply. Her attention was with the whispering beyond the flapping door, with the contempt in Barbara's gurgling laughter as she and Marsden went off together towards the house.

Why, Kate cursed herself, why had she not realized it before? *Starched collar ... tailored coat ... cultivated air;* he belonged to the world of Barbara Canard. She did not. He had mastered her, had claimed her, but he would never belong to her as she did to him.

She waited until their voices faded away, then slipped quietly across the cobbles and away into the night.

He did not come to her that night.

Next morning, the sun rose behind a blanket of louring cloud. Rain lashed her face and flattened Jack's fur against his wiry body as they stumbled up to check the ewes. Kate saw the trampled hurdle gate, even before Jack bounded towards it. She braced herself against a rainy gust, pressing her crook hard into the wet grass, and scanned the hillside.

A dozen or more ewes were sheltering up against the sides of the fold. She could only hope that the others had the sense to take to the copse and had not wandered on to her neighbour's land. After a sleepless night, the thought of another confrontation with Tom Clarke was more than she could bear.

She lifted the broken gate from the muddy grass and tied it in place. The sky was an unrelenting grey; no sign of a break. And as she climbed back down to the copse, thunder rumbled across the hills.

It was past noon before she reached Apescross. She had eventually found the ewes, scattered around the small wood. Many of them were caught in brambles. Three, she found stuck fast in the mud at the edge of the pond, bemoaning their luck. With the aid of Jack's strict marshalling though, she had finally driven them all back to the fold and secured the gate with new posts.

She had stopped off at the cottage only to make an infusion of freshly picked feverfew. Then with a change of boots and stockings she set off on the Kingeswood low road.

The sun had at last broken through the cloud and Kate stopped to trace the arcs of a double rainbow. The vivid spectrum of colour weakened into spectral transparency and vanished into the yellow gorse on the next hill. The sight of Jack tearing up the hillside and bursting through the coloured bands, urged her on again.

When she reached the stableyard it was busy with men and horses. The Grafton coach, its gleaming black paintwork and crest spattered with wet mud stood inside the arched gateway. A liveried footman leaned against the kitchen door, indolently scraping his boots as he watched the grooms coaxing the horses away to their different stables. And through it all ran four noisy children, three girls and a boy, still wearing their travelling cloaks.

Hoping she might complete her business and be gone before her presence was noticed, Kate pulled Jack in close to her and skirted the yard, past the mildly curious footman, towards Prince Rupert's stable. She was just passing the wrought-iron gateway before the stable she wanted, when a harassed matron flew through the opening knocking the bottle of ointment out of her hands.

'Good gracious!' declared the woman, straightening her mob-cap. 'What on earth?' She shook her head at Kate, then chased after one of the noisy children. Kate knelt down to retrieve the bottle, relieved to find that the thick green glass had weathered the impact. As she stood up, Kerry emerged from the stable. She moved towards the groom but a frantic gesture from him made her hold back. Just then Samuel Grafton, his features locked in a censorious scowl, marched out after Kerry.

'That horse had better make a full recovery,' she heard him say. Kerry cracked his face with a semblance of confidence and uttered an assurance. His master dug his hands into his coat pockets, his lower lip clapped firmly over the upper and stared intently at an indeterminate point in the sky. 'Mark my word, Kerry,' he growled, 'I shall check your story with this ...'

'Marsden,' swallowed the groom.

'Yes,' pondered Grafton, 'Marsden.'

Kate waited for the master of Apescross to move away, then slipped into the stable after Kerry. She was pleased to find the Prince up on his feet, limping around.

Kerry held the door shut against unwelcome visitors and snapped, 'Where were you this morning, eh?'

Kate had coaxed the Prince into giving her his injured foot. Ignoring the tetchy question, she uncorked the bottle and poured the soothing yellow infusion over the swollen hoof, then sealed it with another layer of green ointment and bandaged up to the fetlock. Kerry held the horse while she eased an open-ended horn in between the Prince's side teeth and poured the rest of the infusion into his mouth.

The horse showered her with disdainful splutters. 'Tastes like mouldering mangel-wurzel, don't it lad?' she laughed. The groom smelled the empty bottle and scowled.

'Filthy stuff ,' he said, spitting into the straw. 'How a gentleman like Marsden came to mix with the likes of–'

'Half a crown, you said,' Kate cut in coldly.

Kerry tilted his head insolently. 'Worth a half-crown of any man's money?' he mimicked, with a suggestive glance towards the far corner.

'I don't suppose Master Grafton would favour witch medicine,' she said, her eyes narrowing, ''specially where his favourite hunter's concerned.' She held out her hand. Kerry stared at it for a moment, then ruefully dug into the pocket of his breeches.

'What I want to know,' he grunted, flicking the coin into her upturned palm, 'is how that spike came to be in there. These eyes are as keen as the next man's.'

Kate closed her fingers over the coin and gave him a knowing smile. 'You know well enough, William Kerry.'

'Ah–' he began, but an uproar outside in the stableyard cut him short. There had been a piercing squeal – a child's cry of alarm – then a surge of angry voices and a yelping, barking dog. *A dog.*

Kate spun round. The stable door was ajar and Jack was gone from beside the brick pillar where she had left him. She flew outside, just in time to see Jack's black and white body weave through a knot of shouting children towards the wrought-iron gate. She screamed his name but he was too intent on escape to hear.

Behind him rushed a mob. The Grafton children had been joined by stable lads and some of the fitter grooms. Clenched fists, stones, brooms, even a hay-fork converged on the fleeing dog.

Kate attempted to reach the partially open gate before the others but was overtaken and shoved aside. She screamed at Jack to get through. He heard her voice and turned. Then an unseen hand slammed the gate shut from the outside.

And he was trapped.

With the first pained yelp, Kate's panic turned to fury. She burrowed into his assailants, throwing the smaller ones aside, wrestling with the men until they too were behind her, She found Jack, pinned against the iron scrolls of the gate, a huddled, slavering mass of bared teeth and hurt.

'Get away from him!' she shouted, turning on the startled faces behind her. The furore had drawn many more servants from the house. They pressed around her, demanding to know what was happening.

'That cur,' exclaimed the footman, quitting his vigil by the kitchen door, 'savaged Miss Caroline! See–' He lifted one of the Grafton children into his arms and moved into the space between Kate and the indignant crowd. At a whispered cue from the footman, seven-year-old Caroline pulled back the sleeve of her travelling coat. Across the chubby arm were three raised weals. There were murmurs of, *'Shame!'* and the girl promptly burst into pitiful sobs. The footman rested his case. He stepped aside. The others pressed in on Kate. Behind her, Jack growled protectively.

She winced as a small foot kicked out viciously at her ankle, and shook herself free of hands that would have pulled her clear of Jack.

'You dare lay another finger on me or my dog,' she hissed. 'I'm sorry the little girl was hurt. But you can all see it's no more than a playful scratch!'

She was answered with snorts of derision. Then the cry went up, 'Do you hear that? The Gurney woman threatened us!'

'Witch's bastard!' screamed another.

'Her dog did this,' added the footman.

Kate knew they were beyond reason. That she had to make her move now. She turned to scoop Jack into her arms and came face to face with Barbara Canard, smiling at her through the iron railings. She knew at once whose hand had closed the gate, barring Jack's escape. Who, even now, stood between her and the open fields.

'You are no more his kinswoman than I am,' Grafton's niece taunted. She clamped her hand down on the gate-latch and raised an eyebrow towards the house. 'He is up there, watching all this.'

Kate resisted the urge to turn and look towards the house. She forced the latch through Barbara's tenacious fingers and with Jack drooping under her left arm, threw herself through the gate. Sharp nails raked her free arm as Barbara attempted to stop her. Kate swung the arm at her opponent. Barbara gave a startled cry and staggered backwards into a bush of overblown yellow roses. Kate ran.

Skirting the slower cobbles, she burst through a gap in the shrubbery lining the path and fled towards the open grazing land beyond the next hedge.

For a moment the only sound was her own rasping breath. Then came the angry shouts of pursuers. She forced her aching legs across the open pasture, jolting Jack as she leapt thistles and dung. When, at last, she reached the cover of Kingeswood, the pursuers had thinned to a single panting voice.

Too winded to go on, she set Jack down. As the dog limped smartly on ahead, she snatched up a stout stick and waited in the shadow of a twisted oak.

The footman did not see what hit him in the shady wood. He remembered chasing the woman and her dog. After that, nothing, until he found himself face down on a carpet of damp oak leaves.

That evening....

William Kerry woke to find himself lying in the crook of a sycamore tree. Above, the sky – clustered with flickering stars – clung to a bright harvest moon.

With a shiver, he rolled himself out of the tree and winced as his bare feet collapsed the sharp wheat stubble underfoot.

A few pots of ale with Marsden, that much he did recall. Then a shot of rum – or two. He clutched his aching, wondering head and stared through the tree cleft, across the shorn field dotted with stooks. Then he saw the Gurney woman.

He shook his head in disbelief.

She was wandering through the stubble, completely naked. Her feet seemed to glide through the sharp stalks as if it were a carpet of down. The white glow of her skin emphasized the darkness of nipples and vaginal hair. And she was surrounded by a fiery aura, from bare feet to her long hair.

Kerry clung to the tree, and swallowed hard as she stopped by the bundles of sheaves closest to him. He heard her murmur as though to an unseen companion. Watched as she first stooped, then stretched herself out in the close-cropped straw.

Kerry's head tightened lightheadedly. His eyes blurred. Then as his focus returned, he saw her reclined body rise a foot above the stubble. He drew breath sharply.

'You want her don't you?' said a low voice, over his shoulder. Kerry jerked round, wide-eyed with terror.

Marsden clapped a hand over his open mouth, and coaxed him back round. 'Don't you?'

Kerry stared at the figure by the stook. She was back on the stubble again, her hips moving gently towards him and away. He watched, mesmerized by the swollen breasts and slightly parted thighs more than wanting.

He felt a dull moan at the base of his skull and through the pain in his head, a voice that urged, 'Take her.'

William Kerry emerged from the shelter of the tree, unaware of the sharp stubble under his bare feet.

# Part 2: Aer

# Gifts...

*'T'is more than a body can fathom, Grafton suffering her to stay on up there, what with that creature of hers savaging his little one.'*

*'Cured his horse, they say.'*

*'Some witchery, to be sure.'*

*'They say Marsden took her part – has the master's ear that one.'*

*'A gentleman of good intent, no doubt. Easy pickings for one such as her.'*

*'Claims kinship, she does, distant cos or some such.'*

*'Her sins will find her out.'*

*'They will.'*

*'T'is that feckless lad I fret for; alone up there with her.'*

*'May the Lord keep him from taint.'*

*... whispered the tongues.*

A lazy January wind carried the peals of Sabbath bells up to the cottage. Kate glanced up from the lumbering ewes, heavy with lamb, at the heavy evening sky and stood up to stretch her aching back.

All the pens inside and adjoining the crumbling outbuildings were full; ewes and singles, ewes with twins, two sets of triplets and a ewe that had lost her lamb – full of redundant milk, bellowing above her sisters.

Where she stood, a handful of expectant mothers jostled around the trough for crushed nuts and hay. All except one, a shearling, which paced restlessly round the fold, pausing only to paw the damp grass. Kate noted the sagging abdomen. This one was for the lambing pen.

It was a sapping business; the fetching, the carrying, the birthing, the suckling; sleep snatched in a draughty barn; food taken on the wing – if she was lucky. Time stretched, time condensed, time meaningless, save for the anchoring chime of far-off bells. And overhead, the sky poised to throw down its blanket of snow. Kate was weary fit to drop, yet she smiled.

She had not hoped to see this lambing; had all but sold the flock the week before the Michaelmas rents fell due. And then he had come to her.

There had been no rest that night either. He had met her misery with gentle coaxing, bullied her from hopeless resignation. He had lifted her far beyond fear of mortal things to a plane of sensual euphoria that lingered for days afterwards. His coming snuffed the rankling jealousy she felt about him and Barbara Canard. He had shielded her from the wrath of Caroline's father and at his leaving he had given her the brooch.

'Have it valued in Bristol,' he had instructed, as she stared at glowing emeralds worked into gold scroll. 'Take the best price you can. What use a shepherd without sheep?'

Next morning he had sent out the boy Ned to her, to tend the ewes while she made the ten-mile trip to Bristol. She had gone to the teeming city; had wrangled with one silversmith after another and taken the best price. But not for the brooch.

In this she disobeyed him, much as she feared his anger. She could not bring herself to part with so beautiful an object; the only thing she had of him. And so, what the silversmiths pored over with their eye lenses was her only other treasure – a chased silver larum watch, the only thing left of her mother.

The enamel-faced watch was her only clue as to who, or what her father might have been. The watch ... the brooch. What was gone ... what he had liberated her from ... what was and might still be. She kept the brooch; sewed it into the hem of her shift and had only to touch the bulge of it under her clothes to feel again the keening vitality his presence brought, to quell her impatience for his next unpredictable night visit.

All her life she had been imprisoned by the need to persuade others that she was not like her mother. Parson Ellson had instilled the need. She had danced to his tune, in a vain quest for acceptance. Then Marsden had come and made her realize that the villagers' scorn was in truth a mask for fear, for awe. The knowledge had given her the confidence to meet the stares of the people at market with amusement. She relished the quickly averted eyes, the unnerved glances, and grudging respect they now paid her. The strength he had promised her had come to pass. She was strong, and free, and more than happy to tackle the rigours of another lambing.

A chilly blast shook the folds, drowning for a moment the blaring of the ewes. Then snowflakes filled the air, stinging Kate into action. She bellowed for the boy then, with Jack's help, separated the agitated shearling from the others and took it through to a half-covered lambing fold between the cottage and the outbuildings.

Jack coaxed the young ewe under the thatch. Kate scrambled under with them and after several bids, managed to turn the distressed ewe on to the bed of straw.

'T'is snowing,' grunted the boy, staggering bleary-eyed in beside her. 'I'm chilled to the bone.'

She glanced at the blue knuckles and bloodless fingers, snatched up a hessian sack lying in a corner of the fold, cut holes for his head and arms and sent him off to fetch a lamp and more lambing oil from beside the kitchen fire.

When he came back, slopping oil over the sides of the kettle he carried, she cupped her hands around the warm vessel and said, 'Pour some over my hands and arms, like I showed you Ned.'

'This 'un ready?' asked the boy, squatting beside the panting shearling. Kate gave him a wry smile. Ned was slow-witted, in many ways much younger than his dozen years but she was glad of his young legs and his child-like interest in the work. When old Will Tunnicliffe had been struck down by palsy last harvest, she had despaired of finding a pair of willing hands.

Ned had come to her raw and suspicious, but not afraid. He was as much a misfit as she, it seemed. His innkeeper master had been more than willing to rid himself of the gaupus potboy with an irritating stammer – even to the Gurney woman.

Curing the stammer had been as easy as curing a wart. She had lured it from him with subtle doses of kindness and patience. And when the boy realized that a beating did not lurk around the next corner, confidence did the work for her. In return, Ned worked willingly, was her daily companion, and her ear to the village gossip.

'Won't she do it by herself?' yawned Ned. Kate murmured to the contrary, sensing the struggle the inexperienced ewe was having. There was quickening but no sign of a birth yet.

Dipping her hand into the oil again, she eased her way carefully into the uterus. She probed the tangle of shoulders and legs, until she found the heads.

'Three,' she gasped. 'Ned, bring the lantern, quickly!'

She worked her hand round to the first head, down over the shoulders to a leg, lying beside the chin. She stopped as the ewe strained, murmuring reassurances until the muscles relaxed again. Then she stretched her aching shoulder and gently moved her bruised knuckles in search of the other foreleg. There was no turning back now, she knew. If she withdrew without the lamb, the ewe would swell and four lives would be lost.

'Hold the lantern steady,' she croaked, as Ned craned eagerly over her. The ewe kicked nervously as Jack snarled at the gusting snow. Kate snapped at the dog to get out.

She found the neck ... then hooves. The ewe pushed again. 'Soon now girl,' she soothed. Cupping the head in her palm, she drew on the neck and legs, easing the lamb along a curved path to birth. A moment later, the first glistening lamb slithered on to the straw. Ned lurched forward to rub the limp body with hay, then with trembling fingers and a clean wisp of straw, gently cleared the nostrils of mucus. The lamb's first sneeze and snatched breaths were his reward. Beaming, he laid it beside the mother's nose.

The remaining two lambs came in quick succession.

'Not this one Ned,' said Kate, wrapping the last in a rag and pushing it inside her coat. 'She'll not miss this one. See to it the teats aren't choked, then put those two to suckle.' She snatched on her hood, listening to Jack's muted barks between snowy gusts.

'Where you taking little 'un?' ventured Ned, but his words were drowned by the blizzard.

Keeping her head down and clutching the crying bundle, Kate ran towards the barn. Jack intercepted her, barking agitatedly and straining towards the dip. She stopped, squinted her eyes through the dense whiteness and saw a dark irregularity in the outline of the chaffinch hedge. No more than that but she knew, as Jack knew, who it was standing out there.

Skinning the dead lamb was the work of a few minutes, even with painfully cold fingers. She cut holes in the skin, unwrapped her bundle and slipped the live lamb into his new coat. The dead lamb's mother stopped blaring and backed suspiciously away from the surrogate.

Ned rushed in, coughing noisily and showering Kate with snow. He stared wide-eyed as the ewe dropped her head and pawed the ground close to the stumbling lamb.

'Go gentle,' Kate whispered, as the lamb struggled towards the hanging teats. The ewe bleated indignantly and knocked the lamb aside. The little one tried again but the adamant ewe lifted a hoof threateningly. Kate held Ned back, calling Jack to her side. The dog knew what was expected. He skirted the pen, hackled raised. The ewe's instincts took over and before Jack had completed a second circuit, the lamb was snug under the belly of its adoptive mother.

Instructing Ned to tend to their needs, before retiring to his pallet, she dropped the dead lamb's remains in the lime pit behind the outbuildings, drove the last four expectant ewes from the snow into the shelter of the barn, and only then made for chaffinch hedge.

The snow drove straight at her, whipping back the hood a dozen times before she finally let it hang. Blowing on her hands, she began to run down into the dip, every step sending painful shudders through her swollen feet. She met the incline on her hands and knees, clawing her way past thistle and hawthorn towards level ground, growing colder every minute. An icy blast sent her staggering backwards into prickly thorns. She shouted his name, pulling herself to the top, consumed by cold.

Suddenly, her head began to swim. The statuesque figure in front of her spiralled into the whiteness. She dropped to her knees....

*And the white turned to black. It was a heavy, suffocating darkness that laid heavy on her lidded eyes; crept into her mouth and nostrils; formed a wedge between her parted legs. It crushed her arms against her chest, into the wild heartbeat beneath; chilled her very marrow. The dark gritted between her gnawing teeth, it squirmed against her naked flesh.*

*She was in death but alive. Taken into Mother Earth's crushing embrace while the senses still rebelled in pain.*

*She curled her fingers up away from the drumming beat towards the light she knew lay beyond, but the muscles of her arms were too weak to deliver the necessary thrust. Instinct levered open her jaw but there was no breath to cry out, only dark to fill the void ... and mind-numbing terror.*

*And him....*

Marsden had watched her collapse in the snow. He stood over her now, all but his eyes swathed in a thick muffler. His gloved hands turned her face upwards and brushed the snow from her hair and mouth. He spattered brandy over her blue lips, then carried her back to the cottage.

The vision had left Kate to a disturbed drowse. The brandy, fire on numb lips and gums, had chased away the dark – brought back the white.

He laid her on the rough wooden table beside the kitchen hearth and stoked the dying fire. He wrenched off her boots and chafed her numb feet until she winced with the pain of hot-aches. She heard him climb the stairs. Moments later he came down with blankets and set about removing her saturated clothing.

Too late she remembered the brooch. She saw the quizzical twist of his features; heard the tear of material and the rumbling growl deep in his throat as he flung the brooch across the shady room. She dragged herself up on an elbow and met the full force of the blow that sent her down into the quarried hearth. She fell heavily, cracking her head and shoulder on the stone.

He threw the table clear, dragged her up with a handful of hair, then struck her a jarring back-hand blow through the shield of her hands.

'Ah Kate.' The words were soft, no more than the hiss of damp wood in the grate. A wisp of cold disappointment that frightened her much more than his anger. She reached out to touch his face but he caught her fingers and crushed them until she dropped to her knees. 'What now of your promise of obedience, eh?' There came a sharp fizz from the smouldering logs. 'You went to Bristol?'

She nodded, her throat cracked dry, and murmured, 'Yes.'

'And returned with money enough to satisfy Steward Clarke. Gained how, if not with that, eh? By whoring?'

'No!' she pleaded. He pushed her derisively with his foot then unbuttoned his coat and draped it carefully over the up-ended table. She made as if to rise but he stopped her with a warning finger. He took the high-backed fireside chair, rested his elbows on its curved arms, and stared pensively into the flames.

The terror of the vision returned to her. It pierced her like a glass shard. Then was gone.

The crackle of the flames filled her ears. Her tongue probed the bloody inside of her cheek. She stared at his dark, shoulder-length hair gleaming in the flickering light, willing him to free her from the awful silence. It seemed an eternity before he invited her to explain. Then her words tumbled into the censorious opening. The brooch, the watch. Her desire to have something of him. And through it all his unnerving, unblinking stillness.

At last he pointed at the coat. 'Take out what is in the inner pocket.' She rose stiffly. Conscious of the lambing oil trapped under her nails, she delved carefully into the layers of fine black cloth and came out with a furry warmth.

'A kitlin!' she gasped, as the cowering white and ginger bundle mewed for the first time.

'The one survivor of a drowned litter,' he said off-handedly. 'Rear it, or kill it, as you please.' He swung himself up and snatched it from her, dangling its neck between his thumb and forefinger. When she moved after it he caught her throat with his free hand. 'That,' he growled, 'is the last time ever you will disobey me. Believe me. I will have you completely, or not at all!'

'I'll sell the brooch,' she swore.

'You will keep it,' he countermanded. 'Wear it openly.'

'It is too fine ...' she protested. 'They'll be sure to want to know how I came by it.'

'A silver larum, or a brooch. What difference? Have them know it belonged to your mother,' he said, tossing the kitten at her and reaching for his coat.

'Stay with me,' she begged. 'Don't torment me by leaving me now–'

He pulled on his gloves, scrutinizing her anxious face, then said slowly, 'I'll not come again until I have proof of your obedience.' He snatched his sleeve from her urgent fingers, and tied the woollen muffler around his neck.

'What can I do?' she choked, following him to the door. 'For pity's sake, tell me–'

The door swung out of his hand and they were enveloped in a snowy blast. He paused, then forced the door shut again.

'One thing alone,' he conceded. 'The child, Caroline Grafton, is to have a birthday feast, after matins two weeks hence. Take a gift to her–'

'The girl Jack scratched?' she asked incredulously.

'By way of an apology ... a weaned lamb would be fitting. Insist you give it to her in person.'

'How can I return to Apescross?' she reasoned. 'I'll get no further than the gates–' The words gusted back at her and the only reply came from the hapless kitten.

The evening of the second Sabbath....

The girlchild twisted fretfully in her sleep, her dreams a mismatch of broken images:

*The witch woman's mouth drawn into a tight smile – being chased by the slavering dog – her father shouting at Samuel, the butler – the lamb's fluffy tail wagging furiously – nurse pulling back the witch's hood – wet eyes looking at her in the mirror – red weals on her arm – Prince Rupert limping with a great spike in his hoof – the witch woman's twitching eyes and outstretched arms – her father's face red with anger – her friend, the footman bowled over by a spirit force – three lines on her arm – frightened eyes in the looking-glass – searching the hall for kind Mr Marsden – the black lamb sucking blood from the scratches on her arm–*

'Mr Marsden! Barbara!' she screamed.

The boy sharing the bed with her, stroked her sweat-matted hair. He kissed her hot cheek and assured his little sister that it was no more than a nightmare. When, at length, he had lulled her back to sleep, he crept away to fetch cousin Barbara.

*The girlchild watched the watching crow; saw it wipe its beak in the tree moss; stretch its great black wings in satisfaction. She watched it flap away ... felt her eyes drawn down, down to the cowslip meadow beneath the tree.*

*Down to the horror of the little black lamb with no eyes.*

# Gull-Catching ...

Not since the excitement of his breeching at Christmas, had Francis Grafton been so conscious of the onset of manhood. That his father should grant him the privilege of dining with the adults was honour indeed, especially when the company included Mr Marsden.

He sucked the dregs from his wine glass, moulded his shoulders – stiff in the blue silk jacket Mama had insisted he wear – into the curve of the chair and peered out under his fringe.

Marsden and his father were busy discussing the likelihood of war with Holland. He listened eagerly to snatches of talk about the relative strengths of the two navies, longing for the day when he, like Mr Marsden, would take part in a great sea battle. Soon though, the men removed from the table with their glasses of porter, abandoning him to bursts of feminine laughter and the clatter of plates as Hannah cleared the table around him.

Aunt Henrietta leaned across him, her perfumed yellow wig sprinkling his breeches with specks of powder, as she listened, head cocked to his mother's confidential whispers. The old lady pressed her fan to her lips and withdrew with an enigmatic smile.

Beyond his mother, Cousin Barbara laughed with the older ladies, brushing imaginary crumbs from her cleavage with an embroidered napkin. Her attention was elsewhere however. Disguise it as she might, her eyes had been on him all night. Which might have irritated Francis but for the fact that Marsden, unlike the London beaux, had been only mildly attentive to his cousin, whereas on several occasions he had been at pains to draw him into conversation.

Francis wound his fingers around the tassels bordering the tablecloth  and imagined the others already in their beds: Joseph, Cissie and Caroline, all feigning sleep until nurse went to her bed ... until he came.

'Come Francis!' cried his father, starting him from sated lethargy. 'Play for us.'

He rose, brushing the powder from his breeches, cheeks flushed. His mother nudged him, impatient as ever that he should do nothing to vex his father. He stumbled over the hearth and his stumble coincided with another titter. Francis righted himself, slowly turned and made a sweeping bow to the ladies.

Marsden joined the ladies' laughing approval of the young man's bravado. This show of spirit pleased, even surprised him. His eyes followed Francis to his inglenook seat; watched the soft, boyish hands first tune, then begin to play, the lute. The melody was sweet, the execution accomplished, but the accomplishment was completely overshadowed by the first boy-soprano notes. The unexpected sound shuddered exquisitely through him.

Grafton refilled his companion's glass. 'Francis had the benefit of a renowned London lute-master – tutor to the king's household.'

'I recall there was an accomplished lutist travelled with His Majesty in exile,' said Marsden, turning to his host. 'Eckeburg – I first met him in Holland.'

'The very man, sir!' exclaimed Grafton. He ran his finger around the rim of his glass before venturing, 'You were even at that time in the king's service?'

'I regret that I may not disclose such information – even to so staunch a Royalist as you sir,' said Marsden, under his breath. 'I trust you alone, as a generous host and a man of principle and honour, to know that I am in the county on the king's business. For both our sakes I dare expand no further.'

'Nor would I expect it,' said Grafton quickly. 'Be assured that you are welcome under my roof so long as business detains you here. It is not often I enjoy the company of a man of affairs and intelligence out here in the country. It seems you have made a great impression on the entire household. My wife informs me that the children talk of little else but *their* Mr Marsden.'

Marsden's eyes came to rest on the ladies, now seated at a card-table. He briefly acknowledged Barbara's pointed glance, then turned to stare through a casement window at the moonlit courtyard below. 'I believe you should be concerned for young Caroline's state of mind,' he said with obvious reticence.

'Ah, Caroline,' Grafton said gravely. 'Some childish morbidity since that Gurney woman upset her. It will pass, in the way of such things. Ellen had told me how the child called for you again this evening – says that the girl is afraid to close her eyes, unless you are there, or some such nonsense. We are indebted to you for your condescension–'

'I fear, Grafton, that this is more than mere childish fancy. I have observed in Caroline a deep disturbance of the mind. It may signify no more than a common childhood ailment; an imbalance of the humours, but such cases demand careful attention.'

'It may yet prove to be Caroline's way of claiming more than her share of your attention,' said Grafton with a wry smile.

'Ahh!' interrupted Barbara, laying a careless hand on Marsden's arm. 'Uncle, I wonder, could you spare Mr Marsden? We need a fourth hand for shuffleboard–'

There came a sudden jarring chord from the lute, a sharp intake of breath and Francis's squeal of pain. The maid, Hannah, walking past with a bowl of apples, lost her grip. The bowl shattered on the stone hearth and apples rolled across the patterned rug. Ellen Grafton scolded the maid as she rushed to her son, who sat palm pressed against his left eye.

'Whatever–' she gasped. Her husband quickly assessed the situation.

'Don't fuss Ellen. Can't you see that a string has snapped?' He inspected his son's injured eye.

'I'm not hurt, Mama,' Francis pleaded, embarrassed by his mother's concern.

'Quite right,' added his father dismissively. 'Nothing a cold poultice and a night's rest won't restore.' With that he guided Francis towards the door, laying the lute on a pedestal table as he passed it, leaving Ellen to trail after them.

Barbara linked her fingers behind her back and leaning her head against the cool window, gagged a laugh. Aunt Henrietta was staring myopically into a mirror, straightening the wig which she had knocked scrambling under the table after an apple.

'A broken lute string!' sighed Barbara, trailing her fingertips down the sleeve of his jacket. 'Is this the limit of country amusement? How much you must have seen and done ... how many women you must have bedded.' She giggled at her own daring.

'Are you so discontent with country life?' he asked quietly.

'I swear it will be the death of me,' she sighed. 'What is there for me here? There is no gaiety in the company of aunts and a stiff-necked guardian. It is not in my nature to be a docile creature. I crave London life – the theatres, the balls, the gossip, the river-boats, the noisy street vendors who wake you at the crack of dawn–'

'The sordid underbelly?' He glanced sideways at her animated face; saw the challenge in her hazel eyes.

'And that,' she agreed. 'One day I shall just up and go.'

'Alone?'

'I'll ride to Bristol, sell my jewels, take the first coach to London,' she enthused.

'And there?'

She smiled. 'I'll lodge with an acquaintance until my fortunes progress.'

'A gentleman acquaintance?'

'I didn't take you for a prude, Mr Marsden. *Virgo intacta* is not my intention. I shall follow the route of Barbara Villiers and actress Nell.'

'The king's bed no less,' he said with a wry smile. A frown marred her enthusiasm.

'Am I not beautiful enough?' she demanded.

'That is not in question,' he replied, casually taking out his pocket watch and flicking back the cover. 'What surprises me is your willingness to lie with an old rake like Charles Stuart – a man who has already used up one Barbara and a dozen others besides. London's brothels are full of whores who began as fresh-faced innocents.'

'Ah but there's the difference,' she said with a lazy gurgle. 'I'm no innocent, Mr Marsden. Why else would Uncle Samuel have banished me to Apescross a month before the family came home?' As she spoke the door opened and her uncle strode purposefully towards them. A barely perceptible start belied her air of confidence. 'The summerhouse, by the orchard,' she breathed, her hand slipping over his as though by accident, 'in a half hour.' She edged away, making much of a yawn, and enquired after Francis.

Marsden braced his arms against the window jambs. In the courtyard below he watched a boyish figure flit through the shadows to the stables. He clicked the watch cover shut and turning towards Grafton, enquired, 'Francis suffered no serious injury, you say?'

Hannah had not meant to spy on them. What with dropping the apple bowl, then Mistress Grafton barking at her to leave the clearing up till morning, her mind had been in a fearful state. She had been sobbing in the scullery when Master Francis had hurried through to the kitchen door. She had rushed after him with some vague notion that if he put in a good word for her, she might be spared a thrashing next morning when the butler heard about her clumsiness.

She had slipped into the stables as the door swung to and hearing hushed voices, had crawled into an empty pen. She could hear Francis talking. Then several young voices replied, some she recognized. Hannah crept closer.

A lantern had been hooked on to a beam. Under it the children had formed a circle. Francis, Joseph and the misses Cissie and Caroline wearing no more than their cotton night-shifts, Ben the housekeeper's boy and Ollie the stable lad, all kneeling in the straw, their heads bowed as though in prayer.

Hannah pressed herself into a dark corner and watched.

Caroline, her back to the corner, rose unsteadily to her feet and moved to the centre of the circle, carrying the black lamb. The girlchild closed her eyes, turned twice, then lay down in the straw, pulling the lamb close to her side.

The others closed ranks and linked hands, in silence. Even the lamb was quietly expectant.

Francis turned to Cissie on his right and whispered. His sister nodded gravely and repeated the message to Ben, who passed it on to Joseph. Hannah closed her eyes and sighed with relief. It was only a round of whispers; a secret, silly game. And it would serve them right if she peached on them, scaring her so.

The whisper had been twice round. It reached Francis and blossomed into a chant:

> *Earth, air, water, fire.*
> *Over nadir, under zenith,*
> *Come, oh spirits lend thy might;*
> *Come, oh come to us this night!*

Over and over again the words themselves seemed to have no beginning, no end. They pulled at Hannah, drew her out of the shadows. Numbed her mind to all but the girlchild.

Fived mouths voiced the incantation. Five hands cupped head, shoulders and slippered feet. Lifted the sleeping child from her bed of straw. Hannah watched and Hannah saw them turn and leave her hanging there.

Barbara had tired of dancing a courante on the springy boards of the pentagonal summerhouse. She lifted her skirts and slumped down on the slatted bench-seat by the window overlooking the orchard.

The spring scent of currant bushes lingered on the night air. And everywhere branches of apple and quince and pear were hung with moon-washed blossom.

She pressed her temple against the window frame and searched the glittering sky for the star-configuration Marsden had pointed out to her the night astrology had become the subject of after-dinner conversation. But soon abandoned the search. She had, after all, been more attentive of him that night than of what he had been saying. And had been again tonight when she suggested this assignation.

Even by her standards that had been a brazen move. Until now she had always basked in the want of a man, responded to his desire, flattered by the image she saw reflected back at her. But now, knowing for the first time what it was to really want a man, she had turned hunter. And forced the lock on her own latent sensuality.

She rubbed her breasts, tingling under swathes of cotton and silk, against the windowsill and willed him to come....

She responded with languid restraint to the hands that began gently to massage her shoulders from behind; to the lips that wafted warm breath along her neck. She gurgled his name and sank back against him, heady with the strange aromas that enveloped her.

'I knew you would come,' she said throatily. 'We understand each other, don't we Mars–'

Spread fingers pushed her dark hair forwards over her eyes, cruel nails ploughing ridges over her scalp. Knuckles jammed between her teeth, choking her pained squeal. She pulled blindly at the clenched fist holding a knot of pulled hair over her eyes and nose, fighting to breathe. The unseen hand pulled the knot of hair still tighter, binding her eyelids open, straining every root in her scalp to its painful limit. It jerked her off the bench and sent her sprawling across the wooden floor. Then crushed her face down where she lay.

Her head had come to rest on her left arm. She attempted to lift it, aware of a dull sensation across the bridge of her nose. Aware too of her own frightened sobs. A blow from behind cracked her forehead down against the boards.

'Dear God, please let me go–' she wailed. A hand forced down on her neck while another dragged her skirts up over her head and tied the loose ends over her head. 'I beg you!' she howled, but held her tongue to listen to a muffled sound; a rumbling, mirthless laugh. 'For pity's sake,' she choked, 'you're not Marsden ... who are you?'

For a moment she lay quite still, listening intently. The sound had ceased and there was no weight holding her down. She scrambled to her feet, slipping a shoe and flailed against the improvised sack over her head.

The hands found her again. Tore at her underclothes until cold air rushed at her bare skin. She screamed as the first pin pierced the tender skin of her inner thigh. The more she writhed and tried to escape, the more intense were the cruel stabs to back and buttocks and legs. Fierce jabs behind the knees made her buckle and fall. The unseen tormentor gave a cold laugh and above her sobs, intoned, 'The whore says she is bored ... t'is easy to bore a whore, ha, ha!'

'Devil, leave me!' she wailed. Rough hands lifted her up, dragged her still trussed and staggering in one shoe out of the summerhouse, down the steps, along the gravel path. Running across through the orchard grass until she could run no further, she tripped over uneven ground and curled into a ball on the dewy grass. She knew it was there, legs straddled across her. Knew by the pungent odour it exuded, the deep rasping breaths. She held her breath in horror, listening to the rhythmic breathing and the nearby bubble of a stream.

Hands seized her shredded clothing, dragged her to inclined ground, then sent her rolling into the babbling water. Far off the voice called out to her, 'The devil never leaves – only takes what is his.'

Her trembling hands found the leather thong, wrenched until the skirts fell away. Her eyes searched the orchard, the soughing trees behind. Then, in stockinged feet, she fled half-mad towards the house, terrified that the unseen thing might be lurking in the dancing shadows. She burst into the courtyard, staggered across the sets towards the kitchen door and there collapsed into the arms of Marsden.

Jessie Harris, nurse to the Grafton children, bustled distractedly into the baby's room. She set down her candle and clamped her plump fingers around the oak crib, her eyes staring at but not seeing the wailing infant.

Negligent, Samuel Grafton had called her, negligent! And she never off her feet! What did the man want – that she should keep a bedside vigil? How was she to know that the little imps would steal off like that? She had left them quiet in their beds – or so she had thought – without even an inkling of mischief. And all this nonsense about fiendish rhymes. The only fiendish thing was Hannah's imagination – spells indeed!

Jessie sighed deeply and lifted the almost hoarse child into her arms. 'There, there my little one,' she cooed, 'a mite colicky are we?' She dabbed a streak of vomit from the corner of the child's mouth and gently stroked its temple. By degrees nurse and baby drew quietude from each other. Jessie cupped the downy head in her hand and lowered the quietly purring child into the crib. And doing so touched something hard and tacky. She quickly removed the infant to Caroline's bed and brought the candle close to the cot sheets.

'Dear Lord, what devilry is this?' she cried. There, scattered within a pool of semi-dried milk vomit, lay a half-dozen round-headed pins and small crystalline lumps resembling coal. She touched the foreign objects in horrified fascination. 'Not possible–' she said, shaking her head. 'Some mischief–' Then she groaned, 'Please God, not the children....'

Samuel Grafton was angrier than the children had ever seen him before. Angrier by far than the time Joseph drank a whole bottle of wine and fell through a glass window into the shrubbery. Even angrier than he had been when Cousin Barbara had tried to run off with a navy captain. His anger turned their stomachs to water, their legs to jelly. It ignored their tears and muddled their minds.

He had caught them leaving the stable; had marched the six of them up to his study where Hannah already waited, head bowed by the bookshelves. He refused to listen to exhortations on their behalf, either from his wife or nurse Harris; had expelled both women from the room. Then lined the children up before his escritoire while brow-beaten Hannah retold what she had seen.

'Who put you up to this sorcery?' he demanded, stern eyes fixing each child in turn. He left Francis till last. 'And you.' His voice was dangerously low. 'To slope off so deceitfully and lead your youngers into God knows what! Is this what I am to expect of my son and heir? Was it you taught them this devil verse?'

Francis swallowed hard and reasoned, 'It was but a g-game, sir.' For his pains, his father seized his scruff and threw him across a chair. Far worse than the birching that followed was the unbearable humiliation of having his precious breeches wrenched down. He howled for shame until his father tossed him aside and set about the other boys.

Grafton repeated his question, 'Who put you up to this sorcery?' And when no explanation came forth, he had first Joseph, then Ollie and Ben lie across the dreaded chair to receive one strike for each year of their age.

It was left to the youngest among them, the girlchild, to begin the rebellion.

Unlike her sister Cissie, who hovered nervously over a puddle of urine, Caroline had stood passively throughout, her tousled head meekly inclined towards the woolly bundle in her arms. That is, until the angry father attempted to take the lamb from her.

Then calm turned to fury. She flew at him, all flailing limbs and bared teeth, screeching guttural curses and vile oaths. Grafton's appalled inertia lasted but a moment, until the demon child sank its teeth into his leg.

The sight of her father swinging Caroline off the floor with a handful of hair was too much for Cissie. She collapsed into a writhing, screaming fit. Francis dropped to his knees, head lolling on one shoulder, eyes rolled upwards so that only the whites showed. The fingers of his right hand pointed towards the bookcase against which Hannah, clutching her head, had pressed herself.

'Devil take her prying eyes!' he cursed. 'Cast her down to cleansing fires ... under nadir under zenith–' Hannah screamed. Grafton roared. Joseph, Ollie and Ben began to throw themselves crazedly against the walls and furniture, yelling garbled obscenities at Hannah as she ran the gauntlet in a desperate bid for the study door.

Marsden crossed Hannah in the doorway. He cut through the squally chaos towards the escritoire on which Grafton had managed with one hand to pin the squirming, spitting girlchild. From his other hand, blaring in protest, dangled the lamb. The father glanced up at Marsden, eyes no longer blind with rage but humble with dread and imploring. Marsden turned to see Ellen, the mother, standing wide-eyed in the doorway, her lips slowly parting in a soundless scream. And knew the time had come.

He stepped over Cissie and moved towards the lectern by a shuttered window. Closed, then lifted the heavy Bible. Breathed life into the words, 'In the name of the Father, I command you, be gone from this God-fearing house, from these innocent children. Leave them in peace....'

They would later say there had been something like a rush of wind no more than that. Words experienced, not heard. Words that formed themselves in the minds of the children, their parents, the knot of servants huddled around the door. Strong words that drove out terror ... becalming ... beguiling words.

The children lay where they had fallen. Some slept, others quietly wept; their nervous energy spent. Marsden instructed the servants to carry them off to their beds. All except Caroline, whom he personally carried upstairs. He watched from the foot of the bed long after she and Cissie were fast asleep. He put an arm of comfort around Jessie Harris's trembling shoulders and listened while she unburdened herself and softly wept about the *things* in the crib.

When, at last, he returned to the study, Grafton was crouched round-shouldered over the unmade fire. Marsden decanted two glasses of wine, then broke the news about Barbara and the baby.

After a long, clock-filled silence, Grafton looked up and with a ragged sigh, said, 'Marsden, you learned the physician's art–'

'An art I have sadly neglected,' Marsden demurred.

Grafton persisted, 'Could it be that they have all been struck down by the same sickness? Some affliction of the mind? Earlier, when you spoke of Caroline–'

'I hoped it was no more than a bodily imbalance,' Marsden reminded.

'But even then you suspected something more insidious ... if I had but listened. Now it has come to this. Dear God, what am I to do?'

Marsden set his empty glass on the desk and taking Grafton's elbow, coaxed him to his feet. 'You must send for a priest, without delay.'

'You believe they are possessed?' Grafton said, his voice jagged with emotion. 'Bewitched? What else would explain this ... this evil that has taken hold under my roof? The words you spoke–'

'The children were afraid. The words gave them an outlet for their fear – a safe harbour, I used a simple metaphysical technique, that was all.'

'Do not take me for a fool sir! There was pandemonium in this room until you invoked the name of God.'

'It may yet prove to be hysterical delusion,' Marsden said evenly.

Grafton seized the other man's collar and jerked his face close to Marsden. 'Was it delusion induced my children to utter incantations in a dark stable?' he flared. 'Lured my niece to a summerhouse and stuck her with pins? Am I to believe that an old stalwart like Jessie Harris was deluded about the baby? Dear Lord–' He fell back, his face suddenly drained of colour and stared in horror at the hands which seemed to have assumed a will of their own. He begged Marsden's forbearance – pleaded with him to remain in the manor, to guide the family through the trials ahead. He would not go for the priest until he had that assurance.

Marsden opened the shutter and watched him go. The master and his Prince, galloping pell-mell into the darkness. Questing for a peace of mind that he alone could grant.

He refastened the shutter and sank into the padded armchair by the escritoire. Then poured himself another glass of Grafton's best Bordeaux.


First light....
Caleb Peebles eased his Prayer Book shut and with age-crooked fingers blessed the sleeping babe. *Suffer the little children,* the Lord had said, *et libera nos a malo....*

The priest mournfully shook his head and glanced around at the murmuring onlookers. During the long years of his parish priesthood he had seen many tormented souls. He had driven out demon spirits, rested unquiet bodies but never before in children so young, or so many. It was as if the Grafton household had been visited by a pestilence of evil.

He had witnessed the girlchild's wild aggression; the boys' self-inflicted wounds. He had suffered their blasphemies and vile obscenities; had provoked them with his prayers.

But this wordless babe? This infant he himself had baptized only days after its birth, to purge its soul of wicked influence. Had evil truly cast its net over this one too?

He raised his hand for silence and directed the nurse to slide the bowl of water beneath the crib. Waiting for the swaying liquid to come to rest, he drew three knobbly oak-apples from a pocket deep within his sleeve, placed them on the water's surface and stepped back.

Let the galls float and the infant was safe. Let them sink and baby Julia was in as much peril as her siblings....

As the last oak-apple plopped beneath the surface, Ellen Grafton lurched towards the child; her cries of disbelief raking the awed silence. First Cissie, then Joseph, dropped insensibly to the floor.

'Bewitched,' groaned the priest, visibly bowed. Clutching the crib, he lowered himself down to his knees, quoting, *'Deliver me a woman that hath a familiar spirit....'*

# Shades ...

Marsden had clawed his way out of the dream. He lay face down in a breathless, semi-clothed sprawl, chemise and hose cold with sweat.

It had been so long since the last time the dam had haunted his sleep. Why should she come now, just when it was all in the palm of his hand? He had buried it deep; left it far, far behind. He had crushed the emasculating hold his mother had once had many times over ... only for it to be exhumed in the image of the shepherdess.

He slashed back the curtains of the guest bed and swore irritably until, at last, the worn flint of the tinderbox sparked. While the candle flames drew life, he rummaged through the dresser for paper and charcoal pencil. Then he sat before the oval mirror and began a frenzied sketch.

*Alone in the cottage, Kate lay on her pallet, staring beyond the darkness of the ceiling timbers. She was keenly aware of arousal; of the musky warmth of her body. With palms stretched taut she coursed the pulsing contours. Finding the bruised pain in the slightly distended stomach, she knew that the moon was upon her and exulted in the overflowing sap of her womanhood.*

*She had dreamt of stars, of standing on Blackwood Top and staring into a heaven full of them; some in winking cliques, others jaded in their isolation, new stars bright with wonder – and one most brilliant star of all.*

*The glowing ascendency was still upon her – it throbbed through her veins. Such burning intensity, she knew, such physical elation, would have its price. But not yet ... not yet.*

*She trailed her fingers over the kitlin's back as it brushed past in the darkness, stretched vitality into her neck and limbs, then reached for her cloak.*

He was absorbed by the sketch. Adrenalin spent on the savage outline strokes, he lost himself in the detailed shading; his art a raw, untutored talent; the germ, as ever, unvented passion.

He dropped the finished piece against the mirror and stood back. This was the dreamt Kate – the naked shadow-danced splendour; flaming swords of sunset radiating from behind, her arms upstretched, neck arched back and her legs astride some abject form....

He felt a tightening at the base of his skull. A sudden draining impotence. She filled his head, disabling every other thought, forcing his attention – even in wakefulness.

A gentle breeze rippled across the drawing. It made the candles gutter and within the picture seemed to ruffle her loose hair. He saw, as he knew he must, the glistening red trickle streaking the creamy red of her thighs. He watched it spill from her navel, shuddered as it spread over the ill-defined being beneath ... as the red filled his sight.

He howled hoarsely, wiping the running wet from his eyes and forehead. He stared at his trembling hands – *no blood on them, no red – only sweat.*

He looked up, past his creation, at the mirror-reflected self; at the sweat-matted, chest-heaving image of himself. He slipped the knife from his boot and struck the bleeding navel, carved the burning image out of his head and left its strewn shreds on the guest-room floor. Then he went out into the night.

Ned was perched on the edge of his straw mattress in the hayloft, waiting for a wave of stomach gripes either to subside or once more propel his shaky legs down the ladder to the nettle patch outside. He gritted his teeth and hurled a stone down at eyes that glowed eerie green in the dark. Then curled up and sank into the goose-feather pillow, his head swimming for lack of sleep.

Above the gnawing of his stomach he heard sounds across at the cottage. He listened keenly above the straw-rustling of rats below him, to the clicking of the door latch and Kate's whispered commands for Jack to stay. He rolled over and spying through vents in the brickwork, saw Kate, wearing no more than a chemise under her parted cloak, close the door and hasten past the barn.

Ned snatched on his boots, buttoned his loosened breeches and swarmed down the ladder after her. Keeping his distance, he followed her out of the yard, down into the dip beyond the chaffinch hedge and the folds to the next hollow. When she stopped halfway down the furze and thistle incline, he wondered if he ought to go down to her, wake her. He could not imagine a body walking barefoot through thistle and thorn unless it was in sleep. But as he went to move he wrenched his foot on the uneven ground and staggered into a tangle of brambles. Swearing venomously, he ripped himself free and sat rubbing his sore foot.

Kate stood quite still, holding the flapping cloak tightly to her – stood and stared up at the ridge beyond. Ned followed her gaze ... and seeing the profile of a man on a horse silhouetted against the night sky, rose unsteadily to his feet.

He watched open-mouthed as the horse reared, like some rampant figure from a coat-of-arms, seeming to hang there for many moments before finally leaping over the ridge.

Ned heard the pounding hooves and the snorted breaths; realized with horror that it was hurtling straight at Kate. Knowing that he was too far away to reach her before it did, he opened his mouth to shout a warning – but the sound died in his throat.

Just when it seemed that Kate could not but be trampled under the mass of heaving horseflesh, she turned her head aside. As though facing a brick wall, the horse swerved violently to her left. In passing, the dark figure slipped from the saddle, leaving the horse to race up the slope alone, almost knocking Ned over in its flight.

Below him, Kate let the cloak slip off her shoulders. Ned latched on to the stark white of her chemise. He saw her walk towards the stooped figure of the rider; watched as the dark thing sprang at her, knocking her down and enveloping her white in its dark wings.

The boy inched closer. He heard the creature's racked, spasmodic moans; saw Kate's arms entwined around it. Then he clutched his head and ran away.

# Part 3: Aqua

# Discoveries ...

Kate stopped singing to listen. Above the bleating of the ewes and lambs, the lazy underpinning of wood-pigeons, she had heard a brief rumbling; a sound ominously out of keeping with the bright spring morning. She scanned the hillside and saw nothing but Jack, snorting with the effort of rolling in some wild animal scent.

The ewe under her shifted, straining at the deformed hoof Kate had trapped between her legs, dragging her back to the task in hand.

*Distant thunder perhaps.*

She pared the twisted hoof shell back to the new growth, smeared it with ointment, then let the ewe hobble back to her calling sisters. Drawn by a huddle around the water-trough, she waded through and was taken aback to find it was dry save for a murky puddle in the drain outlet. She felt underneath for the wooden plug and pulled it out. As the stagnant liquid sluiced through her fingers, something small and firm dropped into her palm. Drawing her hand out she was saddened to find it was the bedraggled body of a wren; tip-tailed even though its eyes were glazed with death. As she closed her wet fingers around the tiny corpse, she heard again the strange rumbling sound.

Grabbing the bucket from its hook on the side of the trough, she climbed over the hurdles and picked her way down to the stream. There in the flowing water she opened her hand and watched the wren wend its way downstream.

There was something in the air. Something to do with Ned not filling the troughs. She had looked in on the hayloft before coming out; had thought nothing of his not being there. He was often up and about at first light, seeing to the feed and water. But Ned was too rigid in his habits, too jealous of her good opinion, to let the trough run dry.

With a sense of foreboding she scooped a bucket full of water and made her way back to the trough. She was replacing the plug when Jack swooped to her side, his hackles raised.

Out of the sunlight, three horses suddenly leapt through the chaffinch hedge scattering the sheep. After them, a jostle of men and boys noisily pushed their way through the broken hedge. Jack, a quiver of muscle and bared teeth, rushed the first horse but was stunned by the flick of a galloping hoof.

Clenching her fingers around the knife in her pocket, Kate rose slowly to her feet. She stared at the malevolent faces ranged around her. Samuel Grafton glowered down from the horse she herself had nursed. Bailiff Tom Clarke sat beside him. Kerry the groom was there and the footman who had chased her. There were lads she had seen that day in the courtyard and men she recognized from the village. But of all the faces none bore more malice than Barbara Canard. Glaring down from the saddle of a dappled palfrey she spat, 'Take the witch! And her dog!'

Kate knew her time had come – as she had always known it would. As it had come to her mother before her. What she had not known though, was that it would come so soon. Why now, when she was only just discovering so much within herself? Before she had begun to explore her own awakening powers? Now that she had him?

She watched them muzzle Jack as he lay semi-conscious beneath Grafton's horse. Saw them truss his floppy legs so that he could not escape. Everyday concerns flooded her mind. Who would tend the sheep, look after kitlin, see that the cauldron she had left on the range did not boil dry? Not one person here, that was certain.

She met their stares. In that look defied them to lay a finger on her. Not one moved, though several murmured. She lifted the bucket and emptied the clear water into the trough.

'Katharine Gurney, you are to come forthwith to my house, to answer the charges laid against you,' Grafton commanded.

Kate turned to meet his gaze. 'What charges?' If he replied, she did not hear. For standing shame-faced beside Barbara's palfrey, she had spotted Ned.

She was vaguely aware that Grafton had issued an ultimatum. Felt hands reach for her arms. And their violating touch unleashed her fury. In that moment she determined not to play out the part they intended for her. She pulled out the knife and slashed at anyone within arm's reach. They all leapt back, wary eyes slavishly following the bloodied knife.

'If any man so much as touches me again,' she raged, 'so help me God, I'll run him through!'

Grafton dismounted and pushed into the inner circle. He said severely, 'God punishes murder Gurney, He does not abet it.'

She surveyed the mud-splashed boots, the braided velvet coat and plumed hat. And was struck by the inconsequence of the posturing man within – him *and* his cowering pack of henchmen.

'Unless the murder be of a witch,' she said grimly.

'From her very mouth!' cried Barbara. 'The witch condemns herself–'

'Of what am I accused?' demanded Kate.

'We all heard your curse that day in the courtyard!' railed the footman. 'Heard you damn the house of Grafton.'

'Been nothing but witchery ever since!' shouted another.

'Those poor afflicted children,' said the footman with a dismal shake of his head.

'Enough!' snapped Marsden. Turning to Kate he said, 'You are coming to Apescross–' Before the words were spoken, Barbara, brandishing her crop, had spurred the palfrey through the huddle of men and boys, knocking her uncle aside. Kate took the first blow on her raised forearms. As the crop came down again she caught it squarely and snatched Barbara from her mount. In a moment of confusion Kate threw herself into the saddle and jerked the reins. The small horse reared in panic, then something clubbed her under the shoulder blades. Gasping for air, she turned to see Tom Clarke arcing a heavy stick at her head.

She would later remember falling off the horse, the knife being ripped from her fingers, grit-toothed faces laughing as she put up a futile fight against Grafton's merciless beating; as she howled her defeat.

She lay, hands and feet tied, staring up from the damp grass at ribbons of moving cloud. And while they argued about the best place to swim her, she watched a bee dance past and envied its lack of pain.

A post, ripped from the hurdle fencing, had been thrust between her tied hands and feet so that she swung under it like a stuck sow as grunting men lifted the ends on to their shoulders.

Kate closed her ears to the raucous shouting and sank into her pain. When she reopened her eyes, Ned was staring down at her.

'What did you tell them, Ned?' she murmured.

The boy's eyes shifted uneasily. 'I-it was the Evil One,' he blurted. 'I couldn't sleep – belly-ache, see. Heard you come out ... thought you were done for.'

'You followed me last night?' she breathed.

'Leave the lad be, witch!' spat the footman, thrusting Ned aside.

The boy tugged his sleeve. 'Lying with him, she was ... only came up on Mr Marsden's say-so ... should never have taken me from the inn.'

'Hush Ned,' Kate groaned.

Thrusting himself between her and the footman the boy snarled. *'Witch! Whoring witch!'* Others took up the taunt, pressing their bodies closer. Unseen fingers poked and pinched her bruised flesh – began to tear at her clothes.

'Come away!' bawled Grafton.

'Aye!' shouted the footman. 'Let the water decide.'

'She'll float, sure as day,' said William Kerry.

'And you should know,' Barbara added slyly. 'Eh, Will?'

Grafton shot his niece an angry scowl, then driving Prince Rupert through the angry men, cleared a way through to the captive. 'We've idled long enough,' he barked. 'You, Kerry, take one end, and you,' he stabbed at a burly villager with his whip, 'you take over the other. We're taking this woman straight to Apescross, do you hear?' Over a storm of protest he shouted, 'To Apescross, I say. Didmerton millpond is out of our way.'

'True sir,' yelled the footman. 'But I have a lad here says he knows of a place close by.'

Minutes later, Ned had guided them through the wood to the secluded pool where, only weeks before, he and Kate had scrambled across the ice to rescue a stray ewe. There they unhooked and propped her against the mossy bark of a fallen tree.

Grafton cast a critical eye over the gently rippling water. He shook his head dubiously, turned to Tom Clarke and suggested the pool was too shallow for their purposes. The footman craved Grafton's pardon; insisted he could not help but hear what had been said, and by his master's leave would gladly test the depth himself.

Clarke dismounted and attempted to take charge of the scramble of gibing lads who, urged on by Miss Barbara, had already untied Kate's hands and feet. But they were too incensed to listen.

They stripped her of all but her chemise, then, with much shoving and infighting, bound the thumb of each hand to the big toe of the opposite foot.

Kate sat cross-legged, her hunched shoulders trembling involuntarily. She watched the footman wade in up to his armpits. He had been too impatient even to take off his livery coat. It floated all round him as he turned and called, 'Goes deeper yet, Master Grafton!'

She stared emptily at the disturbed water, wondering why, of all places, it had to happen here. Where before to float staring up into the sky had been her secret pleasure, not a crime. And this the very log on which he had delivered her absolution ... *Caelis in es qui noster Pater* ... words reborn. New doors unlocked, old ones closed forever. Here in this tranquil place, which they now raped with their clumsy vengeance.

Rough hands lifted her above the water. They carried her beyond the reeds, past the footman as he waded back to the bank, and when they could hold her no more, tossed her head first into the murky pool.

The water rushed at her ears cutting out the jeering voices. She sank deep into the welcoming dark....

*And saw dogs clustered under the trailing branches of a willow. She saw their frenzied clawing – leaf mould and soft earth tossed between their hind legs; heard their whining gasps and jealous snarls as the thing began to take form. The worm-eaten, flesh-rotted thing....*

Kate fought the vision. She writhed against her bindings and the tangle of weeds; pushed and paddled until she burst through to the light. She gulped air, then crashed back under.

She did not want to see it again. Cried out against it, but the cry floated away on a cloud of bubbles. And it was here; waiting for her among the waving tendrils, lurking in the muddy dark.

*Putrefaction laid bare beneath the slavering jaws and twitching snouts; the remains of a woman, carelessly buried. Earth-filled mouth stretched with the horror of death.*

*Kate shrank into her terror. It was a woman no older than herself, sharing her build – tossed into a grave unmarked save for the dog-luring stench of decay. The image buckled her reeling mind, lured the breath from her aching lungs. Beckoned her consciousness.*

Marsden had come unnoticed. And while they jostled and jeered Kate's first break for air, he cut Jack free. He watched the terrified dog career off into the wood then, unbuttoning his coat, strolled towards the crush of bodies by the water's edge.

'Damned creature isn't coming up yet!' yelled Tom Clarke, with an anxious glance at Grafton.

'Give her time!' snapped Barbara.

Marsden pushed between niece and uncle. 'Would you see the wretched woman drown?' he asked, kicking off his boots and throwing his coat at Clarke.

'Wait man!' Grafton called after him. 'We must know–'

But Marsden broke free of the hands that tried to detain him and splashed into the deeper water. When he could no longer walk, he dived under the surface and combed the mud-stirred bed until, at last, he found her caught up in the weeds. He grabbed a fistful of loose hair, tugged her free, then dragged her up towards the light.

Kerry alone waded in to help him haul her to the bank. Kerry it was who cut her free and pummelled the water from her lungs. The others looked on in shifty-eyed silence while she spluttered back to life.

Marsden walked away, his features twisted grimly, and pulled on his boots. Grafton laid a hand on his sleeve.

'Damn it man,' he blustered, 'you know as well as any what is at stake here ... the pot-boy saw her cavorting with an evil spirit.'

'The allegations of a weak-minded child?' Marsden flared.

'My decision to fetch this woman wasn't based purely on the boy's testimony,' insisted Grafton. 'So much points to her, surely you see that? And still does.'

'Ah,' sighed Marsden. 'So swimming her has done nothing to convince you of her innocence. Perhaps your mind refuses to accept such a possibility?'

'Your intervention saw to that, sir!' bridled Tom Clarke.

'She refused to come to Apescross,' Barbara cut in, 'bloodied three of the men–'

'And knocked Miss Barbara to the ground,' Clarke added quickly. Barbara spread her fingers with a conclusive smile.

'Is that the reaction of an innocent woman, Mr Marsden?' she asked.

'Would a hare lay down to the hounds?' he asked, dousing her smile with a cold stare.

'Mr Marsden,' she retorted, feigning protest, 'we did not hunt this creature, merely requested she answer the charges against her.'

Grafton shifted uneasily. 'Your concern for the Gurney woman is admirable to a fault–' he said testily.

'Who else will speak for her kind?' Marsden asked.

'Tell me,' said Barbara pointedly, 'is there truth in her claim that you are her kinsman?'

Marsden drew a deep breath. He thrust out his lower lip and shook his head.

'Surely, you can see my point,' urged Grafton. 'My first duty is to Caroline and the others. Since this woman refused to see them, what option is left to me but force?'

Kate lay on the log, stuttering air into her lungs, knowing that he had come. She stared at his mud-soiled shirt, showing pink where the wet material clung to his skin. Felt his hands cup hers.

'Come with me Kate,' he said. 'To prove your innocence.'

'They want a scapegoat,' she said, fighting the urge to cough. 'Their fear ... they'll kill me like they did my mother.'

'Perhaps they will,' he agreed. 'But not yet, we still have time.'

'I saw–' she began, shivering with remembered terror but seeing Grafton and the others peering over his shoulder, clutched his wrist and whispered, 'Don't leave me.'

'Well, will she come freely?' demanded Grafton. Marsden stood up, and taking his coat from Clarke, answered, 'She'll come.'

They had left Caroline till last. Last for what, she was not quite sure. Five times the polished doors into the hall had opened and five times an older child had followed Parson Peebles' beckoning finger and been sealed in by the click of a lock.

She tried peeping through the keyhole but the escutcheon plate inside, blocked her view. She squashed her face against the cold floor tiles in an attempt to see under the door but the narrow gap was cluttered with grit and dust. So she pressed herself against the wainscoting idly scuffing her heels against the oak panels and wishing with all her heart that she had been born before Cissie, or Ollie, or Joseph and had not been the last to go in.

The sharp click of the door handle made her stomach lurch. She clenched her tingling fingers and pushed harder against the panelling.

'Come child,' said the parson, nodding encouragement. Caroline frowned at him.

'Am I to be punished,' she asked warily.

He held out his wrinkled hand and said gently, 'No child.' Then he took her reluctant hand in his and steered her through the doorway.

After the dimness of the corridor, the brilliant light of the hall hurt her eyes. She squinted into the brightness and saw many attentive faces; some seated, others standing behind. All of them were staring at her in silent expectation.

Last of all she saw the woman – caught in a shaft of sunlight as she stood on the centre mat where the table usually stood. Caroline saw and turned panic-stricken to the priest.

'Do not be afraid,' he said, gently pushing her towards Kate.

The girlchild's eyes darted around the circle of faces; at Cissie and her brothers, sitting cross-legged on the floor; at her father's unyielding mask; at her mother's white anxiety. She felt the first tears spill on to her burning cheek.

And the witch woman smiled her jagged smile; knelt and tempted her with soft words. But the girlchild knew it was only a witch's ruse and backed away. She yelped as strong hands barred her retreat. Turned and clung to the neck of her friend, Mr Marsden.

'Caroline, my girl,' he whispered, stroking her hair, 'Go to her. She will not harm you while I am here.'

'I-I dare not!' she whimpered. He prised her arms from his neck, clasped her burning face between his hands and stared into her frightened eyes.

'Go to her,' he breathed and with his finger smoothed the furrows between her eyes. The girlchild sighed as a breeze fragrant with meadow grasses seemed to cool her face. She turned and found the faces gone. No walls, no silent expectation. Just bird-song meadows and tethered to a tree not far away, the lamb. She rushed joyfully towards the basking creature, buried her face in its black wool, curled herself around its warmth.

A harsh cry startled her eyes up into the leafy boughs. She saw the swooping blackness, screamed as its talons raked the flesh of her arm. She knew it wanted the eyes of the lamb, and threw herself against it, kicking and scratching.

For several stunned moments, the Grafton household watched the small girl's frenzied attempts to scratch the woman. They looked on helplessly as the other children became embroiled, shattering the quiet with the violence of their affliction.

Kate fended off her attackers until there were too many flailing limbs, from too many sides. Then she buried her head in her arms and dropped to her knees with a groan.

Barbara sprang from her seat, pointing at Kate. 'Her imp attacked me in the orchard!' she ranted. 'What more proof do you need?'

Marsden knocked her aside. He pulled Francis off Kate, swung him round and struck him sharply across the face. The stinging blow cut a swath through the raving voices. All at once the screaming stopped. Francis touched his face and stared at Marsden in open-mouthed confusion. Ellen Grafton cried out. Her husband rushed forward to catch Cissie as she crumpled insensibly towards the mat. The girlchild stumbled back into Joseph and Ollie, who had pressed themselves against a wall.

Kate slowly lowered her arms and uncurled her bruised back.

Parson Peebles marshalled the quietened children into a straight line. He passed from one subdued face to the next, willing each in turn to meet the challenge of his eyes. But none did. From injured Francis, to pouting Caroline, not one stood up to his scrutiny for more than a few seconds before blinking away. And that worried the old priest. He sighed gently, then turned away from the bowed heads.

'Would you deny the evidence of your eyes?' Grafton demanded tetchily.

The priest bit his lip, then said softly, 'It takes more than a sharp slap to rout an evil spirit.'

'What are you implying?' hissed Grafton. 'Imposture?'

'The children are susceptible to influence,' Marsden said quietly. 'There is no suggestion of wilful deceit.'

Grafton glanced across at the children, then at Kate, who was attempting to draw together the torn parts of her bodice. 'Whose influence?' he asked. 'Was it the blow restored them, or the scratching? Look at the woman – her face, her arms all scored by their nails.'

'And now they are rid of their torment,' agreed the priest. 'It may well be that Katharine Gurney is responsible, Samuel, but we must be certain of it before we commit her to the law. What will it benefit the children if she is not their tormentor?'

As he spoke, the butler stepped between him and Marsden.

'For pity's sake, Samuel, what now?' snapped Grafton.

The servant cleared his throat uncomfortably, 'The petty constable requests to see you, sir ... a serious matter.' He nodded towards the doorway where two men stood holding their hats. With a broken sigh, Grafton stalked towards the visitors.

The constable acknowledged him with a respectful nod, untroubled by the scowl etched into the man's face. There were things in this world worse than a man's displeasure. And he had just seen one of them.

'A woman's body? Where?' asked Grafton.

'Pack of hounds dug her up in Freeman's Spinney,' answered the constable.

'That is not my land–'

'No, sir,' agreed the constable, 'but her people are tenants of yours ... this gentleman,' – he glanced at his companion – 'is Master Sutton, landlord of the Chequers Inn, Didmerton way. He identified the remains as Polly Trenshaw, his taproom girl – went missing before last harvest.'

'Trenshaw ... I see,' said Grafton.

'Lovely girl, Polly,' put in Sutton, 'reckoned she'd done a flit – never thought no more about it.'

'Is it known how she died?'

'Carved up, sir,' said the constable grimly. 'Buried alive, by the looks of it ... a terrible business.'

Though she was standing away from the doorway, Kate could clearly hear the constable's voice. He was a man, it seemed, more used to raising the hue-and-cry than holding a private conversation.

A woman murdered ... buried alive. She felt the blood drain from her face. Understanding, at last, the things she had seen; the killing, the dark terror, the dogs. All three linked to this taproom girl, this Polly Trenshaw ... and him.

She looked across at Marsden; saw the girlchild break ranks and throw her chubby arms around him seeking comfort. Kate watched him stroke her hair then casually look up.

Over the head of the girlchild his eyes found hers. It was there in his face, in the flicker of weary disappointment. Dear God, it had always been there, if only she had chosen to see. His rough questioning when she had her first vision of the girl; the promise he had extracted that she should keep nothing back from him. *Withhold the most trivial of details,* he had warned. At every turn, the signs were there. No vision of the girl came to her but that he had been there.

The truth had screamed out at her, the girl had cried out to her. How could she not have seen? Marsden had murdered Polly Trenshaw. Her lover, the man she had sworn to obey, had mutilated and buried alive a woman younger and fairer than herself. She had seen through the eyes of the killer, had known the victim's suffering and comprehended nothing ... because she loved him.

Trusting in him, she had delivered herself into the hands of her accusers; stood passively while they played out the charade with the children – trusting completely in him.

But now she knew. And he was aware of her knowing. His dark eyes had drawn a chilling blank. No trace of concern in his tight-drawn lips. The illusion had crumbled and with it Kate's last hope of salvation.

'Sweet Jesu!' she wailed. But no one heard save Marsden. Keeping his eye on Kate, he leaned over the girlchild and whispered in her ear.

Kate sensed what was happening. The children were as much his vassals as she had been. He meant for them to destroy her. She backed instinctively from him and the girlchild, spun towards the door and fled – straight into the arms of the footman.

'Thought you'd slip away? Eh witch?' he sneered, hurling her across the mat. She fell heavily on her hip but despite the pain staggered to her feet and lunged past the hostile faces. Something caught her foot and she fell across Grafton's vacated chair. Then she felt nails digging into her back, heard the girlchild's hysterical screams–

'She killed it! She killed it! She killed it!'

Kate swung the demented child off her back. She lashed out as the others rushed at her. Suddenly, arms locked around her chest, crushing the breath from her lungs. She cried out, 'Let me be!' But a hand jerked her chin upwards, choking the words in her throat ... his hand, she knew.

'What is this?' bellowed the constable, pushing through to her. 'Who is this woman?'

'She has bewitched my children!' sobbed Ellen Grafton, as Joseph tore himself from her arms and fell, writhing to the floor. The constable stared nonplussed at the pinioned woman, at the torn clothes and blooded face.

'She killed it! She killed it!' shrieked Caroline.

The constable caught the child's wrists and asked, 'Killed what?'

'My lamb,' sobbed the child. 'She killed it!'

Landlord Sutton eased himself through the crush, curious about this woman they called witch. He took in the cut lip and bruised cheekbone. Stared at the bared thigh and shoulder, until his mouth watered. Then a glint of green light caught his eye. He pushed forwards and pulling the torn bodice to one side, traced the scroll with a wondering finger.

'What is it?' asked the constable.

Sutton rubbed his mouth. 'T'was Polly's only treasure that brooch.'

# Watching ...

Her mind cried out for sleep ... for death, but there was no mercy in their eyes, no respite from the torment. And the sun was slipping again, depriving her of warmth and light, locking her into the musty darkness, where there was no refuge from the watchers.

In lucid moments she knew she was in the back room of her own cottage; knew the choice of incarceration had been the priest's, approved by his mentor. Things familiar to lure her familiars, to hasten her confession.

She dimly remembered the boy, Ned, lifting clouds of dust as he swept the stone floor around her; the priest not letting him rest until the besom had scoured every rugged inch of the walls. The old man fetched him a stool to reach the furthest corners, till neither louse nor spider remained. And when the boy had done, he had him do it all over again, urging him to kill every last fly he found.

Satisfied at last, he had dismissed the boy and prepared the room with hallowed words and the draughty sweep of his clerical black. Then he summoned to the snare the creatures who did her bidding; the evil beings that of old found sustenance in the blood of a witch – the familiars.

He had enveloped her in his dogma, the aged priest of the musty robes; had suffocated her calm with relentless rhetoric, denying her everything but the route to purgatory. No food for her tight-drawn belly, no warmth for her nakedness, no sleep or mercy or hope.

And Marsden had watched it all, directing the priest when his old mind waivered over the details of the investigation. The mentor, the tormentor, the witchfinder sanctioned by the constable at Grafton's insistence.

By the pond he had said, 'Come with me, to prove your innocence – we still have time....' And she had given him obedience, put her trust in him believing that what lay beneath his mask was partly hers, never once linking him with the visions ... until understanding was thrust upon her.

Then he had sprung the snare.

And there was no escaping his dark presence. Since the discovery of the brooch he had not left her for a moment. He had stood across the doorway of the bedroom at Apescross, while four goodwives, chosen from among the servants, stripped and examined her body for insensible abnormalities. He had heard her screams as they pricked suspect areas with pins; had watched as they shaved every last hair from her body and employed their pins in the most intimate parts of her, searching for the Devil's mark – the teat from which a familiar could suck blood. And when they shook their heads, unable to find a single place, she had heard him thank them and say, 'No matter, it is not essential that she have them, for the Devil might easily move his badge.'

Her memory of what came after was hazy. She recalled the jolting of a cart and bindings that rubbed a sackcloth cover into her irritated flesh. And Ned's face as it peered down at her. She saw him as he had been the night he delivered his first lamb; the bright-eyed wondering Ned, and smiled. But the boy kicked out at her and reaching up to the driver gasped above the rattling wheels, 'Mr Marsden, sir! She's at it again!'

Marsden had carried her into the cottage, across the yard and through the fire-dead kitchen. He cut her bindings and set her upon a stool, while the priest directed the boy to sweep. And listened while the old man drilled her, over and over again, day in day out ... watching not for witchery, but for treachery.

In moments of distraction she had called on God, and the priest condemned her blasphemy; when she called on her mother he decried her sorcery.

Every nerve in her strained against the sun's sinking, willing it to stave off the terror of the dark but the shadow of the watcher by the window moved as imperceptibly and inevitably as the hands of a clock. It stretched to the foot of her stool, crept across her trembling nakedness....

'Awake, Katharine Gurney!' ordered the priest. 'No rest for you yet, no rest for any of us. Stir yourself!' She gave a feeble groan of protest as between them Marsden and the old man untied and lifted her cramped legs from the stool, then began again the dreaded walking.

'Before sunrise, your suffering will be at an end,' declared the priest. He pointed to the ceiling. 'A soft mattress to rest on, freshly roasted pullet, new bread–'

'How many nights?' she asked, wincing as they forced her split and blistered feet across the rough stone between hearth and window. 'How long?'

'Do you not know, child?' quizzed the old man. Kate shook her head. At length he said, 'This will be the third night.'

'And on the third day He rose again–' she recited emptily.

The priest stopped abruptly. 'The articles of faith come ill from the lips of the Devil's mistress. Confess it, he has oft-times come to you in the guise of a man, lain with you here and out there in the fields!'

Kate looked away from his burning eyes. 'It is no great sin to lie with a man,' she murmured, steadying herself against Marsden.

'You have an incubus, a demon lover ... declare it!' snapped the old man. 'What did he promise you? Riches, power, eternal life?'

Hoarse with thirst, she squealed, 'Leave me be! I want only to sleep–'

'Confess and be done with Lucifer's schemes!' blasted the priest. 'Admit that you are an agent of the devil; that you sent your imps to torment Caroline Grafton and the other Grafton children; that you sent it in the guise of a man to molest Barbara Canard.'

'They had an attack of the *Mother,*' she raged. 'Were you so blind? Scared witless by tales–'

'*Suffocation of the Mother* – hysteria,' explained Marsden as the priest frowned quizzically. 'It may be so.' He paused reflectively, before adding, 'The Mother often signals the Devil working through a witch.'

Kate heard him and began to shudder with weak laughter. It burst from her lungs with eerie savagery. Perturbed, the priest snatched her shoulders forwards so that her quivering features jerked back to look at him.

'Was it the Mother caused an infant to vomit pins and other vile objects?' he cried, grating his teeth. Incensed, he raised his hand but before he struck the hollow-eyed face, checked himself and dropped his voice to a cracked whisper. 'He has made you his instrument, Katharine; blinded you with lust and fornication and worthless promises. He might promise you the world, my child, for his own evil ends, but he will destroy you who serves him, just as he seeks to destroy the innocent....'

Kate blinked and said with pathos, 'I know.'

The priest glanced at Marsden, then quietly asked, 'Was it to satisfy his lust you murdered Polly Trenshaw?'

The girl's name triggered a rush of blood to Kate's head. She swayed dizzily, remembering woods and twitching snouts and consuming, terrifying darkness. 'I saw her,' she said, gulping back nausea. 'I *saw* her–'

'You saw her,' insisted the old man, 'because you held the knife that severed her throat. Confess it! With the knife you would use to skin a sheep, you slit the skin between the poor soul's breasts, cut down through her abdomen to the pelvic bone–'

'No!' Kate howled, struggling against Marsden's cruel grip on her shoulders.

The priest glanced again at Marsden, then turned gravely towards the window and said, 'One of the most sordid features of witchcraft is a belief in the efficacy of burying live animals. What did you think to gain from Polly's terrible suffering?' His voice was racked with pain and as he tilted his head up and pressed his eyelids shut, Kate watched a tear tumble down his age-dry cheek.

She followed its course in the fading light, no longer able to comprehend the priest's emotion, or the meaning of his words, for the whirring pain in her head. Kate pressed her palms against her bruised eyes, sending flashes of yellow light through her brain. She raked her fingers across her shorn scalp and became aware that she was no longer being held.

She looked up in confusion to see Marsden staring into the old man's eyes. She watched his fingertips stroke the aged temples as he might a child, murmuring soft words that had no meaning for her. Sensing her attention, Marsden looked up but the light was behind him, his expression masked by the darkness. Beside him the priest stood as though in a trance.

She heard no sound. Did not expect it. Then words took shape in her mind: *'I chose you for this ... do not fight it, Kate. Why prolong the suffering when you know there can be no escape? Go with it, accept your fate.'*

She felt the pull of him, the sapping lure of his will beckoning like a beacon across a cruel sea.

'Give me rest,' she pleaded. 'For pity's sake.'

She heard his cold, almost disappointed snort of laughter. Then on the horizon of her mind, far to the right of his siren light, she saw for the first time the faint flickering of another light and knew it for the stirring of a latent inner self.

Her breaths came rapidly, her hands fell from her ears. She turned as the door to the kitchen groaned ajar. She sighed and the unformed notions spilled into the still room – curling themselves around her and Marsden and the priest – flooding her mind with living pictures....

*She saw orgasmic bodies locked across a tombstone; the tonsured head of a young priest, the sweat-matted curls and desperate gasps of a woman.*

*She heard afar a child's quiet prayer. Drew nearer to the kneeling figure and cried aloud with remembered grief at the sight of her own young fingers holding back the minute hand of the silver larum watch. She buried her head as the church bell began to toll, then saw again fat fingers drawing obscenities in the dust, and her mother's eyes asking why and why and why.*

*Far off she heard Priest Peebles' startled shriek, but she was surrounded by bloody mutilation; absorbed by the sight of soldier bodies strewn across a quaggy field, still save for the furtive scavenging of looters. She looked down and stared into the weeping face of a boy-soldier, unable to move his head for a gaping wound to his neck and shoulder. She saw the pleading turn to horror as a flashing blade axed through his neck; knelt beside him, touched the severed head and looked up into the face of the executioner....*

'Murderer!' she hissed, throwing herself at Marsden. He caught her trembling fists and forced her to her knees.

'The word of a witch!' he breathed. 'Bound for the gallows.'

'Hold her fast!' gasped the priest. 'I have it....'

Kate knew by the startled mew what the old man had caught. Kitlin was bound to come to her sooner or later. The priest held it up in triumph. Kate wrenched herself free and lunged at the dangling cat. Startled, the old man tottered back against the open door and lost his grip. The young cat arched its back and sprang towards the window, straight into Marsden's waiting hands. With one practised flick he broke its neck and kitlin's sleek body dropped on to the flags with a soft thud.

'It will do no more harm,' said Marsden, flicking the limp bundle with the toe of his boot.

'I-indeed,' stammered the priest, clutching his forehead with trembling fingers. 'Dear God ... had I not seen it with my own eyes – it came as a man, every inch the mortal man, save for the vile odour it carried. I heard its step on the floor ... saw it reach for her until you sir, subdued her. Before my very eyes it was transformed into this ... this cat.' He eased himself down to his knees and looked over the limp animal in horrified fascination.

'Katharine Gurney,' he cried righteously, 'confess before your examiners and before Almighty God that this thing was your familiar, that you did fornicate with a demon man and do his evil work. Confess also that you have another familiar – a dog known to you as Jack.'

Kate folded her arms about her and frowned distractedly. 'See to it my sheep are tended,' she murmured. 'They have had naught but lean grazing these past days–' She shrank back from hands that reached for her.

'Only confess,' insisted the priest.

'Do not fight it, Kate,' breathed Marsden.

The old man pushed the open door to and as the latched clicked into its keeper, shook his head and urged, 'You are doomed, child, there can be no escape. Divest your soul of its evil burden before it is too late.'

'Let me rest one last night in my own bed,' she pleaded softly. 'One last night in my mother's house–'

She lay upon her pallet, waiting for fugitive sleep, conscious of Marsden's sentinel presence at the bedside.

'Why did you choose me?' she murmured into the void.

He stretched his interlinked fingers, cracking the knuckles. 'To give you purpose,' he answered, 'to colour your empty existence.'

'You have dealt me destruction.'

'That was your destiny. Better by far to explore brief life to its burning limits than grind on through an eternity of hide-bound vacuity.'

'And the Trenshaw woman, did she reach the burning limits?' Kate asked coldly. 'Before you destroyed her?'

'She had no depth,' he said planting himself heavily beside her on the mattress. 'She was a body for sale, a willing woman, no more.'

'Did she warrant such savagery? Could you not, for pity's sake, have finished her off before you buried her?'

'I do not deal in pity.'

'No,' she agreed. 'More fool me, that I should always have known it and still my woman's nature yearned above all else to please you. As you expected it would.'

'The man who is aware of and can satisfy a woman's sensuality, no matter how cruel, draws like water in a desert,' he said.

'Why me?' she repeated. 'Because they feared my blood?'

He shifted abruptly, shaking the pallet. 'Perhaps.'

'An outcast willing to pledge absolute obedience, to be your scapegoat when the time came.' Her throat tightened with emotion. She coughed and felt the weight of his head on her chest.

'You Kate,' he breathed into the coarse blanket. Conscious that he was listening for tell-tale emotion, she stilled the rise and fall of her chest, willing her thudding heart to calm.

'And others before me,' she murmured, burying her cold fingers in the warmth of his hair. His hand wound under the blanket to her naked breasts. The hand which had more than once teased her aching flesh to unspeakable pleasure, now seemed to burn into it. Her stomach lurched in revolt. Her eyelids snapped shut and she clenched her teeth.

This she had longed to know. That her body, like her mind, was no longer servile to his will. She was free of him. And the knowledge cut a swathe through her desolation.

She caught his hand in hers, steering it from under the blanket. 'The others before me,' she persisted, 'were their powers real? Did they have the sight?' He straightened slowly, and strained his ear after the distant cry of a vixen. One by one the faces came to him, old and young, knowing and guileless. Soon this one would join them, very soon.

'No more words,' he was dismissive. 'Your time is come. A clean death, the noose–'

Kate shivered involuntarily. Clean, perhaps, but not always swift. Her own mother had clung to life for minutes, they had told her, dangling high above the ghoulish crowd. But above all she feared they would cut her down and bury her deep under prison earth before she was truly dead. Polly Trenshaw's horror haunted her yet.

She pulled the blanket up to her neck and stared past his shadowy form into the darkness beyond. 'Did ever one go to the gallows bearing your child?' she asked grimly. The mattress flinched under her as he stiffened. Trembling with something other than cold, she said, 'It was for the child I went to Blackwood Top ... it was I summoned you.'

# The Cunning Man ...

Marsden had been in the saddle since first light. He had driven the liver-chestnut gelding over the mellow stone walls of the Apescross estate, across yawning pasture and the hill country around Wootton. He had cantered past drovers steering their flocks over Micklewood Chase; skirted thatched farmsteads and woodland mire; stretched the horse with a two-league gallop downriver, weaving between the clustered cottages of Berkeley village and across the bridge, digging his heels hard in until he reached the banks of the Severn.

He sat, hands folded over the pommel of his saddle, while the sweat-lathered horse drank its fill of water among the stagnant reek of the river-edge. He wore no hat and the untied black of his hair had been blown clear of his wild-eyed face.

A youth astride a cargo of grain sacks on a passing river-boat, spotted him and waved amiably. Marsden raised his hand in heavy salute and watched the disturbed water ripple towards him.

*It was I summoned you,* she had said. He grunted ironically. The shepherdess was condemned, finished business – so he had thought. He recalled Mother Sutton's meek acceptance of her fate, doe-eyed Alicia de Bourg, the pained confusion of Goody Winthrop. Then again of Kate's quiet triumph, her self-possessed calm and gradually the face he pictured assumed another, disturbing identity.

He growled as the old tightness gripped his chest and the base of his skull – snatched at air to quell rising nausea. Though oceans and moons had come between, he could not escape the dam. She was there, ever lurking in the shadows, ready always to explore his weaknesses, to belittle and subjugate. In death as in life.

His childish self had loved her. Though she had sent him from her to be educated by the sisters of the Abbey Alessima, he blamed himself for the separation and adored the Blessed Virgin. To win his mother's favour he had drunk dry every source of knowledge available within the confines of the convent. To win her.

He could not tell, even now, when adoration had become something other; when he had dared to aspire to the unreachable. Scholastic prowess, the onset of manhood – what matter? Her dark beauty had filled his thoughts, clearing his mind of pious clutter. His one fervour, her. And she had been aware of his enslaving passion, had anticipated it, perhaps even nurtured it. Her quiet knowing smile, the touch of her hand as she stroked his face, her skin perfumed with oil of musk-rose. Every smile, every lingering touch exquisite, moulding him until he had no will but hers.

To seal his fate, she had put him on the road to priesthood. To keep him purely hers, she had him take on the emasculating skirts of a priest. And the vows he took, were to her, not the god of the sisters of Alessima.

He jerked the gelding's still dripping head from the water, skewed round and up the narrow path towards the forest track. The horse snorted with the effort of the climb, stumbled sideways in loose gravel, righted itself and began to pick up speed.

*Poverty.... Obedience.... Chastity....* Marsden dug in his heels, forcing the flagging horse to gallop harder. A blaring horn from a river-boat faded in his wake. Wiry branches hung with new green leaves lashed his face and neck, their stinging salving the prickling hurt that had crept over his flesh.

The prickling hurt that years before had driven the young priest alone in his cell to strip away the skirts, to flay his ardent flesh and bind his aching member. Chastity. In fevered dreams he begged for release, cowering abjectly beneath her while the blood of her womb spread over him, blinding him. For she was without mercy.

He had hardly noticed the girl at first. She came and went carrying choice wines from her father's vineyards to the cellarer. A tousle of brown curls, bare feet – a nameless face, one among many village suppliers. Then, emerging from the cloisters one morning, he had caught sight of the tanned flesh of her thighs as she mounted a panniered donkey. With a sly smile she hesitated before pulling her skirts across and ambling away. When next he saw her, there was no hesitation. One moment she was standing in the sun-filled doorway of the chapel, the next, they were locked together over a tombstone in a sheltered corner of the cemetery. Not making love but venting a fury; the brown curls matted, the well-rounded body writhing under him, sweat from his temples dripping on to the glistening arch of her neck, over the grimaced parting of her lips. He ground her naked buttocks into the lichen-pitted stone, wanting to see the sly eyes flicker with pain. But they only burned more brightly and the cries that rent the air were his.

After, as he sat head propped against the stone, he felt her lips kiss his tonsured pate, felt her fingers trail over his smooth face. A parting gesture so redolent of his mother. And in that moment as she flitted away from him towards a copse from where she would follow the river back to the village, he knew the dam had sent the girl to test him. He saw then that the girl was living proof of his betrayal.

Death was swift; a sharp blow to the base of the skull before he submerged her midstream. Oyster fishermen found her swollen body four days later, caught in the hanging branches of a willow. Suicide, it was mooted, the guilty conscience of a fallen woman.

The gelding thundered over the wooden planking of the bridge into Berkeley, its haunches rubbed raw by Marsden's thrusting heels. Slackening a little it met the rising ground and trotted through the twilight mill of children and dogs, playing the day out in the rutted streets.

The corpse was discovered and he had gone to his mother, telling no one he was leaving the monastery, knowing that he would never return. The religiosity of the convent had become anathema to him; its tenets sprung from the words of a man whose humble forgiveness had led Him straight to the cross. Emulate, worship, murmured the convent, give yourself up as a lamb to the slaughter, for in weakness there lies strength. Deny yourself in this life so that you might reap the rewards of the next. Prostrate the self, castrate the self, delude the self until there is no self – nothing but a living death.

The girl was dead and there was no guilt in him, not one shred of remorse, no flicker of compassion. Through her he had discovered in himself the existence of a personal power; a life force that could not be contained – not by the strictures of the habit, nor the subtle manipulations of his mother.

On a night sultry and humming with crickets he had gone to her. She was alone when he found her; sitting on a balcony heady with the fragrance of jasmine, beneath a pergola covered with white blooms of camelia. Her hair was soft to his touch and the play of moonlight and shadow across her downy face lent it an ethereal quality. He recalled how she covered her surprise with a slow, welcoming smile, how she had offered up her cheek to be kissed ... but shrank coldly from him when his burning lips found hers.

And for the first time in his life her disapproval had meant nothing to him. Nothing at all. The carved arm of her chair was under his hands. He gripped and hurled it clear of the pergola, launching her against a wrought-iron fence. She had turned, clinging to the rail, the cold glitter of her dark eyes changed to a shifting wariness. She did not cry out, had not demanded explanation. Nor was she afraid, not then. She had held out her hand and waited for him to crumble in the face of her forgiveness, for him to fill the silence with humble words. Had it not always been the way?

He stared fixedly at the outstretched hand, at the diminutive figure before him. So great was his physical advantage that he could have crushed the life out of her with one hand. Yet this was the force that had racked his nights, dominated his days.

He watched her edge towards him, evading the fingers which reached out to caress his brow. Then crushing her wrists between his fingers, he described for her every last detail of his encounter with Therese, the vintner's daughter....

The gelding had come within homing distance of Apescross when Marsden turned its head across country towards Kate's cottage. Bats flitted overhead, wheeling aside as the dark silhouette galloped between a line of overhanging trees. Shadows loomed and fell away. Hunger had left him light-headed and his arms felt too weak even to lift their own weight, But he pressed on, through the copse, driving the spent horse until they reached the clearing and the silvered water of the pool.

He stumbled from the saddle and walked out the stiffness in his legs. He let his cloak fall away. Unbuttoned his shirt and flung it aside, his clammy flesh shuddering as it met the cool air.

He had meant to shock her into submission. Instead she had attempted to turn the situation to her own advantage; to use their shared knowledge to regain control over him. It had been weakness not to finish her that night in the garden. While she lived he could never truly be free. His awakened potency told him that, yet still he had walked away, knowing even then that ultimately one or other of them would have to be destroyed.

It was a mistake he had never repeated. After the dam not one had slipped through his fingers. His journey had been a long time in the making. Across Europe they had welcomed him into their homes, the outcast women. They had taken him for their master, though at first he was no more than a penniless priest. He had learnt to harvest strength, to eke out their age-old secrets; and having drained them of their usefulness, to step aside and watch them succumb to the fate he had set in place – cleaning the slate. Each one had won him new credence, each one had been a victory over the dam.

It had been simplicity itself until last night in that dingy room with the shepherdess – with her quiet knowing. Not that he cared for the bastard growing in her, only that she had control over something of him. No-one since his mother had ever managed that. No one since her had resurrected the cowering figure or the blood. His mother and the shepherdess, their images flitted back and forth in his mind until they merged into one smiling face.

Everything he ever vowed for the dam, he had renounced. He scorned poverty, aspiring to wealth and status; ridiculed chastity in an endless search for new gratification; and as for obedience, now he would have nothing less than complete mastery. All this in defiance of the hold she once had over him, to rid himself of the stigma of the dam. And the greater satisfaction would be in knowing that he had used her kind to do it.

Her spirit might fight him through the shepherdess, but he was stronger yet. A child was it? Then let the shepherdess hang but not yet. Not while she could claim part of him. One way or another the child would be his.

Twigs cracked underfoot as the gelding wandered off in search of grazing. Marsden breathed deeply, stripped himself of hose and boots and waded into the icy water. She had chosen him, she had said. But his would be the final triumph. And his dive shattered the mirror surface of the pool.

# Maleficium ...

Before God and Edward Johnson, Justice in Eyre, they testified:
'I was driven to her, Your Honour; near desperate I was, what with the master expected home from London any day, and the horse chirurgeon out of the shire.... I've tended horses all my life – I'd never have missed a spike like that. I swear there weren't no spike in Prince Rupert's hoof before she came with her chuntering and potions–'

*'Fair mangled she was, what with the dogs and months under the sod....'*

'Aye, Your Honour, fresh off the coach I was, resting up awhile by the kitchen door, watching the young masters and misses sporting in the courtyard. Out of thin air it came, a-slavering and showing its fangs. Great ugly beast of a thing went straight for Miss Caroline ... savaged the poor mite before we could chase it off, then *she* came after us; strength of a demon in her arms and such oaths as you've never heard–'

*'Flesh wound to the throat, Your Honour, insufficient to sever the windpipe....'*

'... so I f-followed Master Francis across to the stables. I was scared see, I'd never done it but for Master Francis being so kind before – I knew if I asked him to he'd speak for me, tell them I never meant to drop the apple bowl ... but t'was like he was in a trance: they all were. I daren't speak to him, not then, so I hid ... I didn't mean to spy. T'was as if the chanting rooted me where I stood, as if they wanted me to see. Oh but I was terrible scared, sir, t'was the smell see, putrid it was – near fainted away, I did. There was the lamb and Miss Caroline hanging in the air as though she were asleep in her cot....'

*'First I was chasing her through a spinney, next I know, I'm coming to under an oak tree–'*

'Walked through the stubble, she did, like it were a carpet of goose-down ... not a stitch on her. Ask anyone, Your Honour, William Kerry is a respectable man: a wife, two girls ... not given to lechery. Bewitched I was.'

'*... a trail of blood-blackened flesh from breastbone, through belly, to her loins....*'

'The rhyme came into my head when I was kneeling next to Cissie. I was thinking about the lady and the lamb so the prayers wouldn't hurt my knees any more ... I told it to Francis because the bad dreams had made me cry ... but I can't remember now; Papa made the bad words go out of my head–'

'*... hands trapped above the chest as though in supplication....*'

'She clearly had designs on Mr Marsden's affections, alleged some vague kinship with the gentleman ... an avowed falsehood. Perhaps she hoped to win him by sorcery and lies. I believe she regarded me as a rival and vowed to destroy me. Twice now she has attacked me and I am sure that she sent her imp to bedevil me that terrible night in the summerhouse. I live in fear of what might happen next–'

'*Sleepwalking as I thought ... followed her into the dip. T'was no mortal horse, he rode, fair flew at her it did, and she a-moaning and a-bucking under him–*'

'Always fingering and admiring that brooch, was our Polly ... often pinned it to her shawl and paraded past us putting on her cheeky airs. Ahhh, a winsome lass she was, said she'd hand it down to her girl, if she had one. Full of life, dear Pol.... To think it should have come to this.'

'*... mouth stretched open, earth lodged in her throat....*'

'As the father of five bewitched children and the guardian of another, I saw it as my duty to apprehend shepherdess Gurney. We came upon her out among her sheep and made a civil request for her to return with us to my home. She had nothing to fear from us, yet she attacked my men with a lethal weapon and unhorsed my niece. Her reaction was wholly unjustified but for one reason ... that she was the witch Parson Peebles had charged us to find.'

'*My opinion as a physician, You Honour, is that Polly Trenshaw was buried alive.*'

'... and that concludes the confession of Katharine Gurney, made in the presence of myself, Caleb Peebles, and my fellow examiner, Mr Matthew Marsden, after three full days and nights of watching. I have read to you exactly as it came from her lips, the words she sealed with her mark, here at the foot of the document. And I have to say that old as I am, and accustomed as I have become to manifestations of evil, the witchery of this woman has shocked and saddened me, beyond anything I can remember.'

'You see here a sorry spectacle, brought low by her own misdeeds and by the privations of prison life. But this is a woman in her prime, who was given every opportunity to learn by the punishment of her evil mother; accepted by the parish; allowed the means by which to earn a living.

'And yet, and yet, she did not spurn the Evil One when he came to her. She welcomed him into her very bed, succumbed to his lust and gave herself up to be his slave. She became his earthly agent, using her power to lay low anyone and anything connected with the house of Grafton ... even to a babe in arms.

'And just as she did Lucifer's bidding, so her familiars in the shape of a dog, named Jack, a cat, called Kitlin, and the black lamb she presented to Miss Caroline Grafton, did hers. We cannot know the extent of her evilness, only God sees all, but there can surely be no crime more heinous in His sight than brutal murder–'

*'I imagined her a woman alone; unprotected and without defence. In the interests of natural justice I felt morally obliged to speak on her behalf. Having heard her confession, seen the apparitions that visited her, I, Matthew Marsden, admit my gullibility–'*

Justice Johnson sounded his gavel a dozen times before making an impression on the courtroom din.

'Prisoner at the bar,' – he shot a censorious scowl at the gallery – 'you have heard the weight of evidence against you, if you wish to speak in your own defence, do so now.'

Kate breathed deeply and pressed her hands on to the brass studs of the rail in front of her. Her eyes trailed from the array of witnesses on her left, over the men of the jury, to the jaded officials ranged around the judge.

'You have me condemned as surely as my mother before me,' she said flatly. 'I'll not waste my breath pleading innocence. I learnt as a child there was no justice.' Her voice rose above the swirl of dissent. 'You must have your witches, for the Scriptures gave us being. If it weren't for us the Bible would have no credence; your faith would crumble to dust....'

'Better for you to repent your wickedness,' said the judge testily. 'You are soon to be tried in a higher place than this.'

Above a swell of outraged voices, she cried, 'I forsake your God, as He has forsaken me!'

And twelve angry men and true howled, 'Guilty!'

Kate twisted her fingers in the tattered cloth over her stomach, and finding *his* eyes, quietly smiled.

Loose ends....

Marsden stood by the water-clock in the gaol yard, fascinated by the ebbing waterline in the graduated glass bowl; by the sparkling column of water draining out of it, taking with it the vestiges of a life.

Over the scaffold, dawn light gave the promise of a warm spring day. And the air, rich with the perfume of wallflowers from a nearby garden, rang with the deep warbling notes of a nightingale.

He waited for the meniscus to reach the appointed level, then turned to see the prisoner, eyes set in an unseeing frown, helped up the steps.

Only days since *her* trial. No mean undertaking ... no mean undertaking at all.

There were few to see the noose tightened; a woman holding a child, a scattering of the idly curious, two turnkeys, a yawning priest, and the executioner. A murmur lifted as the head, shaking abruptly, scorned the chance for last words.

He moved closer to the scaffold, arms folded, his dark eyes fixed on the prisoner. He saw the startled flick of eyelids as the knot jerked against the neck, and concentrated on the eyes – lulling, leading to the final moment.

The air was still save for the trickle of the water-clock and the periodic creaking of the rope. He lingered a moment, following the twisted neck as it swung from side to side.

William Kerry had come to him after her trial, full of innuendos about his dealings with the witch, offering to sell his silence. Foolish man might still have been of use to him. But his feeble mind had a dangerous lack of subtlety, a reckless disregard for self-preservation.

Kerry had come to him in his inn lodgings hard by the court buildings; sweat-beaded lips quivering at his own daring, sure that he would corner his quarry. But confidence had proved a capricious companion, had deserted him in the face of Marsden's hypnotic influence.

Before dusk of the same day, he was crouched in a dank cell, rocking backwards and forwards as he repeated over and over again, 'Blood on my hands, pity my little ones ... sweet Jesu.' While in a candlelit office nearby, Justice Edward Johnson, scanned the contents of a confession newly brought from the gaol.

'... and that while in the thrall of the convicted witch, Katharine Gurney, I, William Kerry, being then employed as head groom at the Manor of Apescross, did murder the woman, Polly Trenshaw ....'

With a parting glance at the bulging eyes and tongue-wedged jaw of the man on the scaffold, Marsden donned his hat and walked away.

# Rebirth ...

*The just shall be wrongfully put to death –*
*Publicly, and being taken out of the midst,*
*So great a plague shall break out into that place,*
*That the judges shall be compelled to run away.*
                                    ...Nostradamus

Beyond the twilight world of the condemned, outside the cold confines of gaol walls, England sweltered its way through the summer of 1665. Eyes across the land bore witness to a lumbering comet and were filled with foreboding. The interpretations of seers and fortune-tellers, astrologers and wizards were in great demand. A sign, came the grim reply, a presage of catastrophe. God had drawn His sword to smite the land, some prophesied, for the wrongful killing of its sovereign lord, King Charles, while others declared the loose morals of the restored court had invoked His wrath.

Slow and heavy was the comet, and the news coming out of London was of plague deaths in several of its parishes. God, warned the soothsayers, had loosed a pestilence that would know no bounds. And the people trembled.

Like wildfire it spread through the capital, despite the best efforts of mayor and magistrates. Examiners were appointed to search for and shut up infected houses; watchmen posted to every door marked with a red cross; nurses to tend the dying; bearers to collect the corpses and death-carts to deliver them, under the cover of darkness, to a communal grave. No public gatherings were permitted, no entertainments. Days were set aside for public fasting and prayer. Every dog and cat was caught and destroyed, poison laid for mice and rats. But still the death-toll rose; tens, hundreds, thousands a day buried without coffin or shroud. Watchmen bribed, watchmen gulled, watchmen violently removed, by every means the confined tried to escape. Some wandered the streets raving with the pain of their swellings, others plunged their tormented bodies into the river. Some escaped through woods to the countryside, others sought refuge in the boats anchored on the river. And the blight that was laying waste London, spread its tendrils ever outwards.

Outside the cold confines of gaol walls, aboard a packet that sailed the glistening waters from Severn to Avon port, came the spectre of death....

Kate wound her fingers around the transom of the small window opening. She pressed her temple against the cold stone, listening to the crickets, and felt the fluttering movement of the new life in her swollen belly.

She had meant to take it to the gallows with her, this thing he had impregnated her with; had kept the knowledge of it to herself, not wanting the execution stayed. But he had outwitted her even in this.

Marsden had come to her on the eve of her execution. He had stood by the cell window, picking at the flaking rust on its iron bars and without a trace of irony, described for her the remarkable recovery of the Grafton children. And of their father's unstinting generosity towards him, their saviour. Then with a sardonic laugh at the world in general, he had touched the spiky new growth of her hair.

He mentioned the child casually enough, at first, but from the moment the turnkey had left them together, Kate knew that it was the only reason he had come. In his eyes she watched latent curiosity ferment into something more intense; a want that filled her emptiness with unhoped for satisfaction.

'I will take it away from here,' he assured, 'when you are gone.' She had laughed then, until the laughter threatened to choke her.

'A witch's bastard, sired by a murderer? You'd have me suffer such a misbegotten creature to draw life,' she had railed.

'I *will* have it.' His voice had been cold with certainty as he rapped the door for the gaoler to come. When the lumbering official appeared, Marsden snapped, 'Unless you would murder an innocent child, this woman's execution must be postponed ... she carries the child of the condemned man, William Kerry. See to it a physician is sent for.' There had been no arguing against the word of a gentleman or the gold noble dropped into the gaoler's hand.

That had been two full moons ago. Two whole months since she had vowed to murder the fruit of his loins before he should have it. She had hated it then, loathed it because it was of him. She had tried, by refusing all food, to purge her body of its parasitic use of her. Then the fever had taken her. For weeks she had been locked into her disorientated mind, kept alive by the rough care of gaoler Bart Halliwell. And with the gradual return of her strength, she found that her hate for the child had burnt itself out. It had come through the sickness with her – it depended as much on her for life as she on it.

And there was no question that she wanted life, now. The fever had ground through the layers of acceptance, consumed a lifetime of conditioning. Out of the ashes had leapt the instinct to survive. She vowed to live as she had never done before, to embrace the special strengths she had inherited from her mother – *in honour* of her mother. The guilt of betrayal, of green eyes across a courtroom, no longer troubled her. Memories of a woman strong and compassionate filled their place. A woman who had used her talents to ease suffering when suffering came to her door, a woman who demanded little but suffered no one to take from her the little she had. Elizabeth Gurney had accepted the mantle of witch, and so would she. Never again would she suffer passively but carve a way forwards for herself and the child. The child had saved her neck and her sanity. The plague, an inner voice told her, would present her with the opportunity to elude the gallows altogether. One by one the obstacles were falling aside, until one alone loomed large: and his shadow haunted her thoughts.

Marsden had murdered Polly, and others before her. His condemnation of her had amounted to the same – almost. Of all living souls she alone had glimpsed the evil lurking behind the mask of Matthew Marsden. And she knew that he would not rest until he had claimed the child and destroyed her. Knowing was her only advantage. Her one hope was that she could elude him until the child was born, until she could build her strength and take the battle to him, on her terms.

Kate filled her lungs with fresh air. Under the window, a pig, surrounded by scratching fowls, foraged in the dust. From behind her in the grim room, the dying woman moaned.

The animals would starve, she knew, when Mistress Halliwell followed her serving girl to the mass grave. There would be no one left to feed or slaughter them, except the dying woman's husband, and Bart Halliwell was too distraught to notice or care.

The plague had sailed into port, Bart had told her, brought from London by a stowaway. Within a week he was telling of how it seared through one parish after another, filling the lime pits faster than the felons released from gaol for the duty, could dig them. He told of once busy streets grown grassy with disuse, of the ever growing number of watchmen and doors daubed with red crosses. His stern, yet not unkindly face, grew steadily greyer and more forlorn with every passing day.

Wilkins, the fellmonger, Gilly, the seamstress and her aging father, Edwin, the baker's boy, Constable Williams, his entire family and servants all dead within a weekend. Turnkeys became watchmen and examiners as one by one their prisoners were conscripted to the death-carts as bearers and bellmen and drivers. Alone at night in the empty gaol, Kate would watch the flickering glow from street-corner braziers and listen for the weary ringing that signalled the passing of the cart to the cemetery beyond the town walls. And inured herself to the terror and the suffering outside as she waited for daylight and the gaoler's return.

Then came the morning when Bart Halliwell did not come to her cell. Not that morning, nor after. Alone save for the doleful clanging of a church bell, without food or water, it seemed that her worst fear had been realized. The gaoler had succumbed and with it her lifeline. She had wept then and prayed away the hours, until at last she was overcome by exhaustion and lost consciousness.

She had not recognized him at first. The cell was dark save for the amber glow of the lantern he was holding over her. But in the seconds it took her waking senses to focus, she had realized that the unkempt figure, with wild staring eyes was gaoler Halliwell.

'She has the tokens,' he gasped, dry-mouthed. 'My poor Rosy is come down–' He braced himself against a pitted stone wall, his rasping breaths filling the cell with urgency. Rosy, Kate guessed, was Rosemary Halliwell, the gaoler's wife.

'Who is tending her now?' she asked gently.

'I'll have no one come,' he choked, 'not surgeon, or nurse, even if they could be had. I've seen what tortures they inflict on ... on .... Dear God what am I to do for her?'

Kate knew too well his fear of the physicians. Days ago he had described for her the treatment he had seen administered to a dying friend. Convinced of the efficacy of bringing the already painful swellings in the man's groins to a head, to coax the disease from him by causing the pus to come away, the physician had first applied a poultice. Finding that this only hardened the boils, he had then attempted to use his scalpel but the tissue refused to give. As a last resort he had attempted to burn into the shell by applying caustics to the lacerated flesh. Agonized, the wretched man had broken free of the straps that bound him to his bed and leapt to his death from an attic window.

'Have you made report of the sickness?' she asked. Closing his eyes, Halliwell shook his head.

'The examiner will shut up the house soon enough – me with it.'

'You clung to freedom that you might come here ... to see me?' she ventured.

'They say you are a witch,' he murmured. 'Agent to the Devil.'

'I am accused of many things – murder among them,' she added warily. 'For all that you still seek my help.'

'If it would but help her I would call on Lucifer himself. God has no mercy for the likes of us,' he said through his teeth. 'For the help I once gave you, come to her now. Do whatever needs must – use the dark forces, only help my poor girl before it is too late–' His voice had risen to a sob.

'You don't know what you are asking, gaoler,' she answered, rising from the pallet. 'No reward ever came of dealing with evil forces. They will lure you with promises meant only to entice, never to be fulfilled and in return they will take everything.'

Halliwell wandered towards the cell door and back again. 'You are afraid for yourself and the child,' he rasped. 'Who knows but that I have brought the infection with me? See I breathe out air fresh from a sick room. My clothes, my hair all shot through with it.'

'My little knowledge of herbs will not save her–'

'Then comfort her, ease her suffering,' he begged. 'You know how, witch. Only stop her cries echoing in my head.'

It was the opening had Kate had been waiting for; not knowing how or when, but knowing it would come. If the gaoler went without her now, he might never return and the opportunity would be lost. So it was that she agreed to nurse his wife.

In the dead of a moonless night she shadowed him out of the gaol. In defiance of the curfew, they skimmed through streets and alleyways, dodging sleepy watchmen to pick their way across the rough pasture leading down to the gaoler's cottage on the outskirts of the town, to a room acrid with sweat and the odour of sickness.

Now another dawn had broken and beyond the window a pig snuffled irritably among the fowls.

'Water,' hissed a voice, with a strangled sob, 'water for God's sake.' Kate took a deep breath before braving the terrible stench surrounding the flock mattress. She emptied the dregs of a pitcher into a cup and knelt beside the gaoler's wife.

There was no vestige of Rosemary Halliwell, the handsome, plump wife who had brought food to her husband's gaol. The hazel eyes were bloodshot and sunken in a face, unrecognizable. Her flesh was marred with black blotches, her groin and armpits disfigured with angry boils, her mind deranged by intolerable pain.

Kate tipped a few drops of water on to the swollen tongue, protruding from cracked lips, and watched helplessly as it dribbled away down Rosemary's chin.

'Leave me, you devil!' squawked the sick woman. 'You've taken my babies, isn't that enough? *Dear God–*'

Kate gently lifted the wasted arms and, untying the compress of oak leaves she had applied, found that the almond-sized swelling in one armpit had grown no larger. The other one, however, had burst, leaking its putrid blackness through the bandages on to the mattress.

Five days she had hung on. For five days Kate had plied the dying woman with vinegars and compress; herb-Robert and ash, feverfew and oak, knowing that it was a futile battle, unkind to prolong the anguished life. But for the sake of the husband, whose last coherent act had been to spirit her away from the prison, whose numbed senses left him staring aimlessly at the dead grate in the kitchen ever since, for his sake she had pitted her wits, risking infection with every breath she took, snatching what sleep she could.

'She called out?' Bart Halliwell's ragged voice startled Kate. She turned to see him stooped under the low doorway. 'Something about babbies. Barren you know, never could–'

The sick woman's breath came in short gasps. She squealed pitifully, then hooked her fingers on to Kate's arm. Kate reached for a pad of wadding, dipping it in a bowl of water and laid it across the woman's forehead, watching a spot of black filth spread across the sheet from another burst boil.

'Aye,' Halliwell cried. 'Had love enough in her for a brood–' He caught a clawed hand and pressed it with his. 'Best this way, eh Rosy gel? Better not to have had them than watch them fail this way. Hell could be no worse. Christus!' He started as his wife suddenly flung herself out of his grasp with a blood-curdling shriek. 'If it had been a dog,' he trembled, 'I'd long since have put it from its misery. You know how, witch, monkshood or some such.'

Her head buzzing for want of sleep, Kate lifted her gaze to meet his bloodshot stare, and murmured, 'Death needs no prompting, it is near enough.' Words sprang to her lips. A childhood prayer forgotten until this moment. 'And if I should die,' she breathed, 'before I wake, I pray the Lord my soul shall take–' She pulled the discarded bed sheet back to cover the woman's exposed legs and lifted the wadding from her head. Bony fingers found her elbow, clenched to make a fist, then there was a gurgling groan and the arm fell limply back to the mattress. And Rosemary Halliwell lay quite still, eyes locked open. 'She is safe now,' Kate said. She left him then to be alone, went down to the kitchen and slept.

Later, Bart Halliwell stood at the foot of the bed watching her first wind the stinking corpse in the soiled sheets, then for want of a shroud, tie it into a blanket. His eyes did not leave her as she washed her hands and dried them on the hem of her coarse prison gown.

'There are guards on the town gates,' he grunted, 'no one may leave until the pestilence has done its worst.'

'Let me try,' she said softly.

'They say you are in league with the Devil,' he murmured, shaking the parcelled corpse as though to stir it to life. 'What do I care for that? You came to this God-forsaken place when I dare ask no other, risking yourself and the child.' He lifted the lifeless bundle into his arms and a deep sob escaped his lips. 'A strong-willed woman, my Rosy ... would never give in without a fight. Licked you this time, eh girl?' he shuddered with grief.

Kate laid a hand on his arm. 'Wait for the cart, it won't be long coming – you will hear the bell.'

'I'll not have her handled by any old Jack!' he flared hugging the bundle. 'We've come this far together – I'll carry my girl to the pit.'

'I shall be gone when you get back,' she told him.

'Take the path down to the river,' he said throatily. 'Go with the flow a mile, two maybe; there's a boat up there, else you could try your luck swimming across.' He kicked the door open and easing himself and his bundle under the sagging lintel of the kitchen door, grunted, 'You'll get nowhere in them prison rags – find something in the chest, she has no more need of them.'

Kate heard the kitchen door slam back against its latch and moved to the window. She watched him scatter fowls and dust, before lifting his load over a rickety stile. As he jumped the last foot down to the town road, she caught his eye. And in his empty stare, saw death ... no more than a glimmer; a sweat-glistening corpse, lying in wet meadow grass – but death all the same, and soon.

She watched until his bowed shoulders disappeared behind the hawthorn hedge, then threw back the lid of Rosemary Halliwell's clothes chest.

The man stooped, slump-shouldered, over the crackling logs of an open fire. Twilight shadow was stealing over the boards of the hut. No more than an abandoned hovel when he came on it that fateful night; rough-boarded, leaky and verminous, but a safe place, buried deep in the woods. A place apart for a man apart. For a restless, wandering man who once had a home, a family, a position of respect and had lost it all.

He coughed and spat a gobbet of phlegm into the nettle patch outside the door. His fingers found the raised scar tissue around his throat and scratched the itching flesh. Outside, trees whispered and the dead things shuddered in a sudden breeze. They hung by foot, by claw, from the crude fencing he had built; hares, rats, shrews, a magpie, a mole, a mistle-thrush, a squirrel and a cat. Some for food, others as warning to wood wildlife. Begone, for here lies a man of stealth and keen-edged blade.

There was satisfaction in a killing well done, in methods honed until there was no longer need of intricate traps and nets. There was satisfaction too in imagining every startled cry, every death squeal to have come from the lips of the shepherdess.

Surprise, he knew, was the only way to take a wily prey. And the witch was as wily and devious a creature as ever stalked among men. Yet even she could not know that William Kerry had survived the noose, that he had regained consciousness lying in a hand-barrow beside a shallow pit; weighed down by a shovel, grit from the barrow biting into his face and lips. The cold had set into his bones, so long had he lain there half-naked.

He shivered and held his hands closer to the smoky fire, remembering. A loud belch had drawn his attention to the grave-digger who sat back facing him not two yards away, swilling down a pie dinner and a pot of ale. His climb from the barrow had been a clumsy affair, limbs stiff and trembling. He could only think that the grave-digger had been deaf, for not once did he turn. Not once suspecting that the corpse of William Kerry would lift the heavy spade and let it fall on his balding head. And more. That a dead man would strip his unconscious form of clothes and feast on the remains of the pie before scaling the gaol-yard wall and fleeing to the outskirts of the town.

At first he could not understand why he had been spared, when everything that he had ever held dear was gone forever. When all that was left to him was a limbo existence. But slowly the answer had dawned on him. The witch had seduced him, just as she had beguiled Matthew Marsden. She, who had cold-bloodedly sacrificed a young woman to her devil master and bedevilled the Grafton children, had singled him out because he had suspected her from the moment she found that spike in the Prince's hoof. The witch-whore had enslaved his body and mind with sorcery, so that he had accepted the blame for the murder and provided her with a ruse for escape.

Pregnant, the turnkey had told him, on the eve of his execution. Pregnant with his child, the man had said, and because of it her execution stayed. Stayed to give her time, for a plague to set her free. For the Devil to loose her and her spawn on to an unsuspecting world.

Understanding had been slow in coming. But he knew now why he had been spared. Surprise was the only way to take a wily creature. Rising to his feet, he stamped out the fire.

# The Dawning ...

It was a sultry night, made warmer by the effort of following a river path grown over with bramble and hog weed, in shoes meant for a smaller foot. Kate found the boat a good hour after setting out from the gaoler's cottage, but it was moored beneath the shifting branches of a willow on the opposite bank of the Frome.

She dropped the bundle of provisions she had brought and turned to look back at the city that had intended she never leave it. The same city that years before had hanged her mother, then burned and scattered her ashes to the four winds. It was suffering now, that pestilent place. Over it the orange glow of well-stoked braziers permeated the night, signalling its distress, and Kate was glad. Her eyes trailed the eerie nimbus over its outline, then turned to the waning moon, with its own misty halo, and smiled.

She waded into a bed of rushes, through the cool of the lapping water, then rolled on to her back to keep the bundle dry as she paddled the short stretch to the opposite bank. She lingered a while midstream, savouring the sensual flow of water over her clammy flesh, then pressed on to the bank.

Kate was not aware of having drifted, until her head struck the wooden hull of the boat. She rolled over and grabbing the boat rail, waded into the stiller water of a reed bed, dragging the dripping bundle behind her.

The sudden shriek of a coot as it exploded from the disturbed reeds, startled her. She staggered back against the boat rail with a gasp. But no sooner had her fingers found the wooden ledge than something heavy slammed down on them.

'Thought you'd get away, eh witch?'

Kate jerked her attention from the fist that had trapped her fingers, up to the moon-glazed eyes of William Kerry.

'Thought I was a stiff, eh?' he hissed, grinding her fingers harder still. Kate took in the gaunt cheeks, the scar-shadowed neck, and said nothing.

'Well so did they,' he grunted, nodding towards the orange glow. With a ghastly laugh he added, 'Aye, they did that, body snatchers they said ... or the Devil come to collect his own ... only it isn't true, is it? The Devil, he protects his own, don't he witch?' The fist came up savagely and caught her jaw. Kate hung on to his arm but it locked around her neck and hauled her into the swaying boat. Kerry dropped to his knees, pinning her to the bottom and slammed his fist against her swollen belly.

'Believed you when you said it was mine!' he gasped. 'Saved your whoring neck!' He clamped his hand on her throat, forcing her head back and strangling her cry. 'T'was a benighted day I fetched you up to Grafton's horse. Then you knew I would, didn't you, sorceress?' He jerked her neck, snatching up her head and let it crack down again on to the planks. 'More than you bargained for, eh? Me, getting away? To make sure you didn't ... oh no, not while William Kerry breathes.' His fingers gouged at her windpipe, choking her cries.

Kate's eyes frantically searched the sky, instinctively knowing she must find the moon. It emerged from behind a stagger of dark cloud, framed with iridescence. And at once its misty tranquillity spread across the havoc of her mind, calming her flailing limbs. Its embrace lifted her through the planes of her being, further even than she had gone with *him*. And every cell in her body suddenly thrilled with vital energy.

She became aware again of the pressure on her throat; of Kerry's crazed grunts. She skewed her head down against his hand, stared up into his bloodshot eyes, and channelled her energy at him.

Kerry's eyes widened in terror. For what had been a woman under his hands now seemed to him a writhing, shimmering coil of serpents. 'Sweet Jesu!' he squealed, recoiling in horror as the scaled bodies swelled beneath him, lifting him out of the boat. He shook his head rapidly, spraying saliva through the air; pushed his arms out against the tongue-flicking head that had parted from the rest; gave a strangled scream as it flung its heavy body around his neck, preventing his leap into the water. And the rippling muscles coursed round and round the soft neck flesh, squeezing out the dregs of a scream. Kerry convulsed as it slid across his lips. His hands jerked upwards, clawing vainly. He could not check the relentless spiral. The turgid body crawled across his sight and Kerry's neck cracked....

Kate stared at her hands, still white knuckled around the dead man's throat. She looked dispassionately at the petrified features; at the rolling head and sightless eyes. And then in the corner of her eye a shadow beckoned her attention.

Intuitively she knew that the sisters had come. They were ranged all around her, in the reeds, on the water. Polly Trenshaw, the face of her visions, was there among scores who had no name. And at her shoulder the face she had last seen long ago, through the dingy haze of a courtroom. A breeze lifted her mother's loose brown hair as, with a sweep of her hand, she took in the others. Kate acknowledged them with a nod. And in that moment a hundred voices filled her head, each unfolding its own moving tale to her. Accents known and unknown, old and young, words tumbling, blending disjointedly. Lives long untold, vying for attention. Then, from the confusion of murmurings one voice emerged clear and soft:

*'For us all, Daughter–'*

And then they were no more. The faces, the voices melted into the night, leaving Kate alone under the moonlit sky, with the shifting reeds and the distant glow of braziers ... and the limp body of William Kerry still in her hands.

She buried her hands in the sweat-soiled armpits of his shirt and heaved his dead weight into the swelling river.

Kate stopped to rest at the foot of Blackwood Top. She dropped wearily into a cushion of dewy fern and eased the shoes off her blistered heels. But there was no rest.

On the eastern horizon the first glimmers of daybreak were permeating the leaden sky. This was the chosen time, she knew. Every step of her night journey had been directed to this place, for this dawning time; for her communion with the spirit of the cunning man.

She put aside the still damp bundle of food and pewter she had brought with her from the gaoler's cottage, and let the oversized gown slide off her shoulders. Then she padded barefoot through the damp grass, keenly aware of the quickening child, and the heaviness in her legs.

The sound of Jack's welcoming yaps spurred her on up the last steep stretch. She did not wonder to see the tail-curled sentinel, she knew he would come. And the warmth of his lean body as he nuzzled against her naked legs – the glad proof that he too had come – restored her flagging energy.

She followed the dog's lead through bramble and thistle to the appointed place. And there bid him be still, while she waited for the fingers of dawn to cleave the slumbering sky....

He came to her through a bank of vermillion poppies. No more than a black dot at first, obscured and revealed by the dancing flowers; a tall man, and heavy and he carried no baggage. And as aurora brightened the sky, so dawned the hour of her enlightenment.

Kate stretched her arms upwards, emptying her mind in readiness. She closed her eyes as energy, raw and elemental, coursed in through her fingertips, as knowing filled the void.

Upon the rustling of aspen leaves in the spinney below, a voice with a foreign accent boasted of its apostasy – taunting her with the deeds of its hatred – unlocking for her its terrible secrets.

A lifetime of secrets.

... She *saw* the tear-stained face of a boy, his dark hair pressed into the sober skirts of a woman; a cold and beautiful woman, her glossy black hair swept back into a coil ornamented with tiny ringlets, her dusky complexion unblemished around glazed red lips and dark-lined eyes. She saw the mother's eyes flick from the child to a bustle of impatient nuns; felt the child's perceived betrayal as hands tore him away – as the mother receded abandoning him to wimpled gloom.

On the voice whispered, through the incestuous infatuation of youth; years rankling with yearning and self-conflict. She saw a man-boy kneeling before a statue of the Virgin, mouthing ritual words, but seeing only worldly flesh and blood-red lips....

A first crackle of thunder resonated the hilltop under Kate's feet. And the images tumbled into her mind.

... A chilly graveyard, beside a stream, a stone set apart carved with rough lettering: *Ignotus ex aquis.* A body unknown trawled from waters far removed from the land of its birth. A body hinted at with childish awe, dead and yet undead ... the body of the dam.

She saw again the tonsured priest grappling with venal ecstasy upon a tombstone; a younger face but his face still, overshadowed by the bell, book and candle of excommunication. She heard his cries of orgasmic baptism, of death and rebirth; witnessed the moment of realization and shifted perspective – the old order renounced, the new boundless and all-powerful. She saw too the river-bloated face of the girl who had brought him to it. *'First blood,'* boasted the whisperer....

And lightning cut a jagged edge through the sky.

... Down the years they came to her, bodies abused and broken. From peasant cottage to battlefield. His strength ever growing, mastery built on knowledge gleaned, onwards and upwards. His goals, power and wealth and status but most of all freedom. Freedom from the dam, from her haunting shadow.

Thunder jarred the air, as its echoes reflected back at her from woods below, Kate glimpsed once more the chilly graveyard, and the inscription;

*Ignotus*
*Ex Aquis*
*Anno Domini 1658*

before the image changed and it seemed as though she was looking down upon herself; upon the belly-blown nakedness and wind-tossed hair. Suddenly the overhead sky flared. A single streak of lightning flashed down and just above her head splayed itself. She saw herself, fingertips and hair forked with silver light. And beneath, in the shadow of her parted legs, was the cringing figure of a man.

At once looking on and being what she saw, Kate's astral being drifted closer to the scene, watching the head-bowed silhouette, and at the same time feeling the trembling body beneath her. Even in dark relief she recognized the tied hair, the deep forehead, only his name was different. The name that came into her head on a blast of wind, the given name:

*François Borri, François Borri.*

The name fitted as Matthew Marsden never had. Not Marsden but Borri. It was the knowledge she had come for – the key to his being.

But in the moment she took the knowledge into herself, the hanging head started savagely. On a violent crash of thunder it rose, not the face she knew, but a malevolence of blood-streaked flesh and fiery red eyes. Tight-drawn lips peeled away from blooded teeth, smiling grimly as his right hand jerked up clutching a flash of dark steel....

'Enough!' It was a far off cry – her own, drawing her back. Back. There was a rushing in her ears. The image receded, dwarfed, until only the red glow of his eyes remained. Then that too was gone.

And she was standing on Blackwood Top, a lark fluting high above her head in a watery-blue sky.

The storm had gone and with it the danger, for now. She breathed deeply, calming her pounding heart, glad of the fluttering protest in her womb. The warmth against her inner leg she knew was Jack. She reached down as she had so many times before, to scratch his ear but there was nothing to feel. It was true then, what priest Peebles had told her during his examination at the cottage. The witch's familiar had been found and killed. She had chosen not to believe, knowing the priest capable of any ruse, if he could but win her confession. Kitlin and Jack were both dead.

Kate turned and began the descent to where she had left her few things, smiling inwardly as the warm muzzle pushed into her hand. She watched Jack bound off into the grass and away towards his old haunts, fingering the beads of saliva left in her hand. And wondered at a world so firmly rooted in this life that it could see no further than death.


At Apescross Manor....

'Master Matthew! Master Matthew!' The first confusion of waking did not slow Marsden's instinct. Slipping his blade from under the pillow, he slid past the bed-hangings and up to the door.

'Master Matthew, please come sir!' He recognized the voice of Hannah the kitchen girl. She knocked urgently.

'What's amiss?' he barked, behind the locked door.

'M-Miss Caroline sir,' stammered the maid. 'No one can do anything for her, ranting and raving like before! Miss Barbara sent for you sir!'

Marsden pushed back the hair from his forehead pensively. The girlchild had had no need of him since the trial; occasionally vied for his attention, yes, but she had not needed him as before. Yet Barbara knew better than to trouble him over a child's nightmare. Instructing Hannah to go ahead, he pulled the embroidered night-shirt over his head and dressed quickly.

'Cissie says Caroline started at first light,' Barbara explained as he sat in the window-seat of the nursery, the girlchild clinging to his neck.

'And where is Cissie?' he asked quietly.

'I sent her off to bed,' answered Barbara, moving to sit beside him. 'One hysterical child is quite enough!'

Standing in a connecting doorway, Jessie Harris glanced at Barbara – still in her night-gown and cleared her throat pointedly. 'Albeit your uncle and aunt are away, Miss Barbara–'

Barbara shot the nurse an indignant scowl.

'Go,' he commanded. 'I will come to you later. You too Harris, I would be alone with Caroline.' He watched them out of the room, then stroked the girlchild's matted hair.

'Tell me, my girl,' he coaxed, 'was it her again?' The child buried her face in the folds of his shirt, forcing warm breath through the cloth to his breast, and nodded furiously. 'Was she here in your room?'

The head shook. Her chubby arm reached out to the window, pointing and her flushed face puckered. 'Please don't let her hurt me or Cissie!' she wailed.

'You know my magic is stronger than hers,' he breathed. 'Tell me–'

'She was bare – I could see her paps and her belly was big and her hair was like snakes slithering in the air and she made the thunder and it frightened me ... and I woke up and screamed but the thunder kept coming....'

'What else? Tell me and it will all be gone.'

'A black monster between her legs and blood everywh....' Her lower lip spread and she exhaled with a sob.

Marsden stared out beyond the park at the distant hills and felt the old tightness take his skull. The familiar nightmare – his nightmare – and now more clearly dominated by the shepherdess. She was gaining strength it seemed while his arms trembled for lack of it. But he need only wait. She would wail at the birthing as all women did. What was there for her but the pain of travail and the noose? Let her fight. She would die as Kerry had died. And he would take the child and move on.

He breathed slowly, once more in control. And looking down, found the girlchild, thumb in mouth and lost to sleep.

# London ...

Kate stood before an oval dressing mirror, tightening the front lacing of her bodice. She glanced past her own image to that of the partly dressed man reclined on the bed behind her. And produced a smile. The Fat Saddler, Cassy had called him. Her smile broadened. Vulgar and breathless he might be, but he was one of the few merchants left in Holborn, and he paid well when she pleased him.

She ran her hand appreciatively over a scarlet cloak worked with black braid, before slipping it round her shoulders and fastening it at the neck. Then she pulled on her gloves.

'You turn a pretty trick, my dear,' chortled the saddler. 'Dash my wig if you don't. I shall have a thing or two to show the lady wife when she comes back from the country – mind, I'm not going to inform her that the plague is abating, yet awhile.' He thrust a clenched fist towards her and dropped a weight of coins into her hand. 'Tomorrow at the warehouse, I'll leave the padlock off–'

'I'll be there,' she murmured, closing the door behind her. She pulled the hood of her cloak over her head and slipped away down an echoing alley. The cool of the November air was welcome after the sweat-reek of the saddler's bedchamber. She savoured its richness; the yeasty smell of ale and freshly baked pies, the odour of horse dung and bonfires, the fragrance of honeysuckle and late roses which rambled neglectedly over the garden walls. The smell of London. The smell of freedom.

Two arduous months it had taken her, the journey from Blackwood Top. She had followed her instincts to London, knowing that few would think to follow her into the plague-torn capital; none perhaps, except *him*. It had been a hazardous and hungry journey, staying with overgrown forest paths to avoid the watchmen and constables who lurked on the outskirts of the towns. Knowing that once arrested the likelihood was that she would be classed a vagrant and passed back to her last legal settlement.

Footsore and furtive, she had braved dogs to steal eggs and milk. She had taken rabbits from poachers' snares, beet from fields and even shared scraps with pigs.

She had given no thought to how she was to enter the besieged capital, knowing somehow that the means would present itself. And it had. They had been wary of her at first, the travellers; had kept her at a distance, afraid that she might be infected with the pestilence they had left behind in their London parishes. But for Cassy they would have chased her away from their tents with makeshift weapons.

A buxom woman with hair of flame and a mind of her own, Cassy had listened. She had examined Kate for tokens of plague and softened at the sight of her belly. The others had argued bitterly against Kate travelling with them, that they were already too many and their provisions full stretched, that the plague could linger long in a body before the tokens showed. But Cassy had stood firm – had found space for a lone woman in her own tent – though it meant removing her shelter to an isolated spot. It was as though Kate was the excuse she had been looking for to assert her independence, to fly in the face of the men who had surfaced as protectors.

'Lord, pay no heed to the stingy beggars!' she scoffed when at last Kate was settled in with her. 'Cock-strutting to impress their womenfolk.'

'You are not of their womenfolk,' said Kate.

'That I'm not, Heaven be thanked!' The redhead laughed irreverently. 'Though I've done a deal more for that motley crew over the years than ever did their womenfolk – if they but knew it.' She met Kate's attention with a mischievous twinkle in her hazel eyes. 'I service their beds, love ... you know, surely there were whores wherever it was you came from.'

Kate smiled and knelt down on a ground-sheet of threadbare sacking. In the eyes of the world this woman and herself were both beyond the pale, a brazen prostitute and a convicted witch. Strange companions. And yet she sensed more honesty and compassion in this earthy Londoner than she had ever hoped to find again after her mother died. She smiled, recognizing in Cassy a kindred spirit and the makings of friendship. 'Yes, there were whores.'

'Where is it you come from? Not London with that accent.'

Kate shook her head. 'My home was in Gloucestershire hill-country ... with a flock of sheep to tend.'

Cassy tilted her head to one side and frowned. 'So tell me belly-blown shepherdess, why are you walking the road to such a

God-forsaken hole as London? Me, I've no choice – I know nothing else, besides nowhere else would have me.'

'I would be safe nowhere else.'

Cassy moved closer and touched Kate's short hair. 'What do you want of the place?'

'Refuge,' murmured Kate, 'a place where my face is not known, where I can earn a living.'

'Aah.' The redhead gave a weary laugh. 'Then it must be Lucifer himself driving you. If by some chance you could get by the watchmen on the gates, where would you stay? Even if you had money, few houses dare take in lodgers – you saw how this lot took to you. And as for an honest living–'

'I have no choice,' Kate said simply. 'There is no going back for me.'

'Not even for the sake of the child?' Cassy persisted. 'I'd rough it out in the forest, sooner than bring a little one into that poxy place. What of the father?'

What indeed, thought Kate. She reached the flapping door of the tent, pulled it across the opening and fastened its fraying ties. Then in the anonymous darkness, in the presence of a silent stranger, she sketched the outline of her life, expressing herself as she had never done before. Completely at ease with Cassy, she described the trial and death of her mother, through the years of isolation to the coming of the cunning man. Long after the other travellers had retired to their own tents for the night, when the only background sounds were of soughing trees, of night creatures and the occasional flap of their tent, Kate's words floated across the darkness, words spoken, words breathed. Until at last, there were no words only a meeting of minds, a transference of thought rich with emotional and factual detail. From Kate to Cassy, from Cassy back to Kate. A relaxing each into the other, until there was no strangeness. Each exploring the being of the other, compressing into a handful of hours, the friendship of a lifetime.

And when at last the telling was done, Cassy reached out for Kate in the darkness. Bonded by empathy and trust, they wound their arms around each other and sank into exhausted sleep.

Kate's first night with the refugees had also been her last. Next morning the two women packed their belongings and quietly quit the camp. 'We'll make for my old lodgings by Newgate Gaol,' Cassy had suggested, as they trudged a frosty road. 'Last I heard, the plague had died down there.'

At her suggestion also Kate had assumed the identity of Amy Farrens, a prostitute friend who had died of yellow fever shortly after she and Cassy had fled the capital with the other refugees. 'Who's to know?' Cassy had shrugged. 'Only the travellers saw me bury her and they won't be coming back while there's a whiff of pest about.'

As Amy Farrens, Kate had slipped by the surly gate watchmen, to enter the capital that evening. And suddenly the gaol cell dream became reality. She who had been half-drowned and stuck with pins, who had been castigated and condemned, found herself a free woman walking the streets of London; along Tyburn Road, through St Giles-in-the-Fields, past the theatres of Drury Lane and the porticoed houses of Lincoln's Inn Fields, around the offices of Chancery Lane. They had walked six leagues that day yet she felt no tiredness, only a heady exhilaration that she, Katharine Gurney, had cheated death.

For a penny they had engaged a link-boy to light them through a warren of tight alleyways to a two-storey building, overhanging a rutted lane. There was an air of abandonment in the flapping boards and cracking timbers of Cassy's lodgings. The damp air inside was chillier than the star-crusted night outside. Pigeons had free access through a broken window-pane in the upper storey and mice had the run of the place. But the furniture – stored in the cellar – was intact, there was a stack of firewood in an outbuilding, and while the landlord was out of town they would live rent free.

They had confined themselves to the kitchen that first night; swept the flags, fetched up mats from the cellar. Lying on the mats, they had supped on warm milk and damp biscuits, their faces aglow in the light of a generous fire.

'Tomorrow,' Kate had murmured, watching the flaring cinders.

'What of it?' drawled Cassy, lifting her head.

'I'll make something of myself, sell the pewter, buy clothes....'

'Save your things; we may yet need them to buy food. If my gowns are over big, we'll take them in. When we find customers, they'll care little for the packaging, only the goods.' She had laughed then, lifted herself up on to one arm and touched Kate's distended stomach. Huskily she had said, 'There are ways of slipping a child....'

'I know,' Kate answered, linking fingers with her.

'Why keep his bastard? Surely–'

'The child is of me, Cassy. I have not come this far to lose it now.'

''No,' Cassy sighed. 'Then we'll just have to work the harder to prepare for your lying in.' She unpinned her hair and flicked it over her shoulders. With a sudden grin she perked, 'Ah it's good to be back, plague or no. God only knows why I went away in the first place – Amy I suppose, always coming down with something....'

'The plague will leave us be,' Kate had said, knowing that just as she knew Cassy's bright grin had masked a deep sadness; a yearning to do not with the child she carried but another, living child – one given up at birth. She had seen it for one brief moment in Cassy's unlighted eyes.

Cassy knelt up and stared down at Kate, her hair a translucent shimmer in the firelight. 'You know about my baby, don't you?' Kate laid her head in the older woman's lap, confirmation in her silence. 'Gawd knows why but I'm glad, only don't speak about it, unless you want to see me blubber. Ah Kate, you're a deep one – by rights you know more than a body ought to; no wonder you gave Squire Grafton the gibbers. Best keep all this to yourself though, eh? What with the plague, London has become as superstitious as the country.'

Neither of them had expected that first night to find work as readily as they had. They could not have known then that the wildfire news of falls in death returns had in the early weeks of November brought with it an influx of people.

That discovery awaited them next morning when they took to the streets. With shears and tongs Cassy had transformed Kate's Puritan crop into a head of curls. She used rouge to heighten her complexion, kohl to enhance her eyeline. In petticoats and the finest gowns the cellar chest had to offer, they ventured into the capital.

From Newgate Street to the wide thoroughfare of Cheapside, the streets so dead the night before, had come alive with the cries of vendors, the bustle of men going about their business, a knot of street urchins playing around the open sewer, every now and then dodging out of the path of hooves or iron-rimmed wheels.

Weary at being so long away from their homes, it seemed displaced citizens had flocked back to the metropolis. In every road, every back way, shops and businesses were reopening. The boards were coming down and with them the defences of the population. The numbers dead of plague were down this week, as they had been the week before. That was enough. No need to trouble the mind with the actual figures – a thousand a week, what of it? Many of them had been sick for weeks. They were the tail end of a horror that was passing; a drop in a mass grave. God's wrath was spent and they were the lucky ones. No need now to shun the streets, to shy from human contact. No need to deny oneself worldly pleasure.

Arms linked, the two women had walked on into Covent Garden, into the sprawling square centred on St Paul's. That the plague summer had done its worst here was evidenced by the many boarded houses, by the sick who wandered the streets, some with bandaged necks, others limping with the sores in their groins. But here too, the taverns and brothels were rowdy with custom; traders' barrows piled high with fresh goods littered the walkways, hawkers plied their wares on street corners, and in the grounds of the cathedral people browsed around the bookstalls.

Avoiding the outstretched arms of a beggar, Cassy steered Kate towards the fashionable houses, towards the porticoed façades and iron railings strung across with glistening spiders' webs, there to renew old acquaintances, to establish who among her old clients was in town, to make known her availability, and Kate's.

By noon sunshine had dissolved the last traces of mist and in less than a dozen house-calls they had secured clients enough for a week. Men, as Cassy had put it, of a better cut; a solicitor, a goldsmith (though see his money first, warned Cassy), a wax chandler, a clerk of the Admiralty, the Fat Saddler, a financier and an old patron Sir Hugh Stanforth. Men of appetite and pocket to satisfy it, men who evidently knew and trusted in Cassy's discretion. Men who knew exactly what they wanted; and when they found it came back for more.

It was a game Kate understood from the first. She was no girl victim that she should go passively to their beds, but a mature woman who had chosen the life, a woman whose experience was gained of a demon lover. Confident in her own sexuality she aroused the most jaded of palates, often intriguing a man by playing out his secret fantasy, though he had never voiced it. There was excitement for them too in breaking the taboo of pregnancy, in exploring new contours, new approaches. She cultivated the art of brinkmanship, of drawing a man to the limit many times over before the final burst. And when it came she would feign mutual passion, conceding to him the final satisfaction.

She made no excuses. With survival at stake, she could not afford to be virtuous – that path had failed her miserably before. She knew the pitfalls. Cassy had warned her about the whore-haters and pimps; about the floggings meted out to so-called penitent prostitutes. But she had no qualms. Every fistful of coin gave her a stronger hold over her destiny, securing a life for her and the child.

The saddler's payment jingled in the pocket she had sewn into the lining of the red cloak as Kate crossed Newgate Street. She skirted the smoking chimney of the soap-works and turned into the now familiar lane.

A green glint of cat's eyes from the shadows momentarily startled her, provoking a kick of protest in her womb. She paused for breath and the splutter of a horse further up the lane, caught her attention. Though the overhanging buildings blocked what little light there was she could see the outline of a coach and the swinging head of a horse blocking the lane outside Cassy's lodgings. She pressed on, past the liveried figure lounging against the carriage, turned her ward key in the lock and ducked under the sagging lintel.

Cassy was standing with her back to the fire, her hem and petticoats lifted to warm her upper thighs. Slipping out of the cloak, Kate flopped into a high-backed chair and asked about the coach.

'For you,' said Cassy grinning. 'Tired or no I wouldn't pass up an invitation to the Temple of Solomon.' She rubbed her thumb and fingers together lucratively. They both looked up at the sound of sharp knocking on the front door. 'A business acquaintance of Sir Hugh,' Cassy explained, 'his coachman has been back twice already.'

Despite the gnawing ache in her back, Kate smiled. For days now a tension had been building inside her, a presaging instinct somehow connected to Marsden. As Cassy spoke, an exquisite burst under her ribs told her that this was it. This summons to the Temple was in some way linked to him. Pausing only to take a swallow from

Cassy's half-empty beaker of ale, she refastened her cloak and went out to the waiting carriage.

# François ...

The coach rumbled through dark lanes, to broader streets bathed in the amber light of public lanterns. It swung hard right by the river, jolting Kate as she stared out at the flickering lights from the river-boats, and away right again through an elaborate gateway into a gravel courtyard. Clutching the coachman's arm, she stepped down on to the gravel and glanced up at an imposing edifice. The dour greyness of the Temple was relieved only by the lighter stone of its cornices and the glassy shine of its many windows. The call of a watchman drifted to her on the still night air, *'Past nine of the clock and a chill winter's eve....'*

'This way–' grunted the coachman, unhooking a carriage lamp and tugging impatiently on her elbow. With a flick of his beribboned periwig he led her smartly across the gravel and into what appeared to be a walled garden. Almost running to keep up with him, Kate followed the chuntering servant along a series of paths; from there into a patch of dense shrubbery until they came upon a leaf-covered stairwell. With a sharp glance over his shoulder the coachman descended the steps and, beckoning her, unlatched a door. Beyond it, in the splay of a lantern, she made out a brick-lined passageway. Gathering her skirts around her, Kate stepped into the dark tunnel and followed the already retreating lantern. Never once slackening his pace, the servant conducted her through the twists and turns of the underground passage to the foot of a narrow staircase. It stretched up into the darkness, a secret way, built it seemed between two wall skins barely a body width apart.

'Please wait!' Kate gasped, burdened by the weight of her pregnancy. She paused for breath, bracing herself between the two walls. The coachman checked and with evident reluctance back-tracked down to her. Peering into her drained face, his brusqueness softened.

'Liven up girl, he's not used to waiting.'

Kate stared through the smoke-charred glass of the lantern at the guttering flame until her breathing grew steadier. This place was linked to Marsden, she felt it. But the man who waited for her up there was not he.

'Who is your master?' she asked.

The coachman tapped his nose. 'Never you mind, girl; a man of influence and unholy temper – that's as much as you're getting. Now shift yourself!'

She followed him up the narrow flight of three score steps or more to a landing stage and a bolted door. He snapped the bolt back and pulling the door inwards steered her into a lavish bedchamber, then quickly retired to the landing. Kate watched the door swing to as he sealed himself out. What had been a door from the landing, was inside concealed as a section of bookcase. She trailed her fingers over a section of ribbed leather book spines, staring for a moment at the strange lettering on them. Then turned.

The curtains were drawn but the high-ceilinged room was ablaze with the light of a dozen candles and a well-stoked fire, which drew noisily as she stepped on to the hearth rug and unfastened her cloak. Her gaze wandered over the mantel ornaments, a lantern clock between matching urns – to a japanned cabinet, its gilded doors opened to reveal wine cups and bottles part filled with brown liquor. Under the window there was a writing desk and chair. A quill pen rested on an open book, beside it several stoppered vials and an hour-glass.

The dominant feature though was a four-poster bed. Its hangings and scalloped pelmet were a tapestry of red on white, matching the window curtains and were – like the window curtains – drawn.

She draped her cloak over the chair and from the desk picked up a glass vial. Holding it up to a candle flame she shook its mustard-coloured contents and watched the disturbed sediment settle. Above the cracking and spitting of the fire, and the quarter strike of the clock, she heard neither the rustle of the bed hangings, nor the padding footsteps behind her.

The man had intended it so. From a crack in the hangings he had observed her progress about the room. He had noted the thrust of her belly beneath the bodice; noted too a certain depth, a self-assurance born he suspected, not of ignorance as with so many, but something more substantial ... more challenging. Another step. And he was close enough to see the scalp beneath her curls, the downy nape of her neck; to breathe her musky scent. Holding his breath he laid his left hand on her shoulder, with his right caught the vial. And was rewarded with a startled yelp.

Pressing close to her ear, he breathed, 'I'd given you up.'

Kate spun round and was confronted with humourless grey eyes. There were streaks of grey in the tied hair and trimmed beard, signs of suffering in the slight body and lean face – above all in the ghastly purple crusts from neck to collar bone; angry scars she recognized at once as scalpel mutilated plague boils. A physician's legacy. She reached out to touch the disfigured flesh and saw his tongue flick across his lips.

'My stamp of immunity,' he said, pushing her hand aside. 'Survivors I am told, run no further risk. So I am safe from you, but what of you? Are you prepared to take the risk?'

'I am here,' Kate answered.

'Indeed you are!' He leaned past her and set the hour-glass running. 'Mine until the last grain of sand falls through the glass.' Smiling pensively he held up the vial. 'We'll begin with this–'

Her eyes followed him to the cabinet, watched as he poured two measures of liquor. Settling them down on the desk, he pulled the stopper with his teeth and shared the contents of the vial between the two goblets. Then he pressed one into her hand.

'The sands of time!' he toasted. With a gesture for her to drink, he quaffed his own.

Holding his gaze, Kate lifted the goblet to her nose. Unable to small anything beyond the rich pungency of the wine, she sipped. The spirit tingled pleasantly in her mouth, singeing her throat. She took a deeper swallow, despite an earthy backlash, enjoying the heady surge of it.

'The apothecary informs me,' he said, replacing the stopper in the neck of the vial, 'that extract of Mandragora effects an interesting shift of perspective ... that it liberates the senses.'

'The man root,' Kate breathed, noting his surprised glance. Though she had never used the potent mandrake, her mother had. She recalled the ritual lifting of the root; the scraping away of earth, twine tied from it to the neck of a dog. The dog chased to tear the root from the earth. The ancients said it shrieked like a man on uprooting, that it was a living creature having the power to strike dead the hand that tore it from the earth. Effigies were cut from it.

Potions for fertility and love and sleep decocted from it. All this she recalled as the warm glow numbed her limbs, as it eased her nagging back-ache and gave her body the lightness of a child's.

The scarred man's surprise had relaxed into an incongruous grin. 'We are quite alone,' he said, pulling the bow at her neckline. 'I alone of the brothers have watch over the Temple this night ... the servants are dismissed. Just you' – he spread the lacing of her bodice – 'and I.'

Kate loosened her skirt and shrugged the gown from her shoulders. Stepping out of its crumpled folds, she stumbled back against the desk. The room had begun to swim in and out of focus. She was conscious of warm hands on her stomach, of him kneeling, his ear pressed against her. She reached for the waist cord that secured her shift and heard him murmur languidly, *'Not yet, not here ... come.'*

The floor seemed to offer no resistance as she moved with him past bed and hearth. He stumbled against the open door of the cabinet. A fluted bottle fell gracefully and floated down before exploding on the tiled floor. And the room was filled with a gurgling laughter she knew was hers.

She watched him untie the leather strap at his waist, then bind her hands with it. His face had lost its grey sobriety. His eyes shone, his lean frame bristling with anticipation. He pulled her past the cabinet towards a wall-hanging embroidered with stars and interlocking triangles. He flapped the symbolic tapestry back uncovering a hatch opening in the wall, and thrust her, head first, into it.

How long she sat there in the cramped darkness – knees drawn up, head pressed down – she could not tell. Her mind had succumbed to sleep when a juddering wrenched her awake. With a sickening rush the compartment began to fall through space. She reached out to where the hanging had been and grazed her arm against moving brickwork. For a few distraught moments she imagined the deranged man had dropped her into a well. Then there was a mechanical creaking above the compartment and she realized that her descent was slowing – to a halt.

Tentatively, she stretched out her bound hands and found the smoothness of wood against the open side of the hatch. There was a vertical crack at the centre as of meeting doors. She pushed and a pair of small doors swung back into the darkness beyond. Kate crawled out, feeling her way across cold marble, around stone columns and lines of benches until she found uncluttered space.

She sensed an aura here, something more than the smell of incense and the lofty chill; a sinister intensity which made her shiver. She struggled to her feet. He was here, the scarred man. She had a powerful sense of his presence ... but not his alone.

The tinkling bells of a wind chime ruffled the silence. Ahead, the orange glow of a lamp suddenly pierced the darkness. Then another came to light ... and another. In the muted light an image took shape. Under a high domed ceiling she saw two great pillars between which were steps leading up to an altar. Behind the altar was a raised throne and suspended high above the throne, a glittering bronze star.

'Women are forbidden the Temple!' boomed the voice of the scarred man. 'It is written.'

Searching the gloom for him, Kate replied, 'I seek the brother guardian–'

'Closest to the beasts is she who bears the child!' he blasted. 'Defiler of my master's house – what say you in your defence?'

She waited for the echo of his voice to fade, then replied, 'My master is not yours, guardian of the Temple of Solomon. I have no fear of him.'

She heard laughter, harsh and guttural, caught sight of movement behind the throne, and the hairs of her skin lifted. The laughter died. 'Then approach the steps, whore!' A dark shape flitted away from the altar to her right, lighting more lanterns as it went. She edged towards the altar steps.

'Not afraid, surely?' mocked the voice.

Bracing herself against the cold and a sudden putrid stench, she placed her foot upon the first step and was instantly thrown forwards under a terrible weight. She crumpled on to her bound fists, striking her head against marble.

He pulled her off the steps, his body pulsing and erect as he turned her and threw her limp arms above her head. For one savage moment Kate felt his weight, a small man made heavy by momentous rhythm. She stared past the heaving flesh into the domed roof, forcing herself to concentrate on the swirl of shadow. Staring, until the shadow resolved itself into the sharp images of stars and triangles, and a central cross – a carnal parody made of their coupled bodies – hers the upright, his the cross member.

And as she stared at the cruciform, she felt a gripping under her skull, a drawing beyond....

*Through the shadow-formed cross she saw another crucifix, set with milky-blue stones. It hung from a leather cord about the sweat-beaded throat of a woman. A woman half-dressed and cowering in the corner of a slant-ceilinged room. Though there was no sound, she was screaming. Her throat muscles strained to it, her mouth and eyes gaped with the terror of it. Blood oozed from a split in her lower lip, streaking her teeth. She pressed her naked back harder against the wall but could retire no further and began to slide down under her own thrust, her arms locked straight in front, distancing, warding. Her tight-nippled breasts juddering as she sank, thighs splayed, on to her heels.*

*Her stretched eyes widened a fraction, her taut mouth slackened. She jerked her head aside, cracking it on the wall, unable to rest her harrowed gaze from the malevolence looming over her. Its shadow stole over her and in the mirror of her eyes assumed the shape of a man. Then it was lost in the flash of a blade, in the impaling of belly flesh on steel, in the searing heat of the blade jerked breastwards.*

*In pain excruciating and interminable.*

*She was prostrate now, the woman; only her head propped up by the wall, her neck tightly curved. Her eyes were mesmerized by the progress of the knife, by the carving of her still live flesh, and the miasmic presence which knew no mercy – taunting her with death but keeping it at bay, stretching her mortality to its terrible limits, to exact every tortuous drop.*

*Kate knew her pain; rent the air with her anguished cries. It was Polly Trenshaw all over again. But not her. The face was more lined, the hair darker but it was the same adept blade – the same evil presence.*

*Him....*

A stabbing thrust made Kate cry aloud again. The vision had faded and she was left staring into the high-domed ceiling, at the undulating shadow of a cross made there. He was frenzied now, the scarred man, gasping in his desperation. His fingers clawed into the softness of her buttocks, his teeth gnawed the tiled floor. He squealed maniacally, then banged his head against the floor in frustration.

'No use!' he whimpered, throwing himself off her. Kate exhaled and closed her eyes, waiting for the discomfort to drain from her. In her mind's eye, she visualized the last grain of sand slipping through the hour-glass constriction.

'Get thee gone from me, whore!' he growled. 'Before I throttle you!' It was the languid threat of a spent body. Kate skewed her head round and stared at his pale limpness, seeing for the first time the purple disfiguration in his groin – tissue more scarred even than his neck. The legacy of his disease, it seemed, went further than mere scars.

'Be gone, I tell you!' he snarled. 'What use are you to me, you bloated harlot?' Kate eased her tied hands down and rolling on to her side, pulled herself clear of him.

'What use any woman?' she murmured, biting at the knot which held her wrists. There was no reply. The soporific drug had taken its toll. He lay sprawled across the temple aisle, saliva bubbling across his lolling tongue.

With one last tug Kate loosed the thong and dropped it on to his chest. She would take her pick of the ornaments on the bedchamber mantel.

That was her due.


Christmas Eve, 1665....
Cassy patted her ample breast with the hem of her jaded silk gown, wiped the matted hair from Kate's furrowed brow. 'Little blighter picked a rum corner to be born, eh girl? In a brothel, overshadowed by Newgate Gaol. And the city laid low by plague, Lord save us.'

Kate snatched at air and clutched her companion's wrist until the contraction subsided. From the alley below came the soulful strains of a street musician, idly playing his flute close to the open window.

'Cassy,' she gasped, 'make him play for us a while–'

The redhead's coarse features broke into a smile as she moved to the window. 'You, piper!' she called, throwing down a coin. 'Give us a tune to lure a little beggar into this God-forsaken place.' She chuckled at some unheard ribaldry, then turned back to Kate. 'Can't say I blame it for wanting to stay put.' She checked at the sight of Kate, hands tight around her ankles, her face screwed up with pain; then started forwards, as with one last effort, the bloody head burst through the dilated passage.

Kate lay listlessly watching Cassy as she bustled around the infant. A lullaby drifted in through the window. And words long ago imprinted on her mind, came back to her now: *Lully, Lulla thou little tiny child....*

'Little tartar,' cooed Cassy. 'Naught to boast but that dark crop of his.'

'And a name,' Kate murmured, fighting to stay awake.

Cassy plumped down beside her with the baby in her arms. 'What name?'

'François,' said Kate.

# Shadows

Sir Hilary Grafton, barr.
Candlewick Street, London

*Deare Father,*

*May this find you well and the gout at bay. It grieves me to have seen you not this twelvemonth, being kept away first by the bewitchment of my children – thank God overcome – and latterly by the scourge which choosing not to evade by coming to us in the country, you did with His gracious help escape.*

*There is, sadly, no news of our profligate ward and niece, Barbara. I wrote last that my man traced her latest elopement to Berwick on the Scottish border. For the sake of her father, my poor dead brother and your son, we can but pray that the Almighty will prick her wanton heart for she is beyond all other influence.*

*Wife Ellen and young Cissie have been much troubled with a quartan ague. You may imagine what fear their illness struck into our hearts. In this, we are once more indebted to the redoubtable judgement of the physician in our midst, Matthew Marsden, who at once settled our minds as to the question of plague and whose chemical physic has driven the ague from them.*

*It came as a great heaviness yestereve, to learn that after so many months under our roof, Matthew is recalled to the capital on Royal business. We shall all feel his loss, Caroline most keenly, but comfort ourselves in the certainty that our loss is His Majesty's gain.*

*I commend this man to you, sir, knowing full well your solitary ways permit few guests but pray you, make exception for this gentleman, until such time as he can establish himself in another safe house. He takes his leave of us two weeks hence, to be in London for Easter Sabbath, the fifteenth inst. God willing, I shall bring my grateful thanks to you in person within the month.*

*Your respectful son, Samuel.*
*Apescross April 1, 1666.*

'How soon is Easter Sabbath?' grunted Sir Hilary, tossing the letter and his eyeglass on to the gate-legged table, next to his bath chair.

The question was directed at the white-smocked blur for whom he was sitting. Nathaniel Taylor, a contemporary of Sir Peter Lely, was a portrait painter of repute and like Lely, favoured with royal commissions. His hooded eyes glanced up from the canvas, accustomed to the irritable severity of the old man.

'Why, sir, this very day. You may recall I came here directly from the mass in the Queen's Chapel. Such music!' He set his brush aside and wiped his fingers on his smock-coat, 'And you sir, are expecting a visitor from Gloucestershire.'

'Visitor be damned! A stranger foisted upon me by my blackguard son!'

'Fie sir! Is this not the day our Saviour was resurrected? A day for rejoicing and sweet temper?' He untied his smock and ignoring the old man's sullen protests, pushed the wheeled chair into the bright light of an oriel window. 'Out there' – he gestured expansively over the rooftops of London, 'the pestilence is but a memory. His Majesty is back in the capital, the sun shines and God is surely in His Heaven! The sitting is done, sir. I am away to the house of my Lady Castlemaine and, unless my eyes deceive me, the coach drawing up bears the Grafton arms.'

In the street below, Marsden pushed the carriage door shut and waited for the driver to unload his baggage. Across the cobbled street, through a stableyard arch, he glimpsed the steelyard. It was an area he recognized; the Mansion House and Royal Exchange but a side street away, the Boar's Head Tavern just around the corner.

'Master Marsden?'

He turned on his heel to see a courtly figure – radiant in green silk tunic and lace-trimmed knickerbockers – emerge smiling from the Grafton residence. Marsden inclined his head.

'A safe journey I trust, sir?' The artist said, saluting him. 'Sir Hilary regrets that he is unable to greet you in person, sir, and t'would seem the servants are away with their families. But come in do, he awaits you in the chamber with the oriel window.'

Marsden tipped his head again. 'My thanks to you, sir.'

The artist pressed himself against the portals, to let Marsden pass. 'An eccentric old bat!' he whispered, flicking his eyes towards the upper storey. 'Too long with his own company–'

Marsden lifted his broad-brimmed hat and swept in. Dropping the hat on a newel post he stood in the dimness of the hallway while his luggage was carried in. Above oak wainscotting the walls were arrayed with a collection of swords and pikestaffs. A dented bugle commanded a shelf between two closed doors and over the entrance door, a frayed banner flapped draughtily. Dust motes hung in the light from an eyebrow window part way up the stairs. Dust and tarnish enveloped the staircase and ornaments. Everything seemed to be steeped in the must of insular old age.

'I'll be on my way, if you please, sir.'

Marsden produced a coin for the hat-doffed coachman. He watched the servant leave, then took the stairs two at a time.

'Lock the door after him!' Marsden checked in mid-flight and squinted up through the shafts of sunlight to the chair-bound figure peering at him over the landing banister. 'You are not in the country now, sir; do as I say and bring the key up to me!'

With a slow but gracious smile, Marsden retraced his steps and closing the front door, noticed for the first time the lock plate – an elaborate work decorated in high relief with the figure of a man on a gallows. As he withdrew the key, the figure dropped symbolically, concealing the escutcheon. Somewhere, he knew, there would be a spring to reverse the procedure. He fingered the bosses inquisitively until he discovered one on the right-hand edge which gave under pressure.

'Three bevelled spring bolts and a night latch!' boasted Sir Hilary.

'A master locksmith,' asserted Marsden, 'with no uncertain views about thieves.' He gave a wry laugh and mounted the stairs.

'Place is awash with scoundrels and whores,' grunted the old man, clipping the key to his belt. 'In here–' He led the way, grunting with the unaccustomed effort of turning the wheels of his chair, into a room lined with bookshelves and paintings. It was a large chamber made small by the crush of furnishings; a bed low and without hangings, a wash basin and chair strewn with towels, a lectern, a desk piled high with documents and dusty tomes, a cabinet, a painter's easel and a gate-legged table set with covered dishes. The shrunken world of a gouty old man.

Marsden wandered past the easel to the oriel window, aware that the old man had picked up an eyeglass from the table and was watching him. He unbuttoned his coat and turning from the bustling street scene to the lip-fast scowl of his host, remarked, 'The gaiety of

Londoners, it seems, is irrepressible. The mortality bill is still in its hundreds, I am told, yet the streets I passed were filled with smiling faces.'

'Intoxicated with their hymns and prayers and the thought of the Easter feast,' said Sir Hilary sourly.

'Ah!' breathed Marsden, gauging the old man's mood. 'The plague was an act of God, they will say, an anger loosed but now spent. Let us rejoice in the risen Lord – in the God of justice and mercy.' He spoke with unmistakable contempt.

The old man snorted ironically, 'No die-hard Christian, are you Marsden?'

'I have faith in myself alone.'

'An arrogant doctrine, sir!' spluttered Sir Hilary.

'I do not deny it.'

'But, I suspect honest enough,' conceded the old man, shifting painfully in his seat. 'As for religion, I have come to the conclusion that only a fool would hanker after a God so indiscriminate in His judgement that he would destroy so many honest lives and yet leave unscathed the infestation of common prostitutes, street criers and impudent drunkards....' He caught his breath with sudden pain, clutched his left knee, then slowly lowered calf and stockinged foot back on to the inclined step of the chair. 'And the court is no better!' he grimaced. 'By all accounts squandering its energy on frivolity and mistresses when it should be raising funds to support the fleet. Deuce take them all!'

He had no need to name the king personally, or the much publicized birth of his third child by mistress Castlemaine, it was more than implicit in his tone. Marsden was well aware too of the state of the fleet, that it had put to sea, a rag-bag of officers and victims of the press gangs, with little enough money to supply the ships, let alone pay wages. It had been a favourite topic of dinner conversation at Apescross. How King Charles had tried to dissuade Louis XIV from honouring France's treaty of alliance with Holland. Tried and failed. So that the fleet had of necessity been divided; part under Prince Rupert, to patrol the French coast, the main body under George Monck, Duke of Albemarle, to take on the Dutch fleet.

'But I forget,' growled the old man defiantly, 'you sir, are an agent of the king.'

'Merely His Majesty's servant,' Marsden corrected. 'Not a spy.'

Weary of peering through the eyeglass, Sir Hilary laid it aside and manoeuvred his chair under the table, knocking awkwardly against the oak legs. He lifted a silver cover from a dish and poked at the blotched red shell of a lobster through a mound of prawns. 'Don't stand on ceremony, man, join me – there's wine in the cabinet; the key is in the lock.'

Marsden availed himself of the washstand and towels before drawing up a chair and unstopping a Bordeaux. Sir Hilary shovelled lobster claws and a handful of prawns on to a plate and pushed it at him. 'So, if you're not a spy,' he barked, picking his teeth, 'what are you, eh?'

Marsden let the dry wine linger in his mouth before he swallowed. 'I am occasionally called on to aid certain negotiations,' he answered with an enigmatic smile.

The old man dismembered a prawn. 'You will not be pinned down, I take it?'

'In short, sir, no.'

'No,' echoed Sir Hilary, chewing thoughtfully. 'Ah well, it seems you have more than impressed my son with your medical skills and in the matter of the witch ... Gunney, was her name?'

'Katharine Gurney.'

'Damnable affair, all that jiggery-pokery with the grandchildren.' He pursed his lips wryly. 'Never thought to see it in my own family.'

'You have come across cases of witchery, though, before the war,' Marsden ventured. 'By all accounts you presided over an impressive number on your circuit.'

'Forthcoming, my Samuel,' grunted Sir Hilary, rough cutting a slice from a breaded ham. He sniffed. 'I recall few cases these days, but I suppose I sat out my share of witch trials ... came in fits and starts. A bind, as I recall. So much hearsay – confessions denied. Never clean cut, more a mess of ignorant tittle-tattle, muddied the waters, you know. From the moment I clapped eyes on a woman my gut told me whether or not she was guilty.'

'A definable quality?' asked Marsden, with interest.

The old man drew a deep and ponderous breath. 'A certain hardness about the eyes, I can't say for sure, but unmistakable and unlike the hardness of a thief who knows he must hang.'

'Malignant defiance, perhaps?'

Sir Hilary cut another slice and dropped it on to Marsden's plate. 'Perhaps,' he agreed, 'saw it often enough.'

'Was ever a woman who passed through your court, acquitted of witchery?' pressed Marsden.

'Can't say that I remember,' muttered the old man, gulping at his wine. 'Safer to hang the devils.' He cut a cube of ham and lifting it to his mouth on the point of his knife, suddenly checked. 'As you mention it, there was one ... name escapes me, ah ... sat at Gloucester. That was it! A woman found guilty; youngish as I recall, condemned by her own brat.' He paused to pick his teeth with the knife, drawing together the white bushiness of his eyebrows in thought. 'One and only time a ruling of mine was overturned – meddlesome fools.' Chagrin gave way to a flicker of amusement. 'Hanged her for all that; diligent sheriff you know – the pardoner couldn't force his way through the throng at the execution!' Sir Hilary barked a laugh.

Marsden lay awake listening to the bubbling crackle of far off thunder. The boon of sleep, Virgil had described it. A boon he was granted less and less it seemed. Good wine and a rigorous coach journey had given him but an hour or two of oblivion. He had been awake again to hear the pendulum clock on the landing strike one, to see the small bedchamber momentarily spotlighted by the first lightning flash.

He turned and the mustiness of the unaired mattress assaulted his nostrils. Another flare of light brightened the room, showing up furniture shrouded in dustcovers, his bag unopened under the window. He swallowed to ease his mouth, parched by the dryness of the wine and wondered where in the capital the shepherdess was this night.

He did not doubt she had come – that she was alive. She had grown strong since he first found her on Blackwood Top. Strong and lucky. Who else would benefit from a plague, not once but twice? Not only had it provided her with the opportunity of escape from gaol, but also allowed her to be swallowed up by the melting pot of

London; into which no constable would dare follow, even if he suspected it to be her hideout. And none had.

It had been left to him to discover that she was gone. And that not until the plague had died down and the gaol had been empty for three weeks or more, with a red cross daubed on its studded gates. Instinct had taken him to gaoler Halliwell's cottage on the edge of the town. He had found the creature, propped against a stile in the garden. The tokens were on him and he could barely speak for his swollen tongue. Halliwell had affected ignorance of the shepherdess at first. But his reticence evaporated when a stick was jabbed against the swelling in his armpit. The words had fought over each other then, squealing for freedom. *She had taken the river path, had spoken of London, dear God take me to Rosy!*

She was leading him a dance was Kate. But even her luck had limits. She could not elude him forever – her or the child, if it had survived the birth. And when he tracked her down she would rue the day she had run from the scaffold.

He rolled on to his back and linked fingers behind his head. It was meet she should have drawn him to London. He had been set on returning to make his mark here, sooner or later. Besides, he had outgrown the challenges of the provinces, his appetite demanded more than whey. And in London was to be found the cream of the land; the monied, the influential. Here the stakes were high, so too were the pickings.

A ripple of thunder, more distant now. And in his mind's eye, he saw the dam; her hands around the bone-handled knife, the darkest of blood welling between her tight-clenched fingers. How many years ago? His wafting brain could not decide. It might have been yesterday the memory was so vivid. And only streets away from where he lay. She had followed him to England, tracked him down, determined either to have him or else break him on the back of the vintner's daughter. And her hold had been too deeply ingrained to walk away. Her very existence drained his. So he had chosen freedom.

His mother ... the shepherdess. Yes, it was fitting that Kate had drawn him to London, for just as here he had gained supremacy over the dam, so here he would destroy her too. Almost of their own accord, events had assumed a gratifying symmetry.

His drifting consciousness conjured a new image, this time a crowded green and Elizabeth, the mother of Kate, being hustled into position over the trapdoor of a scaffold. He pictured a man tearing his way through the crush, waving the pardon aloft; saw the two drawing closer and closer.... But the key was withdrawn and the figure dropped, just like the one in the Grafton lock. There had been no escape then for the woman they called witch. Nor would there be.

He started from dream-ridden sleep, rudely awoken by a resounding bellow. It came again, ragged with torment, and he knew it was the old man. Swinging his legs over the edge of the bed he snatched open the door and stepped on to the landing. He was met at the top of the stairwell by a bleary-eyed manservant. Jenkins, had returned to Candlewick Street earlier that evening after a visit to his family in Clerkenwell – in time to serve supper and dress Sir Hilary's leg before retiring. Tucking his shirt into his breeches with one hand and holding a candle in the other, he squinted up at Marsden.

'I'll take care of the master, sir. Naught to trouble yourself about – his leg's been at it for days.' Standing across the door to the oriel chamber, his hand resting on the doorknob, he stifled a yawn. From within came subdued squawks of pain.

'In that case, Jenkins, your treatment to date has been ineffectual.' Marsden snatched the candle and pushed the servant aside. To Jenkins' stammer of protest he replied, 'Go to your bed, I am a physician.'

'With respect, sir, the master's own physician says there's naught to be done but bleed him and dose him with–' He checked, unnerved by the glowering threat in Marsden's eyes. Checked and stepped back a pace. Marsden opened the door and locked the bemused servant out on the landing.

He moved to the bed but found Sir Hilary sprawled across the floor. His face was pushed down against a rush mat, his gasping breaths overlaid with moans. Marsden set the candle down on the hessian-backed wheelchair and turning the old man towards him, lifted his racked frame across the bed. Despite the old man's screams, he unwrapped the tightly bandaged left leg and let it swing down from the knee joint to rest against the valance. He moved then around the bed and began to knead the taut muscles under Sir Hilary's chin.

'Who–'

'Marsden.'

'B-brandy!'

'Afterwards.'

'Now, damn you! Now!'

Marsden struck him sharply across the chin. A spray of saliva shot from the old man's mouth. 'Listen to me now, or die of it.' There was a pause. Sir Hilary's throat muscles relaxed then tensed again.

'I'm listening Marsden,' he said quietly.

Marsden dug his fingers into the prominent veins of the old man's temples and squatted beside his head. 'Where are you?' he breathed, grinding his fingers hard through skin to scalp.

Sir Hilary shuddered with suppressed pain. 'Where the bloody hell do you think?'

'Go with my voice, float with it ... where are you?'

'Bloody purgatory!'

'Where is the pain?'

'All over!' growled the old man. 'Ears, back, groin, leg.'

'Can you move?'

'No.'

Marsden rolled a pillow up and wedged it under the base of Sir Hilary's skull. Then he snuffed the candle. And walked around the bed.

Through his agony it came, a voice gossamer light, yet strong. Distant at first, no more than a soughing on the fringe of his mind, of his hurt. But little by little it drew strength, words clear yet incomprehensible. Words of no substance yet filling his ears, spinning their filigree web around his pain. And drawing it in; from his limbs, his head. Stronger yet and the net tightened, sucking the hurt from back and thighs. Pain exquisite, concentrated in calf and foot, in foot and toes ... in the joint of his big toe.

A moment's suspense.

And then it exploded from his extremity; a shower of crimson putrescence. Its vile stench caught the breath in his throat, depleting the air in the chamber, threatening to suffocate him. The voice wafted across his new terror, refreshing the air with meadow scents and coolness. He gulped its fresh purity, suddenly conscious of a sobbing ... a venting that came from himself; aware too of the lightness that was his body, of the absolute lack of pain.

And the silence of the chamber.

Sir Hilary lay quite still, listening to the bumping of his own heart. There came a sharp click and a flare of light. He skewed his head round and saw Marsden, tinderbox in hand, lounging in the wheelchair.

'Where are you now?' asked Marsden.

The old man pulled himself up on the bed to face him. 'Will it come back?' he asked hopefully, then quickly added, 'No, I don't want an answer, I don't even ask how you did it.'

'You can help yourself by leaving off the brandy,' suggested Marsden. 'Drink watered wine instead. And put the weight on your legs more often.'

Sir Hilary shuffled himself off the bed and tentatively tried his legs. Swinging his right leg forward, his left buckled slightly, so that he snatched at the bedpost to steady himself. The next attempt though was surer and by clinging to the furniture, he managed the door and staggered back again.

'Lord knows how long it is since I tried that,' he murmured. He lowered himself on to the bed and laid his hand on Marsden's shoulder in wordless gratitude. 'It seems you are a sorcerer, Marsden.' He shrugged a laugh and rolled his weary head onto the pillows.

'Not a sorcerer,' breathed Marsden. 'Not that....'

Sir Hilary Grafton though, was already asleep.


Kate put her basket down between the surface roots of a new-green ash tree. She had set off, an hour before, to walk through Moorfields with François. An early mist had given way to clear blue skies and a sapping noonday swelter. She spread her cloak on a carpet of daisies and ground ivy, and sat down beside the basket, stretching her legs out in front and easing off her buckled shoes.

A young couple in courtly dress, paused to steal a kiss within feet of where she sat. Seeing Kate over her lover's shoulder, the girl recoiled with a coy giggle. Unabashed, the lover promptly pulled off her shoe and made great play of shaking out a troublesome stone before refitting it. Then with a wink at Kate he escorted the girl away.

As they moved off, arms linked, Kate smiled and leaned over the basket. François lay on his side, his sucking thumb glistening with saliva where it lay, fallen from his sleep-parted lips. She leaned back on her elbows, gazing up through a cloud of gnats to the tree. It was hours before she was due to go to the Fat Saddler's warehouse. Time to herself; answerable to no one but the dark-haired bundle beside her.

She sighed contentedly, closing her eyes and relaxed into a rare inner quiet. She was drifting towards sleep when suddenly her mind veered off sharply–

*And she was engulfed in terror – clinging frantically to hands that had her neck in a vice hold, to arms which held her writhing body above the earth. She plucked at them until her nails splintered, forcing the dregs of a scream through her constricted throat. She blinked away the watery blur from her eyes and recognized ... Dear God! The lambing sheds, the yard and her cottage. And him, his eyes intense with effort.*

*It dawned on her then, why her feet would not reach the ground. He had her suspended over the lime pit, over the hole she had dug to dispose of dead lambs and vermin. On fear-founded strength she flailed and fought but her blows were as nothing against his cruel strength.*

*The crack when it came was like the snapping of a dry twig; sharp, clean and sickening. Her arms clung for a moment, then fell away. The death struggle lost; her body insensible though her mind was yet acutely aware of his gritted gasps and sweat-streaked temples. And the rush of air as she dropped....*

*It crawled around her, the half-rotted squirm of the pit. It first found the exposed flesh of face and hands, then burnt through her clothing. And her upturned eyes watched passively as he reappeared on the brink above her, a sack in his hands; fixed on broad hands which curled back the hessian sacking, then began to shake a white powder into the air above her. She continued to stare – though the powder had burned the sight from her eyes – until her quivering body became one with the squirm. Until broad hands filled the pit with shovelled earth.*

Kate's eyes snapped open. She had rolled off the cloak and lay face in the grass, her nails bleeding and clogged with earth, her vitality drained by the vision. Slowly she eased herself on to hands and knees, breathing away the residual terror.

In the basket François was stirring, his tiny fingers reaching out for a passing butterfly. With trembling fingers she lifted him out and bracing her head against the rough bark of the tree, held him tightly.

How much more suffering must there be? How much more death before the demon she had evoked on Blackwood Top, was himself destroyed? She banged her forehead against the tree trying to erase the horror. She had seen through her eyes, shared her experience of fear and pain right up to the moment of death and then she had stood apart and looked upon the marred beauty of her one-time enemy, Barbara Canard.

# Encounters ...

Jenkins had been a witness to it yet he still found it hard to believe. In his four years of service at Candlewick Street he had seen Sir Hilary leave the house exactly four times. Four times he had been wheeled or carried through the front door, slinging insults and cursing the physician who had insisted he should make the journey to the spas of Bath. The manservant scratched his head and, absently wiping his hands on a boot rag, stepped out on to the front steps in time to see the carriage disappear into Fish Street.

Not two nights ago, the old man had been howling with pain. Now he was off gadding about town with Marsden. 'Jenkins, polish my boots,' he had ordered at breakfast. 'Marsden and I intend to take a boat up to Whitehall this morning. No buts if you please.' No buts indeed! He scarcely knew where to look for the boots they had been so long unused. And would have gambled his last shilling that the old man would neither get them on, nor walk in them if he did.

It was as well there had been no one to take the bet. With his own eyes he had watched the old man walk unaided downstairs and out to the carriage he had ordered from the Boar's Head. What was more, the old tartar had actually managed a laugh at some ribaldry from the coachman. Jenkins shook his head bemusedly and went back in.

Poking her head around the kitchen door Sally, the laundress, gave an awed whistle. 'Blow me down! Did you see that?'

'What do you think you're gawping at?' he snapped, locking the door behind him and pocketing the key.

'It's a bloody wonder though, ain't it?' she persisted. 'Us thinking he's about to kick the bucket, then up turns Marsden like a genie.'

'A shady character if ever I saw one,' grunted Jenkins.

'Enough to give a body the creeps those dark eyes of his.' She gave a shiver of pleasure. 'A real gentleman though.'

'Don't you go getting any ideas, Sally Cade!'

'Why ever not?' she giggled, shrinking behind the door as he crossed the hall towards her.

'Because,' he said, shrugging off his leather apron and capturing her wrist, 'I've ideas enough for us both!'

The manservant's expression had tickled Sir Hilary. It had been worth the pained effort of walking downstairs to see his wan disbelief. The old man's chuckles had filled the coach, spontaneous as the resting of his hand on Marsden's thigh.

That had knocked the dullard Jenkins off his laurels! That and his request, the night before that a truckle bed be moved into the oriel room so that Marsden would be on hand during the night. In the privacy of the coach, his hand lingered on the muscled leg, familiar, but not as bold by daylight as it had been during the night.

It had not been pain which kept him awake last night, rather a strange tension which he had not at first recognized. So long had his body been beleaguered by pain, so long his one desire to be free of hurt, that the return of his libido had taken him by surprise. He had lain awake in the darkness, unable to sleep for a poignant sense of the potency lying in the bed beside his. Listening for Marsden's steady breaths, detecting with pleasure the male smell of him. Recalling the heady days of his youth and the soft-featured captain to whom he had yielded his virginity. Piquant thoughts which had finally induced him to reach out in the darkness. There had been a moment of danger and uncertainty; excuses forming in his mind, lest his advances caused offence.

But there had been no offence.

Instead Marsden's hand had found his in the gloom, had drawn it down to his naked breast. Without a word, he had climbed up beside him, knowing his need, embracing his passion, teasing it until he had no sense of his mortal frame, of the aching baggage he had accumulated with age. And the sublime moment had been a kind of death, an exquisite release and renewal, such as he had never before known. Pleasure he had taken for granted in his youth, craved for as lost in latter years, was stunning in its rediscovery.

And the sleep which came after was the deepest, most refreshing, his memory would allow. His appetite for breakfast the keenest for years. Matthew was not merely remarkable, he was a phenomenon. A physician who had no need of physic, a man who understood his need better than he did himself.

'This house is suffocating you,' Matthew had announced over breakfast. 'It is time we ventured out.' The *we* made anything possible, even leaving the safe familiarity of Candlewick Street.

The coach drew up to let a dray pass, then trundled over uneven cobbles into the yard of the Old Swan.

'Well 'pon my soul!' breezed a rugged figure, dipping his head under a sagging lintel and hurrying across to the carriage where Marsden was helping the old man down the folding steps. 'Bless me if it isn't Judge Grafton!' he exclaimed, clasping Sir Hilary's hand and shaking it vigorously. 'Last time you took a morning draught here, sir, I do believe the place was hot with news from Edgehill.'

'So you thought I was pushing up the daisies, eh landlord?' grinned the old man, straightening his coat.

'Well sir, such times as we've had....' The landlord bit his lip gravely. 'Ah but it's good to see the old faces!' he perked. 'What can I do for you good gentlemen? A jug of house ale? We've a fine sack, or porter if you prefer. A plate of beef perhaps? There's a game of billiards going in the back–'

'A jug of buttered ale, if you please,' instructed Sir Hilary. 'My companion and I intend to take the river to Whitehall.'

'Of course, sir; I'll send the lad to enquire at the jetty for you.' He dashed a raindrop from the tip of his nose and glancing up at the leaden sky, led them towards the shelter of the inn.

They had been more than an hour in the gaming room before a boat was procured; had watched the vain attempts of several challengers to wipe the smug grin off the face of the local billiards champion. But none had matched the stocky boatman's accuracy with the mace; his studied strikes which knocked the ivory balls cleanly through the hoops and into the pockets beyond. As they rose to leave he was still raking in the pennies.

Even an hour's wait, it seemed could not secure them the pair of oars ordered by Sir Hilary. The innkeeper's lad scudded along the jetty ahead of them. 'There's not a scull or a wherry to be had this side of noon,' he gasped apologetically. 'It's this or naught!'

*This* was a flat-bottomed hoy carrying a cargo down to Lambeth. The only seat was an upturned crate and that was occupied by the boatman; a weasel-faced character who sat in the gangway draining a tankard of Swan ale. Assured by the lad that there was nothing better in sight they climbed aboard and waited for the indifferent boatman to stir himself.

Nothing, however, seemed to dampen Sir Hilary's spirits, not even the rain which began to drop with heavy directness, pitting the murky water of the Thames. They settled on makeshift seats made from the cargo of flour sacks, sheltering beneath an oil-cloth while the boatman steered away from the jetty.

Cocooned in a mist of rain, the barge hugged the built up north bank, past Paul's Wharf and Blackfriar's Stairs, by Somerset House and the Savoy Palace. As it veered southwards with the river towards the half-mile sprawl of Whitehall, the sky began to brighten and the rain slackened. Pausing only to find an angel for the drenched riverman, Marsden hoisted Sir Hilary on to the Whitehall stairs, then followed, splashing up the puddle steps to a dry colonnade.

The steps drained what little strength there was in the old man's legs. Rubbing his stretched thighs while he paused for breath, he ruefully relinquished his independence and accepted Marsden's arm. Together they strolled through the labyrinth of galleries and gardens, Sir Hilary making verbal note of various apartments they passed, dovetailing what he remembered of the place with the snippets of court news brought to him during his sittings by artist Nat Taylor. He took for granted that a servant of the king like Marsden would know the ins and outs of it all. And Marsden's nonchalance reinforced the notion, though in fact he had never set foot in the palace before.

'Ah yes,' mumbled Sir Hilary, stopping between stone columns to stare across a quadrangle ablaze with spring blooms. 'Over there, close by the bowling green, is the residence of the king's brother, James, Duke of York.' His pointed finger swung a quarter turn to the right. 'And tucked into a quiet corner, past King's Street and the king's beloved tennis courts, the lodgings of his naval counterpart, Lord Albemarle. 'Am I correct thus far?'

Marsden smiled indulgently. 'Doubtless.'

'According to Taylor, the Castlemaine's apartments are now to our right, though they were once by the bowling green.'

'Closer to the banqueting house and the king's privy chambers.'

Sir Hilary sniffed censoriously. 'If our Sovereign Lord directed a little less of his energy towards the Castlemaines of this world and a little more towards his Portuguese queen–' He broke off in midsentence as a woman, prim in high-collared black, emerged from a side door, steering the unsteady totters of a very young child. As nurse and child moved slowly past them, the child's eager blethering echoed across the quadrangle. The two men bowed.

When the tight-lipped woman was out of earshot, Marsden picked up Sir Hilary's remark. 'You suggest the king's virility would be better employed in getting a legitimate heir?'

'Castlemaine produced a third last Christmas, yet in six years of marriage to Queen Catherine, nothing!'

'Then perhaps the lady is either unwilling or unable–'

'Unwilling was never a problem and if the woman is barren, as is said, he'd do better to marry his mistress; it was good enough for brother James....'

Engrossed in his own ideas, the old man seemed unaware that the conversation had lapsed into a monologue; that leaning against the stone pillar, Marsden was having to strangle the urge to laugh into his face. Bigotry, bias and buggery; that was all he was this one-time circuit judge. A fumbling fart who abused the respect granted to the opinions of old age. *Unwilling was never a problem,* he coughed to smother his amusement, trying in vain to imagine old Grafton raping any woman. He had hanged a good many in his time but it would have to be flaunted in front of his face before his codpiece was undone.

'...then I never expected any better of Barbara,' rattled on the old man. 'Had a wayward streak in her since a child. Her fool mother, you know, wouldn't have her strapped.' Marsden's straying attention snapped back.

'It was not her first attempt at elopement,' he said carefully.

Barbara ... foolish Barbara to have chosen such a night to drag him into her manipulative games. The blood had been on him, triggered by Caroline's nightmare.

*You will be there Marsden, won't you?* Caught up in the thrill of slipping past Jessie Harris, of riding away with him into the early hours, she had had no sense of the danger in him. That had been her downfall. *We are two of a kind,* she had said. And the empty-headed impertinence of her words, of the attempt to trade flesh for a hold over him, might have been laughable but for the rawness of his nerves that night.

'No Grafton blood in her,' the old man was saying. 'Canard died at sea you know. I suppose the little hussy went after you, eh?' He sniffed. 'Enough gall even for that!'

Marsden concentrated on the bubbling water of a central fountain. The colonnade was beginning to hum with footsteps and voices. They moved on towards the Stone Gallery, hugging the stone columns. 'Country life was too dull for Barbara,' he said pointedly, 'she sought her amusement where she could.'

'Bound to bolt sooner or later, I suppose,' grunted Sir Hilary. 'But she needn't expect me to take her back this time!'

They turned into the Stone Gallery, a long and splendid hall housing, it was said, some of the finest paintings in Europe. Portraits, land and seascapes; works of battle and love, of pathos and ecstasy. Masterpieces created by the likes of Van Dyck, of Muytens and Lely; part of the great collection of Charles I, fragmented by his enemies, and restored as far as possible by his son.

With Marsden's help, the old man threaded his way through the knots of gossiping courtiers and ministers. It was for this that he had made the journey to Whitehall. He had told Marsden so, as they huddled under the tarpaulin on the river journey; had chafed his hands gleefully at the prospect of hearing first hand the latest rumours, the hottest gossip. After years of dull isolation he longed to be in the thick of it again, to exercise his modest influence, to make his voice heard. Marsden had been right of course, the house had been suffocating him; his personal tomb, waiting on his death, just as Jenkins and son Samuel were waiting. Dear God, he had even given up on himself.

'Why, Hilary Grafton!' The open mouth of incredulity pulled away from a party standing by a large gilded mirror and took his hand.

'Matthew,' Sir Hilary cleared his throat, 'may I introduce you to an old acquaintance from my Oxford days, Sir Hugh Stanforth ... Hugh, Doctor Matthew Marsden.'

Marsden noted Stanforth's polite but dismissive nod. He watched the heavily jowled face turn to the old man even as the man offered his hand, met the clammy limpness of it with a knuckle-buckling grip and watched with growing amusement as Stanforth's eyes jerked back to reassess the *humble* physician propping his old friend.

It was diverting the speed with which he became the focus of the party by the large gilt mirror – thanks to Grafton's unstinting praise. Palates wearied by the telling and retelling of current affairs of court, of hackneyed jests and society scandals, leapt to the challenge of the taciturn Dr Marsden. This square-shouldered man in puritan black, whose voice had a continental edge to it and who, according to the old judge, was both healer and witchfinder, excited their curiosity.

'Come sir, you are too modest,' protested Stanforth, at Marsden's suggestion that he was not entitled to be called doctor since his training was never completed. 'It seems you have more talent than any qualified physician I have ever known. Cured a gout, whoever heard of such a thing?' Behind their fans several ladies in the group chuckled.

'I do not claim a cure,' Marsden politely corrected. 'The illness is in respite – how soon it recurs depends on Sir Hilary himself.'

'All this you achieved with words?' ventured one of the ladies over his shoulder. He turned and brushed against an ivory-coloured gown. His eye was caught by the flash of a large amber brooch in the bodice, by a double string of pearls which hung down from it, hugging the left breast and down to another glittering brooch at the waist. Creamy flesh rose above the low-cut cleavage, shoulders tapering in to a necklace and hung with a single string of large pearls. He smiled into a face, girl round and fringed with small curls, into eyes haughty, yet verging on laughter.

'I believe in the innate power of the human mind,' he answered. 'That we are all capable of healing ourselves to a greater or lesser degree. And that some of us have the ability to release that power in others.'

Wafting her fan thoughtfully, she went on, 'If it is in us to heal ourselves, then is it possible that we are in part responsible for our illnesses? Is it feasible to suppose that a body believing the plague to be inescapable, might induce the disease it so dreads?'

'Lady Aldrigge does so like to tease!' guffawed a young wag in scarlet hose and tunic.

'No, Carlton, I am serious,' she persisted, half laughing and ignoring Sir Hilary's snort of derision. 'I would value Dr Marsden's opinion.'

'I suggest,' said Marsden, 'that the lady speaks from a deep dread within herself.... And that a troubled mind can indeed lower the body–'

'Heavens above!' gasped Stanforth in mock horror. 'Knowing Lady Aldrigge's constitution, that surely beggars my hopes of survival.' As he spoke a murmur surged through the gallery. A short distance from the gilt mirror, past several clusters of visitors, curtains of crimson velvet were drawn aside by guards in cloaks of scarlet.

'The king is early to dine this morning!' breathed Carlton, as a dozen occupants of the gallery converged on the opening doors, their plumed hats and elaborate wigs blocking the narrow gallery. Others rushed up behind, pushing up against the first so that the few who had not joined in the scramble could only guess that King Charles was present by the lulling of voices and doffing of caps.

'What o'clock is it?' Sir Hilary's voice dented the hush.

'Noon bar a minute,' whispered Stanforth pocketing a chased gold hunter. 'Come, take my arm, we'll follow the progress to banqueting hall ... find a seat in the balcony where we can talk and watch the king at the same time.'

Pocketing his eyeglass, the old man turned to Marsden. 'Matthew?'

Marsden caught Lady Aldrigge's eye.

'Dr Marsden and I will follow,' she assured the others. 'Carlton–' she said pointedly. The grinning courtier tipped her a bow and sprinted after the two judges. Marsden noted Sir Hilary's anxious backward glances, searching for him with panic in his eyes. The *we* become *I*.

He knew the feeling well enough, felt the stab of it in a memory glimpsed; of a boy torn from his mother so many years before. He watched until the old man, clinging to Stanforth, his limp more pronounced now, was swallowed up by the crush which was following the royal progress out into the pebble court. An hour or two apart would whet the old leech's appetite, he mused, sharpen his gratitude. One night more, two at most, he gauged before the parasite would be glutted enough to pluck.

The gallery was all but empty as he turned to the woman. Smoothing the curve of her eyebrows in the mirror, she glanced up at his brooding features.

'I wonder that His Majesty is not crushed there are so many petitioners and visitors,' she began idly. 'It is said that Louis of France goes nowhere without his *mousquetaires* to guard his person.'

'Dashing blue cloaks and rapiers,' he said, with a wry lift of his right eyebrow. Lady Aldrigge laughed.

'Yes Dr Marsden, I confess to a romantic streak.'

'I see devilment in your eyes,' he breathed over her shoulder, 'not romance.'

In the mirror, her smile gave way to a querulous, slightly vulnerable expression. She twisted her head over her right shoulder and strained her eyes towards him. 'One does not necessarily preclude the other,' she murmured and looking ahead into the mirror, produced a gracious smile for an elderly gentleman who wandered past, his hands linked behind his back.

'Perhaps we should follow the others,' Marsden said briskly.

Lady Aldrigge turned with a rustle of silk. 'Trust me, sir, all seats will by now be taken....' she hesitated.

'Then you may know of a quieter spot elsewhere?' he prompted.

'My husband has the use of a chamber adjoining Lord Albemarle's lodgings.'

'And your husband?'

'Is very much afloat.'

Marsden lifted her gloved fingers to his lips and gestured for her to lead the way.

After dusk....

Kate braced herself against the velvet padding of the rumbling coach, resisting the slumped weight of the sleeping gentleman beside her. George Whalley, an associate of Cassy's good friend Sir Hugh Stanforth, was a good client; a soft-spoken widower who now and then wanted a tumble but more often than not preferred a responsive listener and a warm knee to squeeze.

As the coach rattled out of Drury Lane into St Giles, the snoozing man's head slipped down into the crook of her arm. She readjusted his wig and rested her head against the carriage window. This evening she had accompanied him to a performance of Shakespeare's *Moor of Venice*. In a box high above the stage of the

Cockpit Theatre, his mischief had stretched to retrieving hazelnut shells from her cleavage, where he had purposely sprinkled them. His boyish humour had done much to relieve the grim tragedy of the play but it had left her feeling vaguely disturbed. And the haunting strains of Desdemona's song still clung to her mind: *The poor soul sat sighing by a sycamore tree, sing all a green willow....*

The song caught in her throat.

Through the rain-grubbed window, beyond a scalloped-brick wall, a dark form had caught her eye. And the muscles under her ribs gripped violently. She scrubbed at the window with her clenched fist but the mass standing back from the road in what appeared to be an old graveyard, came no clearer and the coach was rapidly leaving it behind. Its aura, overwhelmingly strong a moment before, was slipping away from her.

Knowing only that she must get back to it, she burst clear of George, threw open the carriage door and yelled at the coachman to pull up. The startled man jerked on the reins so the sleeping man inside fell heavily against her. She in turn stumbled out on to the road.

'My dear?' George croaked blearily.

Kate pulled up the hood of her cloak. 'Forgive me,' she said, forcing her attention. 'You go on. Next time.... I'll explain next time.' She smiled and helped him back to his seat. Despite an agony of tension, she waited for the coach to drive on, for the puzzled face at the window and the flickering coach lamps to be enveloped by the night. Then slipped her shoes and darted back past a long fence to the scalloped wall.

The damp grass saturated her stockinged feet as she picked her way between listing headstones. The wet squelched cold between her toes and up her ankles.

And it was still there, the dark mass – beneath a hawthorn pale with May blossom, a figure hunched over something she could not see.

She moved closer, pushing her toes carefully through a carpet of pine cones and thistles; aware of running water and spits of rain. Aware too of a low hum.

As she drew nearer still the hum became a voice, indistinct but a voice no less. She froze, pressing her face against a stone angel. The shape had moved and her eyes, grown used to the light, picked out the head and arms of a man. She did not need to see the rugged profile, the tied back hair, to know that *he* had come. The tightness at the base of her skull, the bristling hurt of her skin, was evidence enough.

Driven by a force stronger than her terror, she edged forwards and sat on a lichen-patched tombstone not four yards behind him. She could see now that he was crouched over a small granite stone, set well apart from the rest. He heard him tearing at the overgrowth of grass and meadow flowers around it. And knew that this was the place she had seen in her vision on Blackwood Top.

She knew, though his body prevented her seeing, that the rough-carved inscription read:

*Ignotus*
*Ex Aquis*
*Anno Domini 1658*

And now that the Fat Saddler had translated it for her, she understood that it spoke of an unknown, dragged from the river. A suicide, the saddler had suggested, taken pity on by the parish priest. But she knew as *he* knew that the woman who lay there was no suicide. Knew too that of all the women he had murdered, Ignotus alone haunted him.

'*Fons et origo malorum!*' he snarled, suddenly jerking to his feet and hurling a handful of weeds towards the brook. 'Why could you not let me go, Mother? Why did you have to follow me to England?'

As yet unnoticed, Kate licked her dry lips. She rose to her feet and very softly so as to smother the tremor in her voice, began to sing:

'*The fresh streams ran by her, and murmur'd her moans; sing willow, willow, willow–*'

He swung round, eyes blazing and rasped, 'Mother?'

'*Her salt tears fell from her and softened the stones–*'

'Mother?' He lurched towards her, then froze as she reached out and lightly touched his cheek. His parted lips closed, then reopened. And the featherlight touch wandered over chin and throat, under his hair to the nape.

For one deluded moment his taut features seemed to relax. The next they were seized with pain as the caressing fingers suddenly clawed and dug into his neck. With an anguished howl, he wrenched himself clear and stumbled out of reach.

'A body dead and yet undead!' she hissed, echoing words invoked on Blackwood Top.

'Be gone!'

'But I have not yet begun–'

He groaned, raking his fingers up his forehead and into his hair. Rocked on his heels in floundering uncertainty.

Kate pressed her advantage. 'Not yet begun.... François.'

The name clinched it. Kate watched his crazed flight, watched until the dark blur of him vaulted the wall and melted into the night.

Only then did she move. Trembling uncontrollably, Kate stepped down from the tomb. She tottered a few paces, then collapsed beside the granite stone.

He had come.

# The Rouge Route ...

Marsden ground his already grazed forehead against the jagged mortar of the alley wall. The narrow passage reeked of urine and rotting vegetation but he was not aware of it as he knelt on broken tiles, his shoulders collapsed forwards. Nothing penetrated his angry shame.

He had returned to the grave to lay the ghost – to crush the cowering dream once and for all. Yet, when the confrontation came, he who had never in his life run away from anyone or anything, had crumbled. And the most maddening thing of all was not understanding how or why. Why the potency in him had shrivelled. Why he had fled before that demon manifestation, instead of taking it on. Why, blinded with tears of frustration, he had run along street after deserted street until exertion and tension had constricted his airways and levered up the contents of his stomach. And why he had crawled away from the stench of vomit into the darkness of the alley in an effort to hide his spineless impotence.

He clawed his way up the wall, scraping his cheek and pressed his open lips against the scathing surface as he drew himself up to standing.

'A body dead and yet undead,' he echoed, his mouth sour with vomit. He felt for the wounds to his neck, the weals surely made by her nails. But found nothing though the hurt still lingered.

And he groaned at his own gullibility.

She had hurt him because he had allowed her to. The soft caress and sudden stinging rejection had been figments of his surprised mind. She had no power but what was in him. The cunning bitch was turning him against himself – his uncertainty was her only weapon.

He spat the bitterness from his mouth and wet his lips with his tongue. His chest heaved with the pounding of his heart, his mind raced. Why, after eight years of watching and waiting, should she choose to pounce now? *Why now?*

The answer crystallized in his mind. It beat at his tortured brain – the dam and the shepherdess. The two were inexplicably bound. Kate's escape had been no accident, the dam had seen to that – he saw it all too clearly now. Kate had survived to lure him back to London, to that granite rock, so that the dam could destroy what she had made.

He moved towards the grey entrance, hands flat against the close walls. Tonight had been Kate's doing. And she must suffer for it. If it was the last thing he did, he would make sure she paid for tonight. He gritted his teeth as a sheet of pain sliced through his head. Then he lurched into the dark streets of Holborn.

Anna Davidson folded her arms tightly around her ribs, and shivered. Luke be damned! If the filthy pimp hadn't come badgering her again, she might have remembered to bring her coat, such as it was. But he had come, cuffing and slapping until she was only too glad to turn out on to the streets. Only now that her temper had cooled, she was feeling the nip – now that it was too late to go back. The old whoremonger would break her neck if she turned up empty handed.

She cupped her elbows in her hands and trudged down Cross Lane towards Baldwin Gardens; it was as likely a spot as any. If her luck was in she might catch a clerk or one of those young legal gentlemen rolling out of the Furnival or Barnard's Inn on his way to lodgings by Chancery Lane.

She quickened her pace. He might even buy her a hot pasty. She glanced up – no moon, or stars. Still, there would be street lamps further on, outside the bigger houses. She should know, she'd worked in one for twenty years. Everything from drudge to lady's-maid, she'd done it all in twenty years with the family of John Gerard, solicitor. Twenty years of service and within a cat's whisker of becoming housekeeper when the plague settled on London. The cook and the coachman were the only two the Gerards took with them when they packed up and fled to the country. The rest, including Anna, had been left to fend for themselves; shot like so much ballast.

She had managed for a while, nursing plague victims, tending the stinking bodies no one else cared to, until the ugly face of death became too much for her, and Luke had taken her in hand. Gawd strike the cruel swine dead!

Lost in thought, she overshot her usual short-cut via the passageway between the milliner's and the baker's shop. It would cost her an extra quarter-hour to follow the roads. She swung back again with a smothered oath. The unrelieved darkness of the alleyway was daunting but the prospect of a warm and well-lit inn porchway lured her on. She scuttled past the first blank walls, propelled by the squeaking of rats and a lively imagination. And in the half-minute it took to reach the arched opening at the other end, her face and arms, the exposed flesh of her bosom had begun to prickle with fear.

She curled around the archway into the opening beyond, panting and laughing at herself for getting into such a state. She was standing now at the wide junction of several back entries. Some wound their way past gardens and cobbled yards, others led to shops and warehouses.

From one there came the approaching sound of male laughter and the yellow glow of a lantern. She waited hopefully, straightening the crucifix at her throat, but the voices tailed off behind the slam of a gate. And the light was gone.

She sighed, resigning herself to Furnival's after all, and levered herself off the wall she had been resting against. Then caught her breath – suddenly aware of a figure standing across the entry she would have to take.

Panicked, she stumbled back against the wall, stubbing her elbows. She bounced off again and flung herself back through the archway. But stumbled over her skirts and her wrist swinging up to catch the wall was captured by a powerful hand. She resisted for several seconds, before being dragged back, whimpering and clawing vainly at the fingers around her wrist.

'What are you afraid of?' The sure male voice cut across her panic; a soothing deep sound with a foreign edge to it. She stopped struggling and the grip on her wrist slackened.

'Christ Almighty!' she choked. 'Where the bloody hell did you come from?'

'I could ask the same question of you,' he murmured.

'How long were you standing over there watching me?'

'Long enough.'

'You might have coughed ... or something.'

'And risk startling you?'

'You did that anyway!' she scolded, her teeth chattering uncontrollably. 'You're not the law then?' The shadow-laden features above her widened into a smile. A warm hand touched her shoulder.

'You are shivering,' he breathed. 'Do you have a room we can use?'

Anna closed her eyes and gave a long sigh of relief. This she could manage. And *he* could manage sixpence more for the fright he had given her. 'Half a crown,' she bartered, adding as an afterthought, 'and a pasty.'

It had been a matter of five minutes' walk to the derelict place in Dog Lane where she often brought her men; a large house with boarded windows, which she shared with several other prostitutes, the rightful owners presumed victims of the plague. Warmed by the brisk walk and the thought of a half-crown, she was quite chirpy as she led the taciturn stranger up two flights of stairs to the privacy of the top floor.

'In here,' she called, beckoning him into an attic room and locking the door behind them. Shuffling around in a corner , she found tinderbox and candle, primed the one and lit the other. 'Ah, that's better!'

Unbuttoning her skirt, she caught him scanning the room. She followed his gaze from the cut-away ceiling with its cracked skylight, to the empty grate and stained chimney breast, over boxes and accumulated rubbish stashed away in dark corners ... to the crumpled mattress beneath the skylight.

In the faltering candlelight he too had taken on form. She eyed him curiously. He had the confidence and cultured voice of a gentleman, yet the wrist strength of a farm-hand. And he could hardly pass as a gentleman of fashion, favouring such grim black. Coat, breeches, shoes, all jet black – even his hair, tied back with a black ribbon. No wonder she hadn't noticed him in the alley. Sensing her stare, his eyes darted across from the mattress with such burning impatience that she was compelled to look away and carry on undressing.

From somewhere in the house there came a loud scraping and a ripple of laughter. He looked at her askance.

She shrugged. 'One of the others,' she said, sauntering up to him in her underclothes. 'Mol I expect ... she won't come up here.'

He stood still while she undid his jacket buttons – so still and silent that her nerves began to jangle again, making her fingers fumble with the buttons. Only his eyes moved and though she dare not look directly into them, she knew that they were with her every move.

Half a crown, she reminded herself, and hot food besides.

She slid her thumbs under his lapels and pushed the jacket over his square shoulders. He let it fall behind him. Encouraged, her hands wandered mechanically down his white shirt to probe the front of his breeches. Her nails gently raked the stiffness of thigh muscle and groin. Her fingers kneaded his hard-packed member and found the necessary release buttons. A husky laugh bubbled up her throat; a knowing, taunting sound.

He touched her hair – gently, almost uncertainly at first. With rapidly gaining surety he searched for pins and combed his fingers through the thick brown tumble. While her hands worked, his hands unlaced drawstrings and dragged the coarse white petticoat off her shoulders. His mouth swooped to her upstanding nipple, and she bit her lip to avoid crying out as he sucked and gnawed at the tender flesh. She clasped his rolling head in her hands and prayed that it would be over soon.

Bruisingly rough, his hands forced the petticoat skirt between her legs, pushing and probing until the discomfort became too much and she tried to pull away. With a nervous laugh, she twisted towards the mattress, hoping against hope that if she could get him there, he might not be able to hold back. The sooner to vent whatever mad passion was driving him.

Thrusting away from him, she skewed over her left hip and crashed on to the dusty boards, her left leg folded underneath her. She tried to turn away, but he slammed his forearm across her pelvis, pinning her down with maniacal strength. She gave a winded grunt, her mouth parched with terror. Too frightened to resist, she lay still, watching the downward drift of soot specks from the disturbed candle, trying desperately to distance herself from reality.

But the tearing of cloth wrenched her back. With bare hands he had ripped through the tough material of her underskirt. She banged her head against the floor, splintering the boards with her teeth as his fingers and knuckles set about her again. As teeth pincered her buttocks. Then a head-jerking thud, her own gurgled cry, and the feeling that her insides were being hammered up under her ribs. Pain issued from her in waves of sweat and tortured grunts, in the blood that oozed from her bitten lips.

And she could taste the terrible hatred that poured from him; its malignance suffocated her. The boards blurred and there was no air, only overwhelming pain....

Consciousness returned while the candle still burned. With it came dread and a body throbbing with hurt. She lay where she had fallen. He now stood apart, the indent of his spine a shadow down his naked back, his hands linked in front.

Her stomach lurched, filling her mouth with bitter bile. It had been the slightest of movements, a bodily reflex, but a board creaked under her and his attention was caught. He twisted his neck to glance over his shoulder.

There was a coldness in his eyes, an unfeeling detachment which turned her bowels to water. She scrambled to her feet but her left leg, so long trapped under her, buckled. Sobbing with terror, she crawled towards the door, dragging the numb leg behind.

Suddenly remembering the noise that had come from downstairs she wailed, 'Mol, for God's sake ... Mol!' But the sound was as feeble as her trembling arms, hollow as the screams of her childhood nightmares. And the key was gone from the lock.

'Please let me go!' she pleaded. 'I swear, no one will ever know–' Struggling to her feet, she crossed her arms over her naked breasts. 'I don't want money, just let me go.... *Oh Jesu!*' He had turned towards her, a macabre smile etched into his face and a long blade clasped against his naked chest.

Anna backed away from the door, ashen-faced. 'Please no–' She staggered over the corner of the mattress, jerking her arms forward to ward him off. She squealed as he stepped across the gap, as her shoulders met the corner of the room. Pleading incoherently, she forced herself hard back, flattening her palms against flaking whitewash. Under her own thrust, began to scud down the uneven surface, her tight-drawn nipples jolting until she came to rest on her heels, her thighs spread.

He stood between her and the candle now; a silhouette fringed with amber light; an object of terror looming larger with every tortuous second. Her palms stretched out to keep off his eclipsing shadow. She could feel the air move as he stooped over her. Jerked her head aside, unable to wrench her eyes from the inescapable.

She reached for the crucifix at her neck, feeling round its leather cord until she found it slung over her shoulder. Soon now, she prayed as his arm snatched back, exposing the knife in the light behind. Her fingers tightened around the cross – *Merciful Lord let it be quick.*

But she knew, even as she prayed that there was no help for her; that the enveloping evil had blocked the light from her soul as well as her eyes.

And the gloating malignance that impaled her belly flesh had only just begun.

# The Witness ...

Kate rarely returned to the lodgings before nightfall but an unexpected call on the warehouse by the saddler's wife had curtailed the appointment by several hours. She looked forward to telling Cassy how the flustered man had cut a dash across the office in nothing but his wig; how she – nearly choking with laughter at the sight of his wobbling buttocks – had to snatch her things before being rudely ejected down a rickety flight of stairs to the loading bay at the back; how, between boxes of leather offcuts, she had made herself decent before slipping away. She only wished she had been able to hear the saddler explain away his state of undress.

Blackbirds were chinking in the back lane as she emerged from the alley skirting the soapworks. Above the rooftops the sky was streaked with a fiery sunset; a scene evocative of summer evenings with Jack and the ewes, of treks through the wood to the pool and her soft bed at the cottage. Dipping her head under the overhanging branches of a lilac tree, it suddenly struck her that the poignancy, the wistfulness which had dogged her for months after the trial, had faded since the birth of her son. François had turned her face from the past. Nothing mattered now except securing a safe future for him.

Finding her key, she quietly turned it in the front door lock and latched the door behind her. She dropped her cloak over a bench in the passage, tiptoed upstairs and put her head round the door of the front room.

Hetty, the girl who nursed François while she was working, was draped over the edge of the crib, her loose hair fallen over her face. Kate lit a candle-stub, leaned over the cot and brushed her lips over the infant's sleep warm face. His eyelids flickered briefly, then sank again. She lingered over him for several moments, then pulled the tossed away blanket up to his neck.

Taking Hetty's shoulders, she coaxed the sleeping girl back against the chair drawn up by the cot, noting with a smile the cushion of pillows Hetty had made to soften the hard wood – pillows *borrowed* from Kate's bed across the room. She eased the girl's arms back from the cot rail and brushed the lank hair from her face.

Cassy had found her shivering in the outhouse doorway on a bitter January morning; turned out of her home after her parents died of plague leaving no one to pay the landlord – just twelve years old and scrawny as a child of seven. But in five months with them she had come on in leaps and bounds, still thin but robust now and, above all, devoted to little François.

Kate fetched the quilt from her bed and was tucking it round Hetty when she noticed a crumple of paper in the cot. Holding it up to the candle she could see from the crude woodcut picture on the front page that it was a dog-eared pamphlet. She flicked past the title page through several sides of coarse print, wondering how Hetty had come by such a thing. It had doubtlessly slipped from her fingers as she slept. Curious, but being able to read only a few simple words, she looked more closely at the picture.

What she saw made the blood drain from her face.

Beneath the smudges of dirty fingers there was the rough-drawn image of a partly naked woman, her head propped up against the wall of a slant-ceilinged room, her body mutilated and dark-patched with what could only be blood, and at her throat a large crucifix.

Kate stepped backwards to the bed and sat on it, trembling. It was her, the wretch she had seen in the Temple ceiling. She searched for a date and found it below the gruesome diagram – *the 30th day of April, this year of our Lord 1666.* More than a month ago. The last day of April – the eve of the Mayday frolics. A groan escaped her. The very evening she had come upon him in the graveyard.

Kate exhaled heavily and squeezed her eyes shut. What happened by the granite tombstone had caused this woman's death, she was sure of it. The madness she had stoked, he had vented on this stranger – a woman, any woman.

She opened her eyes and saw that Hetty was sitting up in the chair, staring at the pamphlet in her hands. 'Where did you get this,' Kate demanded. Hetty shrank back into the pillows, her pale face puckering with fear. The girl's reaction instantly softened Kate's anger. She moved from the bed and stooped beside the chair. 'I need to know where it came from,' she said, more gently.

Hetty hesitated ... then stammered, 'I didn't mean to take it, honest, Kate!'

'Take what?' Cassy stood in the doorway, yawning. 'I thought you were out for the night.'

Kate glanced up at her friend. 'So did I.' She held the pamphlet out. 'Look at this.'

'I-it's just I don't get much to read now and it was there hanging out of his pocket,' Hetty gabbled. 'I only wanted to look at it ... I meant to put it back, honest I did!'

'Sweet Lord, this is her – the one you saw, isn't it?' blurted Cassy.

'Whose pocket?' Kate pressed.

'The gentl'man came last Sabbath,' whispered the girl.

'She means George Whalley,' added Cassy. 'What else did you take?'

'Nothing!' Hetty was distressed. 'I don't take things!'

Kate laid her hand on the girl's trembling arm. 'We believe you, Hetty ... don't cry. The picture caught your eye, didn't it?'

The girl nodded balefully. 'And the lettering over it. *A Most Certain, Gruesome and True Discovery of a Murdered ... Whore,'* she quoted.

'Where did you learn to read?' Cassy asked sharply.

Hetty blinked away her tears. 'Father did some farmgate preaching, he made me read his sermons out to him.'

Cassy glanced at Kate and shrugged. 'She'd better read it aloud to us then.'

Kate squeezed the girl's arm and passed the pamphlet back to her. In the crib François was stirring. Cupping his downy head, she lifted him out, blankets and all, and sat on the edge of the bed rocking him. 'Read it to us,' she coaxed, 'and I will buy you something from the bookstalls in St Paul's yard.'

Hetty glanced anxiously from Kate to Cassy and back again.

'Come on, you goose!' sighed Cassy, plumping down on the arm of the chair and tussling the girl's hair. 'I shan't turn you out if that's what you're fretting about.'

'I took it to the outhouse to look at,' explained Hetty, 'but he'd gone by the time I'd done. I would have put it back, *truly.'*

'Never mind that now, read it to us!' Cassy said through her teeth.

'*A Most Certain, Gruesome and ...*'

'We've heard that,' sighed Cassy. 'What comes after?'

Squinting in the meagre candlelight, Hetty ran her finger down the page. '... was found in the attic room of a derelict house in Dog Lane, the horribly mutilated body of one Anna Davidson, prostitute of this city,' she read, dramatically.

'Anna–' echoed Kate.

'... one terrible incision from breastbone to loins, another crosswise to the first, laying bare the fertile regions, which had been plundered. The two savage cuts presenting a dia ... diabolical inversion of the Cross ...'

'Christ Almighty!' shuddered Cassy.

'Go on Hetty,' murmured Kate.

The girl swallowed. 'Though mangled and lying in a pool of blood, the wretched woman was yet alive when discovered by a friend. She expired before the arrival of constable and examiner. Embedded in the flesh of her left hand was found a crucifix ornamented with blue agate; said to have been *given* to Anna by the family of a plague victim she nursed. It is devoutly to be wished that in her final suffering moments Anna Davidson renounced her life of sin, in readiness for the judgement. Hearken all you sinners, the wrath of–'

'That's enough,' Cassy cut in, 'we can do without all that.'

Stroking the baby's head, Kate lifted her eyes and smiled heavily. 'There's gingerbread in the tin by the kitchen fire. Take some to bed with you, Hetty.' She watched the girl's eager exit. Cassy pressed her ear against the closed door, listening for the sound of retreating footsteps then, satisfied that Hetty was gone, dropped into the vacated chair.

'The evil bastard!' Cassy hissed, snatching up the discarded pamphlet.

Laying François on the bed, Kate went to the window and stared out into a sky dusted with stars. 'I have to find the house in Dog Lane.'

'Leave it alone, Kate. What hope would you have against such a monster?'

'There will be traces of him, there,' Kate went on, 'something that may lead me to him.... I know it. If I could find the one who discovered her afterwards, the witness–'

'And what do you mean to do if you find him?' Cassy demanded.

'I will know when the time comes,' Kate answered. 'For now all I know is that if I don't go after him, he will come searching for us.'

Nothing stirred in Dog Lane but the creaking board over the baker's shop and the occasional puffs of pipe-smoke which blew from a casement window, where the watcher kept vigil.

From a mattress dragged beneath the window, the witness gazed down on the empty lane, waiting out one more sleepless night in case the demon should return, praying that he would come after the one who had crossed him on the stairs that night – that he would come to destroy the only one who could identify him. And coming be himself destroyed.

Balancing the pipe on the sill, fingers reached down for the loaded musket and stroked the cold metal of the barrel; reassured, replaced it on the mattress.

He would come now that the initial clamour had subsided, now that the sheriff's men and the pamphleteers, the headshaking priests and ghouls had all but forgotten Anna Davidson. In the wake of all that he would come ... he must come.

The world had put aside thoughts of *whore Anna;* one more death among the thousands in the plague cemeteries, worthy of a moment's notice for its mouth-watering cruelty, that was all.

But the witness could never erase the horrific memory of that night. It clung to the brain as it clung to the attic room above, obliterating all else.

And focused the will.

Nothing stirred in Dog Lane but the creaking board over the baker's shop. The witness drew on the long stem of her pipe and blew a circle of smoke towards the misty moon.

# Witchcraft ...

Cassy knew better than to waste breath arguing with Kate. She had never known a body more stubborn. As for actually going after the murdering devil, that she considered fearless to the point of stupidity. But Kate was not open to reason. She had slipped into one of her disturbingly intense moods and there was no talking to her.

Cassy had seen her like it before; that first night they had shared the tent, then again, one afternoon when she had come back from walking in Moorfields with François, and most recently, the night she limped all the way from St Giles graveyard, having lost her shoes somewhere. It was as though another, stronger self emerged – someone strange and awe-inspiring.

She had long ago accepted the fact of Kate's second sight; that it was, in the main, a curse rather than a blessing but a fact nevertheless. And it was becoming more and more clear that there was more to it than just *seeing*. There was a depth in Kate that went far beyond the normal; something not of the ordinary, safe world.

At first, she had put the strangeness down to Kate losing her mother so young and in such a way – a retreat in times of direst stress – an occasional imbalance which, with patience would pass. With time though, she had been forced to come to terms with the distinct possibility that her friend was – and most likely always had been – what those ignorant villagers had branded her.

Kate was a witch.

Furthermore, she was a witch who had borne a murderer's child. It was a truth she could no longer evade. And being true, she had to believe too, that Kate was right when she said that unless she found this beast who went by the name of Marsden, found and *presumably* destroyed him, he would come after her and François.

All this she had realized as she lay beside Kate on the front-room bed, waiting for the dawn. By first light she knew too that whatever else Kate might be, she was foremost her friend. And if she was hell bent on going after François' father, then she was going to need her help to do it.

Dog Lane was waking to a fine drizzle and the waft of new bread from Hyslop's bakery, when the two women reached it shortly after dawn. Throwing back the hood of her scarlet cloak, Kate strode on ahead of Cassy to the barred gate at the field end. Then she sauntered back again, past several straggling buildings to a two-storey house butting up to the pavement.

She stood on the pavement opposite, waiting for Cassy to catch up and squinted through the spatter of rain. It was a timber-framed house with basketweave brick infills. There were boards over the ground-floor windows, old boards carved with initials and stuck with weather-beaten notices. The higher windows though – those out of range of prying eyes – were unboarded. One directly above the padlocked door, she noticed, was flapping open. Moving to one side, she glanced up at the undulating roof, at the slate-slipped neglect and cracked skylight.

'This one?' gasped Cassy, reaching her at last. Kate took her arm, and stepping over a heap of manure, pointed to a brick path at the side of the house. They followed it round, through a tangle of overgrown shrubs and brambles, past an empty pigsty, to a back porch ankle-deep with old leaves. Cassy lifted the latch of the mouldering door within, and pushed. But it held fast.

'Try again,' Kate breathed over her shoulder. 'It is not locked, only swollen with the damp.' Without hesitation, Cassy put her weight behind it and this time the door groaned into an earthen-floored vestibule.

They stepped inside and were met with the reek of stale urine and damp plaster. Wedging the door shut behind them, they went through the kitchen, scattering mice busy with crumbs on the ale-slopped table, to the light-starved hallway beyond. As Cassy flagged behind, Kate lifted her skirts and took the first flight of stairs two at a time, until she reached the landing above. If her bearings were correct, the blank wall ahead of her fronted the lane, which meant that the open window would belong to the room on her left.

She reached for the doorknob. It was loose and rattled around its spindle several times before releasing the catch. She let the door swing inwards, then cautiously moved into the bright room.

There was a semblance of order about the folded blankets and dirt-free floorboards; about the careful positioning of the mattress under the open window and the pipe and tobacco pouch on the window sill above. The occupant of the room had gone ... but the traces – the presence Kate felt – were very strong.

She stooped beside the mattress and placed her hand on the impression in it. Still warm. Whoever it was had been watching the lane ... no doubt knew they were in the house.

'Not in here Kate,' Cassy hissed anxiously from the door, 'the pamphlet said she was found in the attic!'

Kate leaned across the mattress and latched the flapping window. 'Yes,' she agreed, keeping her unease to herself.

The steps to the attic room were concealed behind a cupboard-sized door. Kate peered up the narrow well. If there was a door at the top, it was shrouded in darkness. Instructing Cassy to wait on the landing, she ducked under the transom and stretching her hands in front, began to climb; with every tentative step expecting to be confronted by the occupant of the room below.

Instead, after only a dozen steps, her fingers stubbed against the hardness of another door. Exhaling raggedly, she felt around and found a latch. And the door fell away from her.

She knew already what lay beyond; the slanted ceiling and cracked skylight, the stained mattress pushed into the angle of the wall. She walked in, her eyes drawn towards the corner to the left of the mattress, to the flaking whitewash, scored by the murdered woman's shoulder-blades as she slipped down under her own weight, and the huge brown stains in the floorboards.

Kate knelt by the mattress and spread her fingers over the largest brown patch. She could see now that the mattress and the bottom of the walls were sprayed with liver-coloured splashes. Closing her eyes, she murmured, *'Anna–'*

A sound barely uttered, yet it swelled to fill the room, boomed all around her, disturbing the heavy silence ... giving leave to the whisperers: voices stretched by lethargy, others cramming words unintelligibly. The early few were rapidly joined by others until her head was filled with their lisping babble.

Kate swayed forwards over her hands, disorientated by a powerful gripping sensation at the base of her skull. Her eyes snapped open but the room rushed out of focus and the terrible tightness in her neck steadily crept over her head. The blurred room began to reel sickeningly. The mattress rushed up at her.

Instinct brought her arm up. It braced against the wall just in time to save her crashing, head first, on to the floor. For several nauseating moments she rested her face on her arm until, at last, the tightness ebbed from her head and her spinning mind regained some kind of equilibrium. Then she summoned the strength to lift her eyes....

*The room had grown dim; the faltering light of a single candle to relieve its gloom – a candle seen only as a flickering shadow on the wall she was facing – on the bloody imprint left there by her hand.*

*Slowly, she turned her palms up and stared down at hands dripping with fresh blood. Felt, before she saw the light reflected in it, the warm swirl of blood around her knees – the essence of Anna Davidson spreading through the material of her skirts, clinging to her.*

*'How long were you standing over there watching me? ... Half a crown and a pasty....'*

*Kate rose and turned to face the one she knew would surely come.*

*He stood with his back to her; naked to the waist, his spine a line of shadow set in well-developed muscle, his neck broad under the tied-back hair, calf and thigh muscles taut beneath tight breeches.*

*She watched him turn to look over his shoulder, his eyes showering cold scorn on the abject thing lying between Kate and himself. She saw the measured twist of his shoulders and hips ... concealing until the very last moment, the knife held with overlapping grip against his chest. She watched the slow blink of his eyelids, the flick of his tongue across parted lips – the pulsing of his penis beneath dark breeches – as the terror-stricken shadow stumbled towards the door. 'Mol for God's sake ... Mol!' Anna clawing at the lock, scrambling away towards the corner.*

*And Kate.*

*She stood now between the demon force and the cowering shadow. She braced herself against its foul exudation – fascinated by the upwards jerk of the blade, by the travesty of a smile on his jaw-clenched face, by hatred unfathomable in his eyes....*

Consumed, she did not fully conscience the voice which screamed her name ... until a winding force hurled her aside and pinned her face down on the mattress. It held her there under its panting weight with no air except that she could force through the mattress. Until she lay still.

Only then did she recognize the screaming voice as Cassy's. Twisting her head round, she glimpsed a tumble of auburn curl and realized with a sinking in her stomach, that the stench and the blood were gone, that the room was restored to daylight.

She heaved a sigh. And the weight holding her down, shifted to let her get up. Cassy sat beside her on the mattress, hugging her knees and trembling violently. 'He was going to kill you!'

Kate knelt up against her friend and hugging Cassy's pallid face against her stomach, stroked her hair. It was the first time anyone had ever shared one of her visions. Not even *he* had managed that.

'He was bloody well going to knife you!' she choked.

'No ... not me.'

'The bastard was almost on top of you! I saw him!'

It had taken courage for Cassy to come to her aid, Kate realized, to come within arm's reach of a demon she believed to be real. She leaned down and kissed her friend's glistening forehead. 'Not me ... *Anna.*'

Cassy shuddered. 'My God! The hatred in his eyes.' She wept then, until Kate's soft whispers quelled the unmanageable fear. But even as she soothed, Kate was remembering the expression on his face as he jerked back the knife. And the words that blew like aspen-chatter across her mind: *This night she will suffer in your stead ... this night you will see.* And she knew that she was responsible for the death of Anna Davidson.

A woman, any woman ... a surrogate she.

She had hoped for more of the attic, had been certain that here she would learn something that would lead to his whereabouts. But the vision had passed and she was too drained to attempt to revive it again today. So, as soon as Cassy was over the initial shock, she guided her towards the narrow stairwell.

Kate emerged first from the small door on to the landing. She held the door open for Cassy then, without warning, something hard butted her between the shoulder-blades.

'Filthy bitches!' It was a tortured howl, deep with emotion and hatred. 'Saw the stains, did you?' The hard object jabbed again. *'Did you?'*

Taking advantage of Cassy's sudden appearance at the foot of the attic stairs, Kate spun round. And found herself staring along four feet of musket barrel at a rusting flintlock mechanism and a finger-curled trigger.

'Just can't leave her be, can you?' She was a thin woman, her eyes casting dark shadows in a sallow face. Her lips were twisted into a loathful sneer. She stood, legs wide apart, bracing herself against the weight of the gun. And forced Kate's chin up with the muzzle. 'Filthy bitch! I ought to blow your head off!' She laughed harshly. 'Would they come do you think, to see where your brains were spilt? Nah ... not spicy enough, eh?'

'You found her, didn't you Mol?' Kate murmured, confident that this was the occupant of the room she had been into, the one Anna had called out to. 'You were the friend–'

'How do you know my name?' The muzzle dug harder into the soft flesh under Kate's chin. 'Who told you?'

'Anna....'

The dark eyes widened with rage. 'Leave her out–' Thrusting the gun up again, her finger had accidentally caught the trigger. Slack-jawed her gaze plummeted towards the mechanism.

Kate watched the dog-head drop towards the steel plate, her hands already swinging up. Instinctively, her mind focused on the flow of energy; on the sound and heat of impact, on friction become spark – coursing into the priming pan, on the violent expansion of the powder as it blasted the iron bullet along the gun tunnel. In her mind's eye she saw it begin to spin, caught on an imperfection in the barrel. She locked on to its spiral flight to the very brink of release – then with a synchronized roll of her left hand, caught the emerging bullet.

For one frozen moment, she held her clenched fist level with her chin. Then Anna's friend staggered backwards, dropping the gun. Kate uncurled the fingers of her left hand and stared at the silver-grey sphere.

'S'truth!' Cassy breathed over her shoulder. 'You caught it!' Kate clenched her fist around the bullet and threw it over the landing rail. As it clattered on the flags of the hall below, she turned to the bemused woman.

'She called to you, Mol ... when she knew she was trapped, she called out your name but the sound didn't carry.'

'What are you?' gasped Mol. 'Who in hell's name are you? Christ almighty, you know where he is, don't you? That's how you know. You're hiding him!'

'No, I don't know where he is ... I had hoped by coming here I would find out.'

'She-devil!' Mol spat, hysterically. 'Should have shot you on sight! By Christ, I'll have him though ... if it's the last thing I do, I'll have that murdering–'

'Not without her you won't!' Cassy snapped, pointing to Kate. 'She is your one hope of avenging Anna, believe me.'

'I must know what Anna said before she died,' urged Kate.

Mol glared at her. 'Why should I believe either of you? For all I know he could have sent you.'

'You fool!' hissed Cassy. 'Do you think Anna was the first he's butchered? Tell her, Kate, tell her that unless you find him, there will be more Annas.'

Mol looked from Cassy to Kate. 'Is it true?'

Suddenly overcome with exhaustion, Kate leaned against the banister and nodded. Mol stooped beside the musket, then glanced up at her. 'The bullet, how–'

Kate shook her head. 'I cannot explain.'

'You saw it though, didn't you?' demanded Cassy. 'Even though you nearly killed her, she hasn't lifted a finger against you. Has she? Tell her what Anna said.'

'What will you do, when you find him?' Mol intoned.

'Whatever she can,' said Cassy. 'Whatever will stop this butchery.'

Mol dropped her head on to her knees and sighed loudly. 'Much good it'll do ... just one word, over and over.'

'Tell us,' coaxed Cassy.

Mol shrugged. 'The shepherdess ... that was all she said, the shepherdess. Sweet Jesus!' A sob escaped her. 'She was in such a state, poor Anna ... poor old girl!' Kate knelt down beside the sob racked woman and stroked a wisp of silvery hair out of her eyes.

'Help me find him, Mol,' she whispered. 'I am the shepherdess.'

*Wednesday 15th August 1666*

The victory salute of the Tower guns had woken Marsden. He pushed back the bed hangings, slid from the soft arms that hung limply over his chest and threw open a casement window.

At the corner of Gracechurch Street and Lombard Street, a bonfire sent sparks and ash into the air. Around it street urchins cheered the lazy brawling of drunken revellers. Snatches of music and bawdy laughter drifted across the rooftops from distant parts of a capital heady with the latest victory over the Dutch.

He had heard the news in a Cornhill coffee shop; 160 Dutch ships taken for a loss of five naval fireships, and a town destroyed into the bargain. It was a good omen, he felt it – the perfect night for his acceptance into the Brotherhood. A night of victory.

There was a rustling of bed hangings, then the naked figure of Cecilia Aldrigge padded to his side. She peered heavy-eyed over his shoulder.

'I can think of better ways to celebrate,' she yawned, pressing her lips against the nape of his neck. 'No doubt Sir Anthony will be in his cups, in a port somewhere' – she waved her hand vaguely – 'no use to woman or beast.' She laughed suggestively.

Marsden stared out across the rooftops to St Paul's. 'Is that any way to speak of a vice-admiral?' he asked with an ironic grimace. 'The more so since he is your husband.'

Cecilia linked her arms around his neck and pressed into the warmth of his back. 'he has only one passion,' she murmured, 'he makes jokes about it when we dine in company; he loves to ride his *Virgin* – the purest, most biddable of ladies. He never tires of the witticism.' She sighed. 'Strange ... he is not unhandsome, yet he prefers plank and sail to flesh and blood.'

Marsden turned in her arms and forced her chin up with a sudden kiss to her throat. 'Beauty should never be neglected,' he breathed, working his lips up to her jewelled ear.

'Later, Matt,' she gasped feebly. 'There is little time before your appointment at Mason's Hall–'

'More than an hour.'

Cecilia pulled away, rubbing her forehead thoughtfully. 'You must have time to dress – I'll send Agnes to the Boar's Head for victuals, then it will be time for the carriage. It is a great honour to be accepted into the Brotherhood.'

'I am not at their beck,' he said coldly. 'They want what I have to offer.'

'And they can offer you much in return,' she reasoned. 'You can not be late tonight.' Undaunted by the darkness of his smile, she went into the adjoining closet, unlocked the top drawer of her dresser and brought out a neatly wrapped parcel. When she turned he was standing in the narrow doorway looking in.

'For you, to wear tonight,' she said, holding it out tentatively. 'I bespoke it of a silversmith, a token.'

Marsden weighed the compact parcel in his hand then untied the silken wrappings. It was a belt; intricately punched leather studded with silver eyelets and a richly worked buckle of chased silver. Holding the buckle he let it uncoil and ran his fingers appreciatively along the leather. He looked up into Cecilia Aldrigge's glittering eyes.

'Bought on your husband's account?' he asked quietly.

'All that I had is his,' she said huskily.

'On his account nevertheless,' he insisted.

She swallowed hard, aware of his dark potency and her own arousal. 'Let us settle the account tonight, after it is done,' she urged. But she knew her will could not match his, did not even want it to.

'Now,' he commanded, kicking the closet door shut behind him. He seized her shoulder and flung her round so that she sprawled across the dresser upsetting combs and perfumes. Snatching up one elegant bottle, he poured musk oil into his palm and rubbed it into her buttocks. Then he brought the beautiful thong hard down on her.

Marsden lifted the curtain from the coach window and glanced up at the overhanging storeys of Bishopsgate. His gaze lingered for a moment on a pipe-smoking trollop who was peering over a balcony rail at him. Then a cloud of pipe-smoke wiped her from his sight and consciousness.

The coach reeled around the corner, spraying filth as the wheels jolted through the street sewer. It swerved to avoid the drunken antics of torch-bearing apprentices, then took the road along the old city wall.

Dropping the curtain, he leaned back into the velvet seat, and smiled. He had gulled them all – the physicists, the astrologers, the mathematicians, the physicians; the flower of English intellect seeking to harness magic with their science; searching with the naivety of children for bridges between the seen and the unseen, for the knowledge that would secure their worldly ascendancy. How simple it had been to gain acceptance and respect; how contemptibly simple to insinuate himself into the company of the rich and influential.

Doctor John Pearson had been his key. He recalled with satisfaction their first encounter at the Crown tavern in St Paul's churchyard. After weeks of patient waiting, he *happened* to be sitting by a window when the doctor and a half-dozen others of the fraternity came in to shelter from a rainshower.

Thinking their conversation about levitation in the African tribes too rarified for the other patrons of the house, they had spoken freely on the subject until the listener by the window intruded upon their discussion with the suggestion that far from being the preserve of ascetics and far-flung tribes, the science of levitation could be mastered by any mind with a modicum of intelligence.

The impudence of his claim had hooked them. They had challenged him to back his claim; had watched with melting scepticism as, with reluctance overcome, he had with soft words induced the potboy to lie precariously across the curved tops of two chairs – one under his ankles, the other under his head. Then with calculated nonchalance he had retired to his window seat, inviting the doctor to withdraw the supporting chairs.

And as the last chair was eased out, leaving the lad suspended against a backdrop of flames from a well-stoked fire, there had been cries of disbelief from all round the tavern.

Despite their clamours for more, he had been careful to leave them wanting. It would have been easy to *cure* the landlord's tic, to fill their minds with conjured images. Easy too, to have blown the impression of himself as a mystic possessing coveted knowledge and be seen as no more than a fairground magician.

He had left them with appetites whetted, assuming a reticence which was only overcome by Dr Pearson's most ardent requests to meet him at a Cornhill coffee house the following morning. It had taken many such meetings and much encouragement on the doctor's part, to *persuade* Matthew Marsden to put himself and the secret knowledge he had acquired during many years of travel, at the disposal of the Sons of Solomon. He had manipulated the doctor with the same subtle cunning he used in making love to a woman – making himself first desirable, then indispensable.

The coach swung into Basinghall Street with a clatter of hooves, past the embers of a street fire. Marsden adjusted the hang of Cecilia's silver-buckled belt and put on his plumed hat.

He had made it his business to become acquainted with the history of the Sons of Solomon. Despite their claims of ancient lineage, of direct descent from the brethren of the Rosie Cross, they had shallow roots, being founded in the unsettled years before the Civil War by one Elias Ashmole and a band of likeminded idealists. They drew inspiration from the Rosicrucian quest for lost knowledge, and took their structure from French and Scottish Freemasonry. They dealt in speculative mysticism, revelling in the secrecy – and élitism – of their society. He knew that they were a conceited band, that their goals were hopelessly idealistic. He knew too that their funds were substantial and their influence great.

Power and wealth. It was a fruit asking to be picked.

He had haunted taverns and brothels, gathering information about key figures in the society, especially the master-general, Sir Jeremiah Palmer. And the fruits of his labour were a gratifying picture of personal weakness.

The coach hugged a wall round into Masons Alley, then eased through the Temple gateway and moved slowly across the cobbled forecourt to the outer doors of the great building.

Marsden waited for the coachman to lower the carriage step, then brushed past the obsequious man on to the shadowed cobbles.

As the coach veered back towards the alley, a torch-bearer and liveried herald ushered him up the steps, through an entrance hall and into the cool darkness of an anteroom.

'The appointed hour is near at hand, initiate,' scolded the herald, tugging off Marsden's square-toed shoes and relieving him of cloak and jacket and hat. 'We may not suffer the master to wait, on pain of–' The reverberating chimes of a clock silenced him.

On the twelfth strike Marsden, led by the bearer of light, moved towards the great doors of the inner temple and deliberately struck the carved wood three times. No sooner had the torchbearer quenched his flame, than the doors began to arc inwards and apart. He waited for them to complete their course, then stepped into the unnaturally quiet temple.

Out of the hush came the tinkling chime of bells and all at once the covers were whipped off a dozen lamps, filling the temple with a phosphorescent glow. Behind him, the great doors ground shut unaided. Ahead, on a raised throne behind an altar, sat the master Sir Jeremiah Palmer, wearing rich blue robes and flanked on each side by a burning candle. The air was heavy with incense and a star, hanging above the throne, twirled on its thread, flashing with reflected light.

Marsden passed under an arch bearing the Greek inscription:

γυῶθι σεαυνόυ

and wryly wondered how many Sons of Solomon *Knew Themselves,* as well as he had come to know them.

'Who is the stranger in our midst?' demanded the master. 'Come forth and show thyself.'

As Marsden walked barefoot across the mosaic floor, the master descended the steps of the throne to stand between him and the altar.

'Who enters the Temple of Solomon?' intoned the master.

'A man with many secrets,' answered a voice from out of the shadows, 'a man worthy of adoption by the Brotherhood.' It was Pearson.

'Your name, stranger?' asked the master, dully.

'Matthew Marsden, your worship,' he declared, prostrating himself and kissing the master's bared foot.

'Are you, Matthew, the son of Marsden, willing to accept the ways of the brethren, to stint nothing in the furtherance of our aims and maintain our secrets?' asked the master.

'I am willing,' he answered, bracing himself as a cold foot pressed down on his neck.

'Then know that the reward for indiscretion is death,' said the master. 'Know too that from the moment you entered the great doors, your bared neck was in mortal danger. Now know that the road to initiation is not for the faint-hearted, it is a testing one and dangerous. Are you willing to take that road?'

Face pressed against the cold floor, Marsden loudly assented. And at once the force on his neck was removed. Hands lifted him to his knees and dragged him to the altar, while a lone contralto voice sang, *'Holy, Holy, Holy: Lord God of Sabaoth; Heaven and earth are full of the Majesty: of Thy Glory ...'*

For the benefit of the neophyte, the master lifted each of the items on the altar, revealing the meaning of each. An open Bible – the Volume of the Sacred Law – the symbol of light above; the Square for duty and moral conduct, the light within; the Compasses for fraternity and services to mankind, the light around.

'Come to know thyself,' boomed the master, 'control thyself, and make thyself noble; for by wisdom and strength and beauty will the temple of mankind be created–'

Marsden looked but did not listen. He saw the crabbed features of Sir Jeremiah Palmer impassioned with noble sentiment and imagined the pained cries of sodomized boys – there were few secrets too closed for the seedy underworld of the city. There was always someone, somewhere, who knew something at a price.

'That the deepest secrets of nature may shine through the darkness and uncertainty,' ejaculated the master, closing his eyes in ecstasy. 'The Great Alcahest, by some known as the Philosopher's Stone; the Elixir, the fount of immortality; and the Sight by which all things are known....'

'Oh Lord, save Thy people; and bless Thine heritage–' urged the precentor.

*'Govern us; and lift us up forever–'* answered the brethren.

And Marsden made obeisance to the master, received the rules of fellowship and swore upon the Sacred Volume to maintain faith with the society or gladly forfeit his life.

They gave him the Secret Word, and the name ascribed to the left pillar of the porch of the Temple of Solomon, the whispered word, *Boaz.* And in return, he drew the palm of his left hand along the ceremonial blade and let three times three drops of blood fall into the Precious Flask.

He watched the rich darkness of his blood wind around the neck of the translucent bottle; watched it coat the inner walls, then drain into the murky pool beneath and was fascinated by the thought that by that simple act he had become blood-brother to so many high-minded, respected and wealthy men; to intellectuals and sophisticates ... to fraudsters, sexual deviants and at least one whose hands were stained by murder.

'But the true secret,' droned the master, linking his bony forefinger around the first joint of Marsden's, and breathing rank breath at him, 'is that which eternally surrounds you, yet is seen by none although it is there for all eyes to see.'

The precentor cried fervently, 'Oh Lord, let Thy mercy lighten upon us.'

And as the brethren answered with the final verse of the *Te Deum*, Marsden mouthed with them the ingrained words: *'Oh Lord, in Thee have I trusted; let me never be confounded.'* But the lord he addressed was not theirs. And he knew that one day that would surely give him mastery over them all. But for now he was content to play the humble apprentice, to abide by their childish rules. It pleased him to imagine how he would taunt them with glimpses of his art; how he would deceive them and extract full purchase from every last crumb of the knowledge he had gleaned from simple women like Mother Sutton and Kate.

Unable even to feign humility, he watched the master repair to the steps of the throne, then proclaim, 'In virtue of the power which I have received from the founder of our order, and by particular grace of God, I hereby confer upon you Matthew, son of Marsden, the honour of being received as a Son of Solomon.' He sealed the ceremony with three strikes of his gavel, then sitting down, smiled grotesquely and said, 'Your trials have been many, my son. Take your ease now, reclothe yourself in mind and body, for the Temple ball awaits.'

Marsden lay in a richly furnished retiring-room, his boots propped carelessly on embroidered pillowcases. He drifted on the warmth of a fire perfumed with sandalwood, idly counting the ticks of the mantel clock.

Cecilia would be at the ball; hungry glances beneath her easy elegance and *savoir-faire* – chastened glances. His fingers found the lacy garters presented to him by the deputy masters after the initiation; garters for the mistress of an accepted one. He twirled them around his fingers and his languid features twisted wryly.

Cecilia would expect him to choose her, then her ladyship was wont to expect ... she still had much to learn.

A sudden creak from a book-lined wall, jarred him from his torpor. He snatched the blade from his boot and watched as the middle section of bookcase swung into the room. In the opening stood a woman carrying a flickering candle. Through the folds of a diaphanous robe he could plainly see the ample outline, the darkness of nipples and pubes. Only the face was concealed beneath the enigmatic smile of a mask and a tousle of flame-red hair.

Marsden folded his fist around the blade and slid warily from the bed. The woman set her candle on a polished dresser and turned to close the panel behind her. 'I am sent to serve,' she whispered, standing with her back to the fire. 'They call me *Comfort.*'

'By the brethren?' he snapped. When the masked face inclined towards him, he snorted derisively and beckoned her towards the bed. 'Then *comfort* me, madam.'

She nodded again, but moved away from the bed towards a drum table set with decanter and glasses. He watched as she poured a generous measure of brandy, and offered it to him, then he clamped his hand around her wrist and jerked her on to the bed causing the dark spirit to slop over the coverlet. She gave a surprised choke but with a deft turn of her head managed to elude the hand which snatched at her mask.

'Not until I know your true identity, sir,' she chided.

'If you are sent,' he said, winding a finger in her fiery hair, 'you will know who I am.'

'Humour me, sir,' she breathed, 'it is the way–'

The bed bounced as he went to the decanter and refilled the fluted glass. '*Comfort.*' He smelt the liquor pensively. 'A rare name for a whore.'

The mask jolted round to face him. 'You are privy to the name of many, sir?' she asked demurely. He gave a short laugh of appreciation, then drained the glass.

'Permit me to propose a game,' he said, watching her provocative gyrations against the spiral bed-post. 'We each invent an identity for the other, the winner to be the one whose portrait is most like.'

'And the prize?' she asked with interest.

'To the victor, the terms of engagement.' Smiling grimly, he moved to a shuttered window, opened it and looked out across Basinghall Street to the leaded lights of the Guildhall.

'Your accent,' ventured a soft voice behind him, 'makes me doubt that you are a full-blooded Englishman.'

He shrugged. 'Whence would you have me come?'

'Oh,' she replied carefully, 'you, sir, have adventured the world over, but I would say you have the blood ... of the Romans in your veins.'

He glanced distractedly at her, disturbed by her accuracy, but even more disturbed by a solitary figure standing in the street below. 'Then why do I have an English name?' he asked coldly. He heard the masked woman's rippling laugh; saw the other woman in the street throw back her hood then turn her moon-silvered face up towards him. And suffered a stabbing pain in his head – a hurt so intense that he clutched his temples in dread.

'Who am I?' he burst savagely.

'Ask the shepherdess,' murmured the woman. '*Ask her* – she's down there, she knows....'

Stifling a scream of fury, he hurled himself at the bed. But the masked woman had slipped away to the bookcase, was already pulling the false panel to behind herself. His fingers caught the edge of the closing door – his nails tore and splintered as he wrenched. But the fleeing woman had the better leverage and as the panel clicked into position, his fingers were trapped. Growling with pain, he prised the crushed tips out and began throwing books aside in a frenzied bid to force the door open. But it had been built to open into the room only. It was fast in a perfect recess – without a hinge in sight. The redhead's escape was secured.

He tore across to the window, searching the street for signs of Kate. Finding that she too had vanished, he drew back his clenched fist and with manic force, punched his arm through a small pane. As his bloodied wrist flopped down against the frame outside, he pressed his face against the glass, and howled with frustration.

And from the corridor outside his door, a small voice urged, 'Brother Marsden, rouse yourself sir! The festivities await!'

# Part 4: Ignis

*Le sang du juste a Londres sera faute,*
*Bruslez par fondres de vingt trois le six*

*The blood of the just shall be dry in London,*
*Burnt by the fire of three times twenty and six*

Nostradamus

# Fire ...


Three weeks of furtive searching, of underworld enquiry and coining of palms, had yielded nothing but a string of goose-chases. And the more shadows he tried to grasp, the more her moonlit face haunted him: *'Ask the shepherdess, she knows–'*

She knows.

He, who had made himself master of fates other than his own, could not abide the thought that she had it in her power to destroy him. He had no appetite for food, or sleep, or even the musky Cecilia. He desired only to destroy his tormentor. And the longer she eluded him, the more consuming was his hatred.

Night after night he started awake in Cecilia's bed, choked with the old dream of her, naked on Blackwood Top, arms upstretched towards the dawning sun, the cowered form crouched beneath her, drenched in her blood.

The fire alone cut across his obsession. Cecilia's prim maid Agnes broke the news as she combed her mistress's hair, stealing glances in the mirror at him, as he lay sprawled over the uncurtained bed. 'Never seen the like!' she gushed, hair-pins trapped between her lips. 'Fish Street no more than a heap of cinders, Thames Street and the Steelyard ablaze, the very church stones catching, they're so parched with drought!'

When, within the hour, the rooftops of Fenchurch Street and the Cheap developed a fiery nimbus, and acrid smoke gusted in through the casements, the fire assumed an awesome reality.

He left Cecilia, clutching her jewel case, as she frantically supervised the removal of her best furniture and hangings to the cellar. He forged a way through the chaotic streets by the Boar's Head Tavern, past carts and coaches marooned in a sea of evacuees, into Candlewick Street. As he passed the blazing Steelyard, he paused to watch a terrified dog tear through the crowds, straight into the fire-licked doorway of a house.

Darting down an alleyway, he broke free of the crowd and made his way by a series of twists and turns, past abandoned houses and soot-blackened gardens, across smouldering Thames Street and down to the crowded wharf.

'Marsden! Marsden, over here!'

Beyond the milling crowds and their assorted chattels, in a boat by a narrow slipway, he spotted a familiar face. It was Pearson and a female companion. He pushed through a gang of excited youths to the water's edge and clambered into the bobbing vessel.

'It was the devil's own job, getting a boat!' gushed the doctor, using an oar to stave off the hands that clung to the boat-rail as he pushed off. 'It is a wonder I saw you in that crowd. Have you, like my niece Jane and I, come for the spectacle?'

Marsden took an oar and glanced at the fresh-faced girl seated in the prow. Beneath the tasselled edge of a lace cap, her eyes shone.

'An exciting prospect,' he said, raising his dark eyebrows at her. 'Fire is so elemental ... so compelling.' A violent jolt, caused by the boat colliding with a flat-bottomed lighter, stemmed her reply. The vessel, overloaded with household effects, dipped precariously below the waterline. Co-ordinating their efforts, Marsden and the doctor manoeuvred past the unwieldy lighter. They steered a course through the barrage of river traffic, cutting through the exodus of goods and displaced people, past squabbling boatmen and a litter of lost goods bobbing unclaimed in the murky waters of the Thames.

'They say,' cried the girl, bracing her arms against the sides of the boat as she leaned towards Marsden, 'that it started at Master Farryner's.'

'The king's baker, in Pudding Lane,' her uncle explained. 'Though there is much mention of French incendiaries.'

'Feasible,' Marsden granted, relieving the doctor of his oar and putting his back into the rowing. 'The City is tinder-dry–'

'Judgement!' yelled a swarthy lighterman. 'Bloody hell-fire and no mistake!'

Marsden smiled. As the bridge came into view he lifted the oars. The flames, keen-edged in the fading light, leapt into the smoky sky above the Fish Street end of the bridge. Their great orange tongues flicked and intertwined, fanned by the strong wind. At Jane's insistence, he rode on towards the stone bridge, so close to the blaze that they were able to observe the dark silhouettes of the fire-fighters overhead. Patches of thick smoke lent the scene a misty unreality. The crackling draw of the flames drowned their voices and the sounds of the river. They glided noiselessly through showers of sparks and ash, the doctor clinging to his intrepid charge, who at the first sign of fire, had leapt to her feet in abandon. Her face, flushed with vitality, had several times sought Marsden's – and her potential was not lost on him.

They passed beneath the echoing stone bridge and out again, towards the crowded wharfs around the market where the smoke was less dense.

'A fearsome thing,' exclaimed the doctor, coaxing Jane back into her seat and plucking at a hole burnt in his coat sleeve by a cinder. He shook his head. 'And difficult to envisage how such a monster might be contained, the streets are so combustible.'

Marsden felt Jane's foot touch his under Pearson's seat. He rubbed his own against her ankle, and pulled on the oars.

'There is a way,' he suggested. 'If the blaze could be surrounded by a moat of clear space.' As he spoke, his eyes, which had been trailing along the line of faces on Botolph's Wharf, suddenly darted back to a figure standing apart from the rest.

'Blow up the houses?' mused Pearson. 'I doubt the militia is well enough organized to execute such a strategy.'

The oars scudded over the surface of the water. Marsden stared through the smoky haze at the lone woman. He saw her hair fly in the wind, watched her head dip and nuzzle the bundle in her arms. A side wind caught the boat and nudged it towards the wharf.

'Mr Marsden?' said Jane, with a half-amused, half-querulous frown.

'Someone you recognize, Marsden?' asked the doctor, laying a hand on his sleeve. 'There is room for another–'

The ill-defined face looked up from the bundle. And across the murky breach she whispered, *'François....'*

'Sir, are you unwell?' Pearson's concern roused him. Without shifting his eyes from her, Marsden dug the oars into the water, urgently cutting across to the riverside.

'My dear Marsden, what ails–' began Pearson.

'Quite well,' snapped Marsden. He cut across the path of a heavy barge, all but colliding with its figurehead, oblivious to the oaths of the bargee. Alarmed, Pearson wrestled with the oars, but Marsden pushed the protesting doctor back on to his seat. A dozen more strokes and the boat thudded against sand-bagged steps.

Levering himself out of the vessel, he glanced up to where he had last seen Kate. Then with a curt, 'Forgive me,' to the dumbfounded doctor and his niece, he took the steps two at a time.

He burst on to the wharf, clawing through the jostling crowd and vaulted a stack of chairs and chests. But the space where she had been was empty. With an oath, he grabbed a chair from the stack and sprang on to it.

Over heads shifting and curious, he spotted a figure in a brown cloak making towards the fire-torn streets around the bridge. A tugging at his sleeve drew his attention down to an indignant youth who was gabbling about his shoes marking the satin seat. He swooped to the ground, cannoned the chair at the youth, and hurried after the brown cloak.

She went into the dusk, tripping the ash-covered streets, darting between carts, weaving through knots of frenzied house-clearers. He followed her into a church overflowing with frightened people. The sick and infirm carried out in their beds, had been lined up by the entrance to the crypt, blocking the way to the door through which she was making her exit. Grabbing the first bed-post, he jumped from mattress to straw pallet, batting aside a wasted arm that tried to hold him, then out through an overgrown churchyard.

Now hard on her heels, he hurdled the hand-gate. She began to run, hampered by the bundle she carried, swinging from side to side with the awkwardness of it. Across stones that burned underfoot, into a street where overhanging buildings belched flame and smoke.

A figure, wearing the side-striped breeches of a soldier, staggered from an entry, and yelled after her, 'Not that way!' But his words were drowned by a crash of timber.

Marsden chased her into a wall of smoke – so close now that he could hear the braying cry of the child. The child drew him. Its cries guided him under the stable arch of a burning coaching inn, across the uneven cobbles of a yard ... to where she stood waiting for him.

He stopped a few paces from her, blocking escape. The inn, a timber-framed building infilled with herringbone brickwork, was crowned with flames. Fire gushed from the windows, spraying shards of green glass across the yard. He glanced to his left. The stable-block was an inferno; its yawning doorway filled with a red glow, and a small goods door at the top of an external staircase was already seeping smoke. She had nowhere to run.

This time he had her.

# And Consummation ...

A sharp gust of wind cleared the smoke, leaving the two of them a small oasis of vision. Above, a full moon pierced the night's haze. The heat seared his chest, the fire's roar beat at his ears – and she filled his sight.

He was fascinated by the change in her. His mental vision was of homespun and weathered hands, of thick eyebrows and scrubbed cheeks. The rude image jarred with new reality. In a moment of clear moonlight he saw beneath the drab cloak, lace and ruby velvet, a glitter of jewels around her throat, painted lips and a froth of curl. It did not surprise him so much that the shepherdess had turned whore, as her apparent success in the profession.

He waited for a blast of throat-catching smoke to disperse, then focused upon her eyes. He concentrated his mind; luring, penetrating, rending the veil of her confidence. He probed in search of the old moorings and finding them, anchored. She was stronger, he sensed that, but not as strong as he had anticipated. His will was dominant still. Despite the dreams and foreboding, he was master. Relief washed over him in orgasmic bursts.

The child in her crooked arms began to cry again. Timber and masonry crashed in upon itself, sending bursts of sparks over them. But neither gaze faltered.

Hooking both hands in the buttoned front of his shirt he ripped it open and held out his hand to her.

'Come Katharine Gurney,' he whispered. 'Come to me ... I will give you rest.'

Kate rocked the child and took a first faltering step across the breach. Then another. And the closer she moved, the tighter drawn was their smoke-blown oasis.

'Come,' he urged, lightly touching her face and throat. He drew her against his bared flesh. 'Tell me how you came to escape the noose....'

In soft monotone, she told him, of plague and a kindly gaoler; of a swim to freedom and the trudge to London. He wiped beads of sweat from her upper lip, pensively stroked her hair, and asked,

'How did you come to be under my window, that night at the Temple?'

'You called to me,' she said.

The obscurity of her reply shot him through with irritation. Grabbing a handful of curls, he jerked her head back. 'No Kate. You came of your own accord,' he snarled. 'It would have to have been one of the brothers told you – a patron perhaps.' His fingers snatched at her necklace. It broke and fell away. But she said nothing.

'The child–' he said, subsiding.

'A son,' she choked, her eyes watering with smoke.

'Born in gaol?' he demanded, prising the bundle from her arms and releasing her hair.

Kate shook her head. 'In a brothel.'

Balancing the child on his left arm, he loosened its swaddlings and glanced at its genitals. Then, cupping the screaming head, rebound the agitated limbs.

'What do you call him?' he asked, coughing. When the smoke thinned he saw Kate had moved a short distance away.

'Find it in yourself.' A sudden acerbic quality in her voice jarred him. He narrowed his eyes and chewed his lip. *François,* she had called across the river. *Ask the shepherdess, she knows.* She gave a great sigh of a laugh and he knew the anchors were away, wondered if they had taken hold at all. And his hackles rose.

'Tell me about him,' he growled.

'It is a story well known to you,' she said, without a trace of fear. She began to pace slowly round him. 'Father away, mother at play ....'

He turned with her, heat stung eyes straining to keep her in focus. Her pace quickened. He felt a gripping at the base of his skull; a sickening pressure which spread across his brain, momentarily robbing him of sight. When it receded, she was standing before him, enveloped in iridescent light.

Her eyes, glowing like rubies in the firelight, found his. 'One day,' she predicted, 'his mother will give him over to the nuns, but not until she has moulded him, explored him ... drained his soul of goodness.'

He felt again the creeping paralysis in his skull, lunged the spread fingers of his right hand at her face but grasped only sooty air. Turning his head up to the shimmering moon, he pleaded, 'The witch must die!'

'A convent in Italy,' she persisted. 'The sisters will teach the handsome child, bring him to their Master, never suspecting that his soul is already spoken for. The boy will be cunning, you see, was born to be so.'

Arms weak with rage, he dug his fingers into the child's armpits and swung it into the air, letting the shawl slip away. The child's tightly curled toes chafed against each other. It sucked at air until its saliva-wet chin puckered inwards then it gave a piercing scream.

Kate looked up at her baby but made no move to retrieve it. 'A priest they'll make of him,' she said dispassionately, 'but a carnal one; a lusting fox.'

His arms dropped. The child swung down like a rag doll, its feet bouncing off the cobbles. It hung noiselessly from his left hand. His right felt for the blade, and finding it, his features creased into a smile. *'Tuum nomen sanctificetur–'*

Her eyes locked on to the glittering steel. 'His manner will be rape,' she choked.

*'Caelis in es qui noster Pater,'* he intoned, beckoning her with the knife.

'And murder!'

'Whom will *he* destroy?' he growled, moving towards her. 'Tell me!'

'Their voices cry out.'

'Whom?' He pressed closer, slashing at smoke. Kate backed into the stable wall. She pressed her fingers against the warm roughness of perished bricks.

'Listen!' she hissed. 'They call your name–'

His looming figure came into rapid focus. And with the weight of his right shoulder he pinned her against the wall.

'I hear nothing!' he snarled. He jerked the stunned child into his arm and pressed the blade into his belly flesh. 'Give me his name!'

'The son embodies the father,' she winced, 'he is all that you are.'

'The name!'

She ground her head against the wall with a choked laugh. And the roaring air was filled with the drone of voices. Louder, they came, pressing form out of formlessness.

'*François Borri,*' they murmured, voices rising in crescendo. '*Father François Borri....*'

'They are calling for you, François,' Kate said, reaching out to stroke his sweat-streaked brow. He recoiled at her touch. Feeling a peculiar yielding under the blade, he looked down. To his horror saw that the steel had sunk through rotted flesh – between the protruding ribs of a child corpse. Grey putridness sagged against his jacket sleeve, its stench stomach-heaving. The head nestled in the crook of his arm, eye-sockets and toothless gums bubbling with maggots.

Howling with disgust, he levered himself off Kate and lunged towards the stable doorway with a cry of, 'Witch's filth!' he launched the vile bundle into the jaws of the inferno. Then, amid a belch of sparks, he rounded on Kate.

She felt a winding thud against her side. She snatched her eyes from his wild eyes, to the blood-dulled steel in his fist. Gasping with hurt, she caught his knuckles with both hands and swung herself sideways. But the toe of her shoe caught in the hem of the cloak. Her knees buckled and he drove her heavily down to the cobbles, pinning her with his weight. She struggled on to her back, the cloak winding tightly round her throat. She clawed her fingers through his dark chest hair and fixed the cat-green of his eyes with the fiery glow of hers.

'I summoned you, François,' she taunted. The darkness was suddenly shot with a myriad flares. 'And you brought your seed to me.'

'Dead!' he spat, jerking the knife high above her chest. 'That abomination is dead! Can't you smell its burning flesh?'

'Does a witch's bastard die so easily?' she delved.

His laugh was raucous with scorn.

'What you are, I have made! And what I have made is mine to destroy.' The knife had arced down to within a hand of her lace collar when on a blast of flame there came the distracting cry of a baby. He rose unsteadily. Turned towards the stable door. In that split second, Kate scrambled towards the steps which led up to the smoking goods door above the stable. She clambered up the rickety boards, catching her hands on the blistering banister paint. Reaching the top platform she flung her cloak over the rail.

He watched it flutter down and spread itself over the stones; craned his neck and watched her sway unsteadily, bracing herself against the creaking rail. And his eyes found hers, dug into her psyche, tearing down the failing bastions.

Feared swamped Kate's mind. The child's cries came to her, no longer reassuring but undermining – pleading for salvation. And the wound in her side was draining thought and power from her. The heat seemed to be exploding in her chest. And the child – she knew she must get to her baby. She must survive.... but her legs felt heavy and he was offering her rest. *Sweet rest.* The words formed in her mind, leaving her clutching at fugitive thoughts, until they no longer mattered. *'Jump,'* he was urging, *'come to me Kate, there is rest in me. Come....'*

She pulled herself up into a squat on the precarious handrail and rose shakily, resting her fingertips against the hot brick wall. Behind her, the smouldering door threatened to blast open at any moment. Below, he waited; legs spread, hands linked behind his back – an irresistible focus in a swirling sea of smoke and flame.

*'I am your master. Yield Kate, you are weary ... come to me and there will be no more pain.'*

His words breezed through her feverish mind like a sweet summer wind; hypnotically soothing. She sank into her knees, poised to jump. The handrail swung dangerously over the courtyard, lifting her fingers off the stable wall. And in that moment the voices came to her; eddying, spellbreaking whispers: *'The cunning man, the cunning man–'*

There was a moment of confusion. Him saying, *'We will soar together, Katharine, further even than before – only come to me.'*

*'Lies!'* hissed the voices united in venom. *'Lies! Lies! Lies!'*

*'Now!'* he urged. *'One step more–'*

Kate wavered. *'His rest is death!'* they cried. *'Come away ... come away.'*

*'One more step,'* he coaxed, reaching up to her.

From inside the stable there came a splintering crash, the spluttering sobs of a child. Kate's head snapped towards the brickwork. She flexed her knees to swing the rail back over the platform. Her hands fell against the wall, and the goods door groaned with the built-up pressure behind it. Caught by a sudden blast of icy wind, she fell off the rail, bounced off the goods door and dragged herself to the rail again.

He surfaced through the smoky haze; unflinching, patiently waiting. Kate rose to her feet and stared down. A rushing stopped her ears. Flame crowned the edges of her sight. And energy coursed from her fingertips and toes, inwards and upwards. Lightning streams of it, cohered and converged through the lenses of her eyes – on him.

His shoulders slumped forwards with a shudder. His jaw slackened and his face puckered into a frown. He dropped his outstretched arms and with a yell, hurled himself at the steps.

Kate's eyes followed him, every nerve in her racked to keep him in direct focus. She barred her mind to the terror that was rocking the steps beneath her, intent on her destruction. She held her focus, groaning aloud with the effort, snatched breath and held it until her chest ached.

He was halfway up when he fell against the crumbling wall – when with a startled scream, he dropped to his knees and ripped at his jacket and shirt.

Trembling with effort, Kate sank to her own knees on the wooden platform. She watched his fingers claw from one baluster to the next in a desperate bid to get to her. An arm's length away, he squealed with pain; chest heaving, hauled himself up and swayed before her.

A bluish flame issued from the loose skin under his ribs. With grim rapidity it seared upwards into the hair of his chest, downwards into his loins. The enveloped torso writhed. The courtyard reverberated with its pain. Then with a tortured scream, he slumped towards her.

'No!' Kate wailed, pushing him away. Consumed from neck to knee, he hung for a moment, his eyes wide and staring. Then he crashed back through the rail, burning arms flailing the air as he fell towards the cobbles.

Kate crawled to the edge of the platform and pressed her face between the balusters. She watched until the last scream died in his throat; transfixed until the last blue flame flickered and died on the pile of smoking cinders, and the smell of charred wood was masked by the sickly stench of burnt flesh....

'Merciful God, I see her! Over there, look!'

Kate turned blearily towards the street opening and saw coughing figures pelting across the courtyard. Soldiers, she guessed, vaguely recalling the one in the street. They drew nearer and in the light of their torches she saw the gleaming buttons of wet tunics draped over their heads.

The first stumbled through the pile of greasy cinders below the steps. He stooped down lowering his torch.

'Sweet Jesu!' he cried, leaping back.

Two others leaned over the spot. 'There's naught left of the poor sod, save half a skull,' one said grimly.

'Look here!' gulped a younger one. 'Fingers! Three of them!'

Kate eased herself to her feet and began a shaky descent.

'Where's the rest of him?' squawked the young soldier.

'Bits of bone,' said another, gingerly poking the heap. 'Never seen bone crumble to ash before–'

'Good God, he's all here!' yelled the first, sniffing the yellow grease on his fingers. 'Pah! If that ain't mortal fat, my name's not Edgar Hutchinson.'

Kate stumbled into the courtyard and kicked the knife he had dropped during his final assault, across the shadowy cobbles. All at once the tiredness went from her and she was oblivious to all pain. Intent on the grisly heap, the militia did not challenge her as she walked around them towards the stable door. She paused on the threshold, eyes and nostrils tightening in the singeing heat. Then stepped into the conflagration....


'Sergeant Hutchinson?'

Edgar Hutchinson glanced up at the dirt-streaked features of King Charles. The king folded his hands into his reins and with a backward glance at St Paul's blazing dome, gave a weary sigh. 'You speak of a man burnt to dust, and a woman who walked unscathed through a furnace to retrieve her child.' The lean face creased into a tired smile.

'Not me alone, Your Majesty,' stammered the sergeant. 'Corporal Lutchins and Infantryman Stacey.'

The king inclined his head. 'Indeed,' he said absently.

'Lutchins, he saw her go inside. Well we pressed close as we could to the door. The heat held us back, blistering it was.'

Hutchinson twisted his hat in his hands, beginning to doubt his own recollection of the scene.

'You saw her walk through the flames?' prompted the king.

The sergeant nodded vigorously. 'With my own eyes – a good ten feet in, she went.'

'And this incombustible creature re-emerged carrying a naked infant.'

'Yes, Your Majesty. Straight past us as if it were naught strange. Aghast we was. But I shouts after her "Who was he?" meaning the ash heap. And she turns and stares straight into my eyes and says, "A Son of Solomon." Well I'd have gone after her but the door atop the steps suddenly blowed ... it was as much as we could do to save our own skins.'

The king stared for a moment into the soldier's earnest face, then turned his horse's head. 'The blast unnerved you, Sergeant, rest awhile. The City needs every man if she's to be saved.' He moved away and the royal entourage closed ranks. Trotting towards Ludgate, the king enquired, 'What is known of the Sons of Solomon?'


Out of the ashes....

On a hilltop overlooking the burning metropolis, Kate paused to rest. She sat on a small bundle of belongings, pulled the strings of her chemise and put the child to her breast.

As the toothless palate found its goal, she stroked the downy head and quietly hummed a tune remembered of her mother. And her quiet mind drifted back to an August night on a hillside far away with Jack by her side.

'You came to me there, François,' she murmured, smiling as she imagined fields dotted with stooks of oats and a scattering of black-eyed poppies. Time to feed up the ewes, ready for tupping. She laughed softly at her own foolish hankering.

She had willed the sun to set on the old life. Had chosen the evening. She pressed her lips against the gently pulsing fontanelle, and whispered, 'Just you and me now, François.'

And turned her face up to greet the dawn.


The End

THE WITCH is the first book in the trilogy by Cheryl Potter:

THE WITCH

THE WITCH'S SON

THE SORCERER

By the same author:

THE MORTAL WIFE


Visit Cheryl Potter at Amazon

or Cheryl Potter(@rosiebelle10) on Twitter

# The Witch's Son

*Ah Kate, did you think me gone?*

1683: seventeen years have passed since Katharine Gurney – the one they called the witch – emerged with her infant son François from the flames of burning London. Quiet years, lulling years....

But one shade has never gone away, has watched her children grow, waiting for the chance to strike back at her.

The second part of the *Witch Trilogy* is the story of François – his passage from youth to a manhood made potent by hardship and the supernatural powers he has inherited from his mother.

It is the tale of a mother's love, and of a man's struggle against injustice and slavery: of his fight against the legacy of evil that has pursued him from beyond the grave.

# By the same author:
# The Mortal Wife

And it came to pass when the children of men had multiplied that in those days were born unto them beautiful and comely daughters. And the angels, the children of heaven, saw and lusted after them. Rebel angels descended and the fruit of the union betwixt the fallen and their mortal wives were called the Watchers....

The whole of Ruth Madigan's adult life has revolved around the care and wishes of her disabled mother. When her mother dies, Clara, an elderly and otherwise reclusive resident of the Laurels rest home, befriends Ruth. It is a friendship that will transform Ruth's world. But there is a dark side to Clara, a legacy she must pass on before her mortal life is done.

*The Mortal Wife* is a story of loneliness and manipulation, of murder and transformation. It is a tale of mortals caught up in the final throes of an age-old rebellion. And of the souls in the balance.